JUMP INTO THE SKY

ALSO BY SHELLEY PEARSALL

Trouble Don't Last

Crooked River

All Shook Up

SHELLEY PEARSALL

JUMP INTO THE SKY

ALFRED A. KNOPF
NEW YORK

THIS IS A BORZOI BOOK PUBLISHED BY ALFRED A. KNOPF

All rights reserved. Published in the United States by Alfred A. Knopf, an imprint of Random House Children's Books, a division of Random House, Inc., New York.

Knopf, Borzoi Books, and the colophon are registered trademarks of Random House, Inc.

Visit us on the Web! randomhouse.com/kids

Educators and librarians, for a variety of teaching tools, visit us at randomhouse.com/teachers

Library of Congress Cataloging-in-Publication Data
Pearsall, Shelley.
Jump into the sky / Shelley Pearsall. — 1st ed.
p. cm.
"A Borzoi Book."
Summary: In 1945, thirteen-year-old Levi is sent to find the father he has not seen in three years, going from Chicago, to segregated North Carolina, and finally to Pendleton, Oregon, where he learns that his father's unit, the all-black 555th paratrooper battalion, will never see combat but finally has a mission. Includes historical notes.
ISBN 978-0-375-83699-2 (trade) — ISBN 978-0-375-93699-9 (lib. bdg.) — ISBN 978-0-375-89548-7 (ebook) — ISBN 978-0-440-42140-5 (tr. pbk.)
[1. Segregation—Fiction. 2. Prejudices—Fiction. 3. African Americans—Fiction. 4. United States Army. Parachute Infantry Battalion, 555th—Fiction. 5. Fathers and sons—Fiction. 6. United States—History—World War, 1939–1945—Fiction.] I. Title.
PZ7.P3166Jum 2012
[Fic]—dc23
2011024935

The text of this book is set in 12-point Goudy.

Printed in the United States of America
August 2012
10 9 8 7 6 5 4 3 2 1

First Edition

for the 555th

CONTENTS

1. Fifth of May

Whenever something bad happened, my aunt Odella was always quick to say how the end of one thing was the beginning of something else. During the war, she cooked for a lot of church funerals, where any comforting morsels of wisdom you could hand out to grieving folks with a plate of fried chicken and green beans sure came in real handy. Maybe that's where it all started, who knows.

To be honest, the spring of 1945 was so full of endings, sometimes it was hard to make a guess as to what the beginnings might be. It was the end of Hitler, of course, although nobody would fry a chicken's eyeball over him being dead. A lot of people were saying it would be the end of the Nazis and the whole war itself pretty soon, if we were lucky. But the crazy Japs kept insisting no matter what happened, they'd keep on fighting forever.

Seeing how often Aunt Odella handed out her funeral advice to other folks, I shoulda realized the day would come when she'd turn around and use the same words on me. But it was like the Japs sneaking up on Pearl Harbor while the entire country was sleeping. I was taken by complete surprise when she did.

I remember it was early on a Saturday, the first week of May, when Aunt Odella came barging into my room like the blitz. I was loafing in bed, half asleep, half awake, my big feet drifting over the edge. They'd been doing that a lot. Or maybe the bed was drifting out from under them—I'm telling you, I was thirteen with feet the size of U-boats.

My mind was drifting too. I shoulda been thinking about my father, who was serving in the army, and who was still staring at me from the same picture frame he'd been stuck in since he left. Or my best friend Archie's older brother who was missing in action, they said, and who could be dead somewhere over there in Germany.

But I gotta admit I was thinking about girls.

I was wondering if the stocking on my scalp was gonna make any difference at all. Every Friday night Aunt Odella smeared my head with a thick coat of Vaseline and pulled one of her old stockings over my hair, pressing it down smooth. Then I had to wear the fool thing all night, praying like the dickens that there wouldn't be an air raid drill or half of Chicago would see me with ladies' hosiery stretched around my skull.

"You gotta start early if you want good smooth hair when

you grow up, so all those colored girls will like you," Aunt Odella insisted. Good hair lays flat. Bad hair springs up in clumps. *Clumpy hair.* That's what my aunt called it. Lately she'd been worrying a lot about my looks and my future.

I tried telling Aunt Odella how there wasn't a girl who would get within a hundred and fifty miles of me if she knew I wore stockings and Vaseline on my head every Friday night. Heck, no girl got within a hundred and fifty miles of me now anyhow, which was fine with me. "Good to hear it. You be sure and keep it that way," my aunt would say, slapping on some more grease.

So I was lying there with a stocking stuck to my scalp and my big feet dangling over the bed when Aunt Odella came in that Saturday morning and made a beeline for the window next to me. She pounded her fist on the frame that hadn't moved since last November. "Open up." After pushing that stubborn window toward the sky, she took a deep gulp of the Chicago morning stink, turned around, and announced to me and the world, "It's a new day, Levi. And I've decided it's time to start thinking about your future."

Like I said, this was a favorite theme of hers. The future. I gotta admit there were times during the war when none of us were real sure we'd get one, what with Hitler and all. But since Germany seemed to be on the verge of surrendering, maybe there was hope for us yet.

Through my half-shut eyelids, I watched warily as Aunt Odella planted herself on one corner of my bed like she owned it. Which she did, of course. When I'd come to stay in her tiny apartment after my daddy left for the war, she'd given up her only bed and moved out to a cot in the front room, so she could have her space and I could have mine. Who knew she'd be sleeping out there for three years?

Aunt Odella wasn't a small person either. Man oh man, just about every night I'd hear that rickety cot creaking as she sat down on it and Aunt Odella hollering how the whole thing was gonna fold up and squash her flat as a bug one of these times. "I hope you're paying attention to all these sacrifices I've been making for you and your daddy and the war, Levi," she'd shout as she wrestled with the fold-up metal legs, "especially if I die here tonight in this cot."

She called me a sacrifice about ten times a day. I was used to it.

From where she was sitting at the end of the bed, Aunt Odella pretended to be studying a spot on the wall above me. The wallpaper in the room was pink roses, good God. I couldn't tell which rose she was staring at. I tried not to look at them to begin with.

"So, I've gone and made up my mind about a few things," Aunt Odella said in this determined-sounding voice, and I thought, *Oh no*—because my aunt making up her mind was like the Germans deciding to invade Poland. There was no defense.

I figured she was probably planning to sign me up for the church choir. Because of the war, Shiloh First Baptist's choir was often short of men, and Aunt Odella was always threatening to volunteer me to sing. I sent up a quick prayer: *Please, dear God almighty, not the choir.* I could carry a tune, but I'd rather lug hot coals across the Sahara than sing with a bunch of old ladies who wore choir robes resembling first-aid tents.

What Aunt Odella said next was nothing I ever saw coming.

"In life, you know how the end of one thing is often the beginning of something else?" She glanced over at me.

"Yes ma'am." I nodded my stocking-covered head as if this was the very first time I'd heard those familiar words. Part of me wondered if a funeral plate of fried chicken and green beans was gonna appear next.

"Well, this is one of those beginning and ending times, Levi. Because I believe I've done more than my share in raising you. More than most folks my age woulda done." Aunt Odella continued, "And with the war ending soon, I think it's time for a change in both our lives."

That's when I suddenly got a real bad feeling about what was coming next.

I watched as my aunt gathered a big steadying breath, squared her shoulders, and with no more emotion than if she was an officer ordering his men to storm the beaches of Normandy, she said how she knew it wouldn't be easy, but she'd decided the time had come for me to move on. To go somewhere else. To leave.

And, you know, part of my brain just couldn't believe I was hearing her right. While there were days when I'd wished on every darned star and planet in the sky to be living somewhere else, I never thought my aunt—who knew my whole life like an open book—would ever think of sending me away.

2. Queen Bee Walker

Dorothea May Walker was the one who started it all, of course. The leaving.

That's the first thing that went through my mind as Aunt Odella sat there talking. Dorothea May Walker was my mother, but everybody else in town knew her as the jazz singer "Queen Bee" Walker for the honey-sweet sound of her voice. I've been told she sang in clubs all over Chicago and even performed with the great Louis Armstrong and his band once. Who knows what's true and what's not. I got my doubts.

All I can say for sure is my daddy met her one night when she was singing at a nothing-special place in Chicago called the Wonder Lounge. The story goes that he strolled into the club for a quick drink and a song, and came out later with a famous wife. But it wasn't quite so speedy. Aunt Odella would always correct that part of the family story and tell me that my daddy went steady with Miz Walker—putting a mean edge to the *z*—for a few months before they ran off and got married. She was a good-looking girl, my aunt said. "Like the movie star Lena Horne, only a coupla shades darker. Like a hot-chocolate Lena Horne. And if the war had been on back then, I'm telling you, her voice woulda been rationed along with the sugar."

"But don't be fooled," Aunt Odella would always add. "That sweet voice of hers didn't mean she was a sweet person. I don't think that girl had a sweet bone in her whole entire body. After your daddy married her, he couldn't do nothing right in her eyes. Couldn't buy her the right clothes, couldn't take her to the right places, couldn't tell her she was pretty enough times."

According to my aunt, Queen Bee Walker was the kind of wife who was always unhappy about something. "And then one night, just a few months after you was born squalling and crying into this sorry world, she up and left."

I knew the rest of the story. How she drove my daddy's old Ford jalopy to the club one night to sing, left me lying on the passenger seat like a loaf of bread, and disappeared.

But I figure the lady must've had some speck of human kindness in her stone-cold heart because even though it wasn't a real chilly night when she left, she'd been careful to wrap me up in a fur coat my daddy had given to her as a present once. Heck, if she'd wanted to be mean, she coulda run off with that expensive fur coat and the old Ford too, right? Next to me, she left a note written on a paper napkin from the club. It said *I AM LEVIN* in crooked black letters.

She didn't have much education. "Couldn't read much, I don't think, and hardly knew how to write more than her own name," Aunt Odella would tell me. "When your daddy found you lying there with that note in the middle of the night, it confused him for a minute. He thought she was giving you a new name: Levin. And then he realized, 'No, by gosh, the woman is trying to tell me she's leavin', movin' on, gone—'" My aunt would wave her hand in the air each time she told this part of the story, as if Queen Bee Walker had vanished into thin air. Maybe she did. "Never saw a hair of her pretty little head around this part of Chicago again."

But the name stuck.

"Where's that baby Levin?" folks in the family would ask, just joking a little because sometimes in life it's better to laugh than to cry. And my daddy had enough of a mess in his life, with a wife who had run off and a new baby to take care of and all. He needed a good laugh, I guess.

As time passed, Levin turned into Levi.

Finally, according to Aunt Odella, everybody in the family just gave up using my real name of Chester, which had come from Great-Granddaddy Chester with the Paralysis. Aunt Odella herself had to admit I didn't look much like a shriveled-up raisin of a man who'd been born during slavery times. "Guess your name is the one thing your momma got right," my aunt would say to end the story, "even if she didn't mean to."

I wasn't so sure.

Because once those words were scrawled on a napkin, I believe that's when leaving became a permanent part of my life. A curse I had to carry around like a pocketful of rocks. *I Am Levin.* How many times had I heard those words? First from my momma. Then from my daddy, who used them so often, he wore them out. Then there was Granny, who'd died and left me—not that she could be blamed for that fault entirely, being the age of ninety-two when she passed on. Now it was Aunt Odella bringing them up again.

Honestly, where did Aunt Odella think I could go to next? She was my daddy's oldest sister—although no words had ever been whispered about how *much* older she was. His two younger sisters lived in Detroit, but they had their own families to worry about and couldn't be bothered with me. Everybody else was busy with the war.

Still sitting on the end of my bed, my aunt nodded toward my father's photograph on the shelf nearby. There he was: Charles A. Battle wearing his brand-new army uniform with a proud smile. Tell you the truth, he hardly looked real. He had one of those thin Hollywood mustaches, a neck the size of a football lineman's, and shoulders that didn't even fit inside the frame. His army cap was so crisp and perfectly creased, you'd swear it was made outta paper.

Aunt Odella gave a loud sigh and picked at some invisible lint on her dress sleeve. "He's been gone for a long time, hasn't he?"

"Yes ma'am." I nodded, wondering where this talk was heading.

"Probably wouldn't even recognize you now, you've grown so much."

"No ma'am." Tried not to give an eye roll, but I never liked people talking about how tall I was. These days, me and Archie looked like David and Goliath walking around together—me being the big Goliath and him being the puny, tough David who would pop anybody in the knees for nothing. There were a couple of taller boys in our school, but the little grammar school kids still liked calling me "Big Man" whenever they saw me. "Hey, Big Man, come be our tree," they'd say at recess, flapping their little hands in my direction. Their part of the schoolyard didn't have any trees for tag, so if I was feeling generous, sometimes I'd stand there with my arms out, being their tree. Wasn't much of a star at sports, anyhow.

Aunt Odella's gaze returned to the picture of my father. "The war's gonna be over soon and you'll want to be with your daddy when that happens, don't you think?"

I shrugged. "When he gets back, I guess."

He was stationed at an army post in North Carolina, but I hadn't been dwelling on him much lately, I gotta admit. The army moved him around so often, you couldn't really blame me for not worrying about where he was every minute or when he was coming home. Only place he hadn't been sent to was the war itself. Which was one of life's eternal mysteries. All these big battles were happening over in Europe and the Pacific, and he hadn't seen a single one of them as far as we could tell.

My aunt continued, "Well, I been doing a lot of thinking and praying about your daddy, and I decided the time's come for you to see him again."

What? Flat-out shocked, I stared at Aunt Odella.

"With the war ending any day now, I think it's time for you to go and stay with him for a while." Her voice was stubborn. "I done way more than my share of raising you. It's his turn to take over. That's what I decided. There's a train leaving for North Carolina today."

Good grief almighty, was she out of her mind? Did she remember my daddy was still serving in the U.S. Army? And our country was still in a big war? And nobody had surrendered yet?

Everything was so quiet, you could hear the people in the next apartment listening to the radio and the sound of their teakettle wailing away. I think Aunt Odella was waiting for me to say something, to break the frozenness of the air around us, but there were no words. Just the sound of that fool teakettle. Leaving was one thing, but sending me to my father was something entirely different. I kept thinking to myself, *How in the world could she just up and decide to send me to North Carolina? Was she expecting me to stroll down there and show up on my daddy's doorstep at an army post with no warning?*

My aunt's determination melted a little around the edges the longer the silence went on. "I'm only looking out for what's best for you and him," she said in a softer voice. "Don't you want to see your father too?"

I didn't answer because I couldn't even conjure up a picture of what seeing him would be like—to know how I'd feel. Heck, it'd been more than three years since he left. Always told my best friend Archie that missing people in the war was like picking a scab—once you started, you'd wish you had left it alone.

"Boys need their fathers and fathers need their sons in this world." Aunt Odella stood up as if that was her final word on the subject. Tugging on the sides of her sturdy dress, she straightened out the wrinkles that had bunched around her middle and wiped her hand across the little beads of sweat that had gathered along the top of her upper lip. "Well, it's getting late. We better get your things packed up."

When I was little, I used to wonder if my life woulda been any different if I'd stuck with the plain old name of Chester instead. Maybe I woulda had an ordinary family like Archie's, with a momma who cooked beef roast on Sundays and a daddy who cranked homemade ice cream when it was hot and told jokes. Instead, I had a family that had taken off more times than a B-17 bomber.

I think that's what Aunt Odella was afraid of too.

Afraid of being stuck with me if my daddy didn't come back after the war ended. Before I'd come to live with her, she'd taken care of Granny during her illness, and before that, Great-Granddaddy with the Paralysis. So maybe that's why she wasn't wasting any time getting rid of me, you know what I mean?

Not even two hours later, I was walking outta her apartment carrying one suitcase and a paper bag of fried chicken speckled with grease. The suitcase held just about everything I owned in the world—which wasn't a whole lot by the looks of it. From what I could tell, my daddy had no idea I was coming.

3. Scorpion of Death

It's strange how many dumb things you notice about a place when you're leaving it. For instance, as me and Aunt Odella headed out of her apartment building that morning, I noticed for the first time how much spit there was on the steps. There was years, maybe decades, of people's spit on the worn gray stones. Those steps were a spit mosaic. A lot of it was mine and Archie's, no doubt. We enjoyed letting a nice wet bomb hit the pavement now and then. Strange to think how I had to leave but my spit got to stay, you know?

I remember how it was a pretty morning for Chicago too. Sunny. Warm. Big yellow dandelions had sprouted up through the cracks in the sidewalk, and I swear I never noticed dandelions growing there before. You could smell the coffee beans roasting at Hixson's Grocery across the street and hear the faint sound of a saxophone playing, even at that early hour. Probably from the all-night clubs a few blocks over.

I took one last backward glance at Aunt Odella's building before we turned the corner. Never thought I'd feel sorry about saying goodbye to that old place, but I did. It was nothing special—just a plain old brick walk-up, three stories tall, with the usual rickety fire escapes zigzagging up the sides. Aunt Odella's apartment was on the top floor. My window had faced the back and looked out over the tar roof of another run-down apartment building behind us. In the spring, you could see the reflections of clouds going by in the roof puddles, which was the only good part of having a rooftop as your scenery. Sometimes you could feel above the clouds.

Aunt Odella walked faster down the street, like she didn't want to give me time to start dwelling too much. The handle of the suitcase kept sliding in my sweaty hands, and I switched sides every time we stopped. In Aunt Odella's opinion, I'd brought along way more than anybody'd need. "It's probably that winter cap and all those extra things you packed, making everything so hard to carry," she said at one stop. "I tried telling you not to take so much."

Maybe North Carolina wasn't the Arctic, but the cap had been a gift from my great-uncle Otis and it was one of those nice leather aviator ones you see in the war movies. People always said it made me look like a mad African bomber pilot, so I couldn't go and leave it behind.

Aunt Odella hadn't backed down on my Speed Jaxon

comics, though. "You gonna be too busy where you're going to read junk." Even before I'd finished packing, the whole stack of them got yanked outta the suitcase and smacked onto the floor. My aunt said she'd give them to the scrap drive. Paper was in short supply in 1945, but seeing my newspaper comics get sent for scrap just about tore my heart out because they didn't have a mark on them.

Still, I managed to slip in the scorpion when Aunt Odella turned around to fold up some of my shirts for packing. The scorpion wasn't alive, of course—this was a dried-up one my father had sent two years earlier, thinking I'd get a kick out of it for my eleventh birthday.

Back then, he'd been training in Arizona for a big war assignment the army changed its mind about and never sent him to. Which was a story that seemed to repeat itself over and over when it came to my daddy and his service. Archie was convinced my father was a spy for the U.S. Army. Or a secret commando. "No other explanation for how much moving around and training your daddy does. Man oh man, I bet he's a big-time top spy for the Allies," he'd try and tell me. Archie's father was too old to serve, so maybe that's why he admired mine.

In some of his letters from North Carolina, my father had written about jumping out of airplanes with parachutes, and getting his "wings" and "jump boots," but Aunt Odella had her own doubts about those details. There was no way my father—or any other sane Negro she knew—would jump outta an airplane, she insisted. "I grew up with your daddy and he couldn't even look over the railing of a porch two feet off the ground without feeling sick," she said. She thought it was more likely he drove an army truck, or worked as a guard, or something dull and ordinary like that. "He just throws in a few big stories now and then to keep us entertained at home."

Most of the time, I couldn't decide what to believe.

Fortunately, I'd opened the mail the day he sent the scorpion—if it'd been Aunt Odella, she woulda had a holy flying fit. The scorpion had been pasted inside a folded piece of paper with the words *Don't show to Odella. Happy Birthday!* written on the front.

For a couple of days, I was like Moses parting the Red Sea as I strolled down the hallways at school with that thing in my pocket. Everybody moved aside to let me and Archie pass by. All I had to do was wave the scorpion of death in the air and we could get anything we wanted to eat for lunch. Deviled eggs. A cheese sandwich. Some homemade ginger cookies. Wave it around again and the line for the school washroom would shrink down to nothing. Me and Archie were kings. It was one of those birthday presents you never grow up and forget.

Besides the old scorpion, there were a couple of other things I slipped past my aunt's X-ray eyes while I was packing up my suitcase. Took all my father's letters and his army picture—although I don't think she woulda complained about me bringing them along. And I couldn't help throwing in a handful of buckeyes from the nice collection I kept under my bed.

It was a crazy habit I had, collecting those buckeyes. Even being thirteen and being too old for dumb collections, I couldn't seem to stop myself from picking them up. Under my bed, there were boxes and boxes crammed full of the smooth mahogany-colored seeds—some as large as the palm of your hand—from the shady buckeye trees in our neighborhood. I could imagine Aunt Odella's shocked expression when she stuck a broom under the bed and found the rest of them. Buckeyes rolling all over creation.

Gotta admit the scene made me smile.

Walking beside me, my aunt glanced over as if she wondered what in the world was going through my thirteen-year-old brain. "You still doing all right with that suitcase, Levi?"

My shoulder was pounding like the devil, but I didn't admit weakness to anybody. Especially not Aunt Odella. I nodded, hefting the suitcase a little higher. "Yes ma'am."

Right after that, she took a sharp left and headed down another block—a direction that surprised me because I figured we were going to one of the main streets where you could catch a downtown bus. Instead, she started walking through another familiar neighborhood of crowded apartments where me and Archie had shot loadies dozens of times. We were the best around at sending our greased bottle caps flying down those street gutters. Archie had a Dr Pepper bottle cap that had never been beat. I'd blown out the knees of a lot of my pants, kneeling in those gutters and seeing how far I could whip those bottle caps down the metal grooves.

As we passed by more places I knew, I had to keep shaking my head and trying to ignore the sorry-tasting lump that was rising in my throat. Heck, I wasn't ready to leave Chicago. Who would tell Archie and everybody else that I'd left town? And what was Archie gonna do without Goliath? And who would spit on the apartment steps and pick up all the perfect buckeyes from the streets? There was a lot I was gonna miss.

4. Peace on Earth

Aunt Odella didn't stop for breath until we got to my great-uncle Otis's barbershop on the corner of Forty-eighth Street. Uncle Otis was a legend in south Chicago. You couldn't miss the big white-lettered sign painted on his store window: WE CUT HEADS HERE. When anybody asked why his sign said *heads* and not *hair,* he'd say, "One hair cut? What kinda fool would pay for that? You come here, I promise you we'll cut your whole head." If you heard him say it once, you heard it a hundred times.

Great-uncle Otis was also the only person in our family—even counting distant half-white cousins—who was rich enough to own an automobile and buy the gasoline to run it during the war. Didn't take me long to realize Aunt Odella must've asked him to give us a ride. When we got to the barbershop, his big chrome and green Chevrolet sedan was already pulling slowly into the space in front of the store. I'm telling you, it looked like an Allied warship docking.

From the look Uncle Otis gave my aunt, I could see he wasn't too happy about being there either. He was close to seventy, I'd say, short and dark as a stick of licorice.

"Don't know why you in such an all-fire, speedy-hurry about doing this," he whispered to Aunt Odella as he came around to open the door for her. The words probably came out louder than Uncle Otis thought because he was going deaf and nobody in the family wanted to be the one to tell him. "War ain't even over yet."

"Well, it's all but over," my aunt answered stiffly, motioning for me to slide in the back. The Chevrolet was a four-door model with a wide backseat of smooth tan leather that still smelled brand-new. Not a speck of dirt anywhere. Made you feel like you were sitting in a church. Up front, Aunt Odella yanked her door closed with an extra-loud thump.

"War ain't no place for a fine young man like Levi," Uncle Otis said, easing slowly behind the wheel with a lot of annoyed sighing that I could hear even from where I sat. The car lurched backward as Uncle Otis kept talking. "I lived through two wars, you know, and the Great Depression and the Panic of '29, so I know what I'm talking about, Odella."

My aunt's voice rose a little louder. "How exactly am I sending him to the war? His daddy's been training for months and months down there in the middle of North Carolina. Germans and Japs ain't in North Carolina, are they? All this moving around and training he's been doing for years and he ain't fought in a single battle yet, so far as I know." She leaned her head back and rubbed the crook of her neck the way she always does when she's mad about something. "Don't know why I gotta take everything on my two shoulders in this family. When's my brother gonna decide to take responsibility for his own son? When the Pacific goes dry? You and me both know of people who've come home from their posts for a visit at least—but it's been over three years and Levi's own father ain't even *seen* him."

I knew better than to jump into this regular argument with my two cents. Great-uncle Otis and Aunt Odella were worse than oil and water when they were together. Running my own mouth never helped either—although I couldn't understand why my aunt often put the blame square on my father for everything. Why was it his fault that the army had sent him from Georgia to Texas to Arizona, then back to Georgia, and now North Carolina? Heck, none of those places were next door to Chicago, were they?

Plus, most of the boys I knew in the neighborhood hadn't seen their fathers or older brothers since the war started either. Take Archie and his family. His older brother Joe had been in the service for more than two years—and now it seemed possible they might never see him alive on this earth again. All you had to do was look around and you could count the gold stars in the windows of families who'd already lost somebody in the war. At least we didn't have one of those. The star hanging in Aunt Odella's apartment window was still blue, glowing like a tiny speck of hope up there on the third floor.

Uncle Otis wasn't ready to give up the argument with my aunt either. Being a barber, he could talk somebody bald. "How's Levi gonna get along in the South?"

"Same as he gets along up here. He's a smart boy."

See, now my aunt was taking my side in a swift counter-attack. She was sneaky that way.

"The South ain't like Chicago," Uncle Otis snapped. "It's no place for a colored boy from the North who don't know the rules. If Charles wanted Levi to be down there with him, it seems to me he'd have said so."

Still keeping my opinions to myself, I silently agreed with this point. I didn't want to get stuck in the middle of whatever important training my father might be doing down there in North Carolina. In one of his recent letters, he'd written about going through gas grenade drills, which still gave me the creepy-crawlies whenever I read over the details. How you walked into a tent with a gas mask on, then they closed the tent flaps and threw a poison grenade in a barrel, and you had to take your mask off and say your name and rank before you were allowed out, half dead from fumes. *Nobody had any tears left to cry*, my father wrote. *Coughed for a week.*

God knows what would happen if I stumbled into a gas grenade tent by mistake down there in North Carolina. Had anybody in the family considered the fact that my father might be preparing for a serious war mission this time? Or where I'd go if he couldn't keep me? What if I ended up wandering around the country like a war refugee pushing all my belongings in a rattletrap wheelbarrow? Good grief.

In the front seat, Aunt Odella fanned herself with a cardboard church fan from her purse, not saying another word to Uncle Otis. There were two white doves on her fan with the words PEACE ON EARTH written above them, although there wasn't much peace inside the automobile right then. The doves' wings flickered back and forth in the air like little white-hot flames. But Aunt Odella kept the rest of her opinions to herself, and Uncle Otis didn't turn around.

5. Like Joe Louis in a Dress

With it being Saturday and the streets not being too crowded, we arrived in downtown Chicago faster than a German Panzer tank division entering Paris. Uncle Otis could be a terror behind the wheel, let me tell you. He nearly got us killed right outside the train station when he slammed on the brakes in the middle of the intersection and hollered, "Great snakes, thought it was the next corner!" Spinning the steering wheel in a wide arc, he missed a Tip-Top bread delivery truck by inches, or we woulda all been sandwiches.

"Sweet Jesus almighty, Otis!" Aunt Odella shrieked.

I jammed my hands into the seat, waiting to hear every automobile in the city crunch into a pile of twisted metal behind us.

We came to rest in front of Union Station, an enormous building that looked more like a Greek temple stuck in the middle of downtown Chicago than a train station. Huge white columns soared upward. Next to it, people scurried around, looking no bigger than ants.

"We're here," Uncle Otis announced with just the smallest tremble in his voice as he turned off the motor.

Although I'd been to Union Station before, the massive size of the place still made my scalp prickle. When my daddy left for the war, the whole family had come to the station to see him off. I could remember all of us being dressed up in our scratchy Sunday best as we sat together in the Great Hall, waiting on his train to leave. Probably looked like a sad bunch of funeral mourners. There was Uncle Otis and his new wife, my daddy's two younger sisters, who'd since got married and moved away—and of course Aunt Odella. The way she remembers it, she spent the entire time telling me to stop sliding off the smooth wooden benches into a heap of boredom on the marble floor. I was only nine. "You were a handful until I got you straightened out," she'd add. "Your daddy and Granny weren't firm enough when they raised you."

What I recalled most about the day was Wrigley's gum. They were selling gum at one of the newsstands nearby, and according to my aunt, I begged everybody in the family— and even some passing strangers—for some of that gum. "When your daddy goes and gets himself killed in the war, you'll be sorry all you cared about was a pack of chewing gum," Aunt Odella had finally snapped at me, shaking my arm hard enough to rattle my teeth in their sockets.

Her dire prediction stuck in my mind for the longest time. I was sure I'd sent my father to certain death because of a pack of Wrigley's. Never liked the taste of chewing gum much afterward. These days, all the Wrigley's went to soldiers anyhow.

"Hurry up, Levi. Collect your things and get out. We're holding up traffic."

You could tell Aunt Odella wasn't in any mood to stand around gawking at the scenery. She was already hefting my suitcase outta the automobile before Uncle Otis had his door open.

Watching everything with a disgusted look, the old man shook his head once he got out. "That woman is Joe Louis in a dress."

I was pretty sure the comment wasn't meant as a compliment toward Aunt Odella, since Joe Louis was the heavyweight boxing champion of the world. Couldn't imagine him ever wearing a dress—but it wasn't too far-fetched to picture Aunt Odella knocking out somebody with a pair of quick left hooks. Nobody messed with her if they could help it.

"Here, I wanted to give you something for your trip," Uncle Otis whispered. He reached into his pocket and slipped a roll of dollar bills into my hand. Uncle Otis was always sly about money. Sometimes he'd drop by the apartment for a visit and the next thing you know, you'd find a dollar or two stuck in the sofa cushions. Or a quarter left under one of the crocheted doilies my aunt kept on her tables.

"Told Odella over and over, it ain't right to send you down there," he said, keeping his voice low and leaning so close I could smell his familiar cigar and peppermint-candy breath. "But nobody ever listens to the advice of old men like me. Told her sending you down there to the South is like sending an innocent lamb to the slaughter."

He squeezed my arm hard. Even being seventy, he had fingers as strong as a pair of shears. "You run into any troubles down there, you find yourself a colored barber and you have him ring me up here in Chicago. I'll pay for whatever it takes to get you home, safe and sound. You can always stay with me and my wife if you need to come back, you hear?"

I knew Uncle Otis was just being nice, because it was a well-known fact his uppity wife didn't like kids at all. Whenever I came for a visit, I had to take off my shoes and sit on towels spread across their good sofa. No way his wife would ever let me move in and become something permanent.

Told Uncle Otis I'd be fine. Then thought I'd die of embarrassment when he suddenly reached up and patted the top of my head as if I was some toddling child in his barbershop—when the truth was, I was already a couple of inches taller than him.

"You're a fine young man, Levi," he repeated at least three or four times. "You got a wise head sitting on those shoulders. Don't let nothing happen to yourself down there in the South, you hear?"

Well, I wasn't as stumbling ignorant about what I'd be facing as Uncle Otis thought I was. I'd picked up a few things from my father's letters during the months he'd been in North Carolina. Already knew the place was overrun with mosquitoes and nasty sand ticks that could make your hands swell to the size of a Christmas ham, according to my daddy. And there were some problems with snakes too. My father wrote about the fellows finding a large snake curled up in their army jeep one chilly morning, and waking up half the camp as they bailed out.

Now, I wasn't a big fan of snakes, but I wasn't a lamb going to the slaughter either. Could watch out for my own two feet and put up with a few bugs if I had to. Soldiers were dying of a lot worse things in other places.

Aunt Odella motioned at the two of us impatiently. "We gotta get moving or Levi's gonna miss the train. You can head on back to the shop now, Otis. I know you got customers waiting. I'll find my own way home after I buy Levi his train ticket and all. No need to keep holding up traffic."

With one last disgusted shake of his head, Uncle Otis got in his chrome and green battleship and drove away.

6. Barbed Wire Pie

You woulda thought the war had already ended, seeing how Union Station was packed to the walls with civilians and soldiers. I don't know who was left to fight. Everywhere you looked you could see people hugging and waving and crying and holding babies and squeezing through the smallest spaces with army duffels the size of tree trunks. As me and Aunt Odella were heading down the big marble staircase to the Great Hall to buy a ticket, the whole crowd around us suddenly froze for a minute. My suitcase slammed right into the backs of Aunt Odella's knees.

"Good Lord, Levi," she hollered over her shoulder. "You trying to kill me?"

Nervous sweat pooled up in the middle of my back.

At the ticket windows, the lines were a tangle of weary people, winding back and forth. My aunt searched slowly up and down the long bedraggled rows. I knew she was hunting for a few colored folks to stand next to—or better yet, a ticket window with a friendly Negro face smiling behind it. Only there weren't any, so she had to get in one of the lily-white lines and hope for the best. Aunt Odella never trusted whites too much. She used to clean houses for them and one white lady sneaked her clocks backward to keep my aunt toiling away longer.

"A few of them are good folks. But most of them you can't even count on to give you the right time of day," Aunt Odella had told me more than once. "You remember that, Levi."

I hadn't formed an opinion yet and never went along with my aunt's ideas on much if I could help it. A few of my teachers had been white ladies and they were nice enough. Plus, the iceman who came through our neighborhood was white, and on the hottest summer days he gave out free ice chips wrapped in newspaper to the neighborhood kids no matter what color they were.

When we finally got up to the front of the line, our ticket agent was a white fellow with the biggest mustache I'd ever seen. It was hard not to stare. I'm telling you, he coulda painted walls with his face.

"Can I help you?" the mustache man said in a bored voice.

"I'm looking to buy a train ticket," Aunt Odella announced firmly. She jabbed an elbow in my direction.

"For him." My aunt leaned closer to the ticket window, talking even louder. "He needs to get to Fayetteville, North Carolina, to see his daddy in the service. How do I go 'bout arranging that?"

Standing there, I did my best to look like my respectful school self. Polite and serious. Archie used to say I had a face like a silent movie because he could never be sure what I was thinking whenever we were sitting in class. Kept myself out of a lot of trouble that way, so I used the look often.

"There's a war on," the man answered without even bothering to glance up. "Is your trip necessary?"

Don't know if he realized the same words were printed on a war poster behind him, but it was hard not to crack a smile. With his cartoon mustache and the poster behind his head, I swear the fellow coulda stepped straight outta one of my comic books. IS YOUR TRIP NECESSARY? THINK BEFORE YOU TRAVEL. My eyes roamed around the walls—posters about the war were everywhere you looked. LOOSE LIPS SINK SHIPS. IDLE HANDS WORK FOR HITLER.

My aunt's chest went up like words were rising inside her too. Like I said before, she wasn't a small person. "It is necessary," she insisted, sounding as if she was teetering on the edge of taking offense.

"Best you can do is wait and see if there's any open space. Seats always go to soldiers first."

"His daddy is a soldier." My aunt pointed an elbow at

me again. "He's stationed at Camp Mackall, all the way down there in North Carolina. He's a lieutenant in the U.S. Army. His name is Charles Battle."

"What's he do?" the ticket man asked, with just a shade of mocking in his tone.

My aunt hesitated a minute. "He's in the parachute troops."

You could see the fellow's mustache go all twitchy-twitchy as he tried not to laugh at this outrageous fact. "That so?" he said slowly, and you could tell he didn't believe one word.

Like I said, we had our own doubts too—which we'd never share in public, of course. Every once in a while there'd be a story in the newspaper about a Negro learning to pilot an airplane, but it was always described as something rare. Like seeing an eclipse or something. If a Negro couldn't fly a plane, it seemed beyond possibility he'd jump out of one, you know what I mean? When people asked us what my daddy did in the war, we usually said he was in the army and stopped right there.

The ticket agent shuffled through some papers. "Best I can do is sell you a one-way ticket going to Fayetteville, North Carolina, through Washington, D.C."

"Washington, D.C.?" Aunt Odella seemed suddenly confused by this information, and I began to feel the first prickles of real fear tiptoe across my scalp. Man oh man, did my aunt have any idea what she was doing? Did she even know the first thing about where she was sending me?

"Is Washington, D.C., on the way to North Carolina?" she asked, deflating just a little.

I guess the ticket man must've run out of his daily supply of patience by then. Leaning forward, he gave my aunt a look that woulda turned a lesser person into a pile of quivering dust. "Buy a ticket or get outta my line. I don't have time for answering ignorant questions from coloreds."

Now sweat was popping out in cold nickels all over my forehead. You never called my aunt ignorant. No telling what she would do next. Honestly, I wouldn't have been surprised to see her reach through the ticket window and wring that man's scrawny little neck like a chicken.

But her voice stayed dead calm. "Just asking." She slid a handful of crumpled bills toward the man. "Give me a one-way ticket to Fayetteville."

Some change and a ticket slid back to her, and somehow we managed to slip away from the window like two enemy submarines, without causing any more commotion than we already had. Once we got outta earshot of the line, Aunt Odella handed me the ticket and huffed, "Like to give that man a big serving of my good barbed wire pie."

If this was a real pie, my aunt would've had to make a couple of them a day, she gave them out so often to people who made her mad. I was always careful eating her desserts whenever she was fuming at me, just in case she decided to put something metallic in mine.

"Now, I got no earthly idea why this is the arrangement, but the train you're taking goes through the city of Washington, D.C., on its way to North Carolina," Aunt Odella repeated over her shoulder as she moved at a speedy pace toward the platforms for departing trains. Words came out between breaths. "Myself, I never been to Washington, D.C., before, but I'm sure it can't be too bad of a place if the president of the United States lives there. All you gotta remember is not to get off the train until it gets to North Carolina. Just stay on and you'll be fine."

She pulled a crisp white envelope outta her purse. "Once you get to North Carolina, there's money in here for a bus to Camp Mackall, your daddy's army post." Her eyes narrowed, giving me one of her radar stares. "Don't you go spending any of my hard-earned money on nothing foolish, you hear? I'm gonna be praying real hard for you the whole time, so I know you'll be just fine."

My aunt was a powerful believer in prayer. She was also a powerful believer in short goodbyes. Probably because they didn't leave much time for second thoughts or tears.

I wasn't much for boo-hooing either. Kids at school could come along and sock me right in the stomach and it didn't make no difference to me. Their fist would make this *oofing* sound and they'd jump back and rub their hands. They'd have tears springing outta their eyes and I wouldn't have any in mine. *Big man,* they'd gasp, *you're like some kinda strange pillow, nothing can touch you—you absorb stuff.* Sometimes I worried maybe I was missing something, because most of the time I didn't feel much of anything, good or bad. It was almost as if the fur coat my mother had wrapped around me as a baby was still there, muffling everything.

Honestly, I could only recall crying once since my father had left for the war. Back when I was ten or eleven, he'd promised to come home for a quick visit at Christmas from the army post where he was stationed. A few days before he was supposed to arrive, everything was ready and waiting. I'd spent a whole week building a pretty darn good model airplane for him, which was sitting in the middle of the kitchen table like it had just landed there. Paint still shiny wet. Aunt Odella used half our ration book coupons to whip up a Christmas meal fit for a king. And then the telegram had arrived, saying he had other orders. *Sorry. Can't come home. Ordered to new post. Be good for Aunt Odella.*

I'd gone up to the roof of the apartment building, busted up the airplane into little pieces, and sat there by myself until I was almost froze solid, with tears and snot running down my face. Of course, it hadn't done any good to cry. The army didn't change its mind and send him home. Hadn't bothered much with tears since then.

Once we got to the train platform, Aunt Odella reached out her arms to squeeze my shoulders in a stiff hug. All around us, people were hugging and clinging to each other as if the *Titanic* was sinking underneath their feet. Next to them, we probably looked like two uncomfortable statues embracing. Then my aunt took a step back and pretended to search for something in her purse. "You better go and get yourself on that train, Levi, 'fore I fall apart and start crying." She pulled out a perfectly ironed, starched hankie and pretended to pat her eyes, even though there wasn't a single tear there.

The two of us were alike in that way, I guess.

I don't think the torpedo of reality hit me until I started walking toward the train—how I was on my own—how I'd never been on a darned train before—how I'd never been outside of Chicago. As I reached the metal steps of one of the passenger coaches and began thinking all these crazy thoughts, I gotta admit my legs turned kinda weak and shaky. Jell-O legs, Archie woulda called them. Whenever we cut through the South Side cemetery coming back after dark, he'd always say, "Man oh man, this place gives me the jiggly Jell-O legs, Levi."

Heading on board that train, I had a bad case of those legs myself. Tripped over my own feet on the top step of the car and half fell over my suitcase. In front of me, a soldier with a fresh GI haircut turned and rolled his eyes, as if I was some kinda clumsy fool. Wanted to tell him at least I didn't have a head that looked like an egg with fuzz.

It didn't help matters when I saw how the passenger cars

were a lot smaller on the inside than they appeared from the outside too. Ducking my head through the doorway, I tried not to seem shocked by the sight of all the people stuffed inside that narrow space. I'm telling you, the inside of that car smelled like canned people. Everybody was pushing up their windows trying to get some air to breathe before they sat down.

Sliding sideways down the skinny aisle, I started hunting around for an open seat. Even though Aunt Odella'd bought me a ticket, I guess that didn't mean I'd get to sit down. Every row I passed by, people shook their heads and said, "Not here." Or they'd throw a newspaper or a coat over an open spot if they had one and tell me it was already taken.

Pretty soon I could hardly see where I was going on account of the fact I was so frustrated. Sweat was pouring down the middle of my back and my heart was thumping like a mortar lobbing shells. From what I could tell, there weren't any other colored folks in the passenger car except me, and I began to get the strange feeling that's why all the seats were suddenly full. The people in the car wanted to keep it that way. Or maybe they didn't want to sit with a kid. Heck, what did they expect me to do? Did they want me to plop my big self smack-down in the middle of the aisle? Let everybody crawl over me all the way to North Carolina?

Finally, at the far end of the passenger coach, a red-haired lady actually looked my direction instead of turning away. "This one free?" I asked the lady, and she shrugged and told me it was fine so long as I didn't mind riding with a cake. She pointed at a big white bakery box sitting on the floor between the seats.

Tell you the truth, I woulda sat down with a plate of cold Spam at that point. Sliding into the open seat, I tugged all my things into the space with me before the lady could change her mind. Don't know what I would have done without that lady. She was some kinda white angel to me.

7. One White Angel

The lady told me she'd been carrying the cake all the way from the state of Kansas. I didn't know how far away Kansas was, but the cake box sure looked like it was in sorry shape. One corner was mashed in and a blue ribbon around the box had come loose. There was a scuff mark on the side like it had been accidentally stepped on. The lady seemed like she'd been on the train for a long time too, from the number of crumpled Milky Way wrappers scattered around her seat and how the bobby pins were dangling from her nice hairdo.

"My name's Margie," she said with a tired but friendly smile.

She was probably about twenty, I guessed. Her curled and done-up hair was nearly the same shade as the orange powder we mixed with the wartime margarine to make it turn yellow. Orange-red hair. Freckles sprinkled all over her face. With that hair and that name, I thought she probably coulda been a good hit song on the radio: "Margie with the Margarine Hair."

Reaching over, Margie handed me a wrinkled high school snapshot of a fellow. "This is who I'm bringing the cake for," she offered without me even asking. I gotta admit the fellow in the picture didn't look very happy about the fact she was bringing him a cake from Kansas, but maybe it was all the creases that made him seem gloomy and scowling.

"His name is Jimmie Ray. He's from Kansas too," she explained. "He's coming home from the war and I'm going to meet him in Washington, D.C., if this darned train ever gets there." Stretching her arms toward the faded green seat in front of us, Margie yawned loudly. Candy wrappers tumbled to the floor. "How 'bout you?"

I felt warm and tongue-tied. I didn't talk to girls or white people much. "I'm Levi Battle. I'm from south Chicago."

"Levi. That's a name you don't hear too often."

"No ma'am." I didn't know what else to answer, not wanting to seem too talkative. I shifted around trying to find a comfortable place for my legs in the tight space. My old Weather-Bird school shoes hardly fit under the seats.

"So who are you going to see, Levi?"

"My father in the army."

"Is he in Washington, D.C., too?"

"No ma'am." I tried hard to be polite with her curious

questions since she'd given me a seat. "He's down in North Carolina."

"That's a long way away."

"Yes ma'am, it is." I wondered again how far away it truly was. "You ever been there?" I couldn't help asking, just in case.

"Oh no. This is the farthest away I've ever traveled. My family are all farmers."

I pictured Margie's family growing outta the ground like carrots—an entire orange-haired family like her. It reminded me of how Granny used to grow onions on the fire escape when I was little. I could still remember those floppy rows of green onions growing like magic outta an old metal washtub filled with dirt. That was the closest I'd ever got to farming. Granny believed in using onion soup to cure everything, from colds to death. Seeing how long she lived, I guess you could say it must've worked pretty well.

I think Margie was lonely for somebody to talk to because one question kept leading to another. She asked me what Chicago was like, and I tried to come up with a simple way to describe where I lived. It's hard picking out things to say about a place you know so good you don't even notice it half the time.

I thought about describing Lennie's Restaurant, with the green bubbling jukebox that played six tunes for a quarter, or Hixson's Grocery, where you could stick your finger under the molasses barrel spout and steal a dark, bittersweet drip or two before old Mr. Hixson chased you out with his broom. But for pure memorability you couldn't beat the crazy lady in the apartment building next to ours who always got blind drunk on Saturday nights and stood on her fire escape in a bright pink dressing gown and raggedy feather boa, belting out songs like she was Ella Fitzgerald herself, even though she was wide as an elephant and tone-deaf as a tree.

None of those stories was fit for telling to a stranger, though.

So I ended up describing how Chicago was a place where the cold could kill you in the winter if you weren't careful and the heat melted everybody's brains into puddles in the summertime. Told the lady how there was a good-looking river that went through the middle of the city where you could catch catfish the size of cows, according to my uncle Otis. I said the downtown was full of more automobiles and people than you'd ever seen in your life, although I didn't get to go there too often myself.

"Sounds like a place that'd be real nice to visit someday," Margie said—just being polite, I think. Her voice had a soft kinda roll to it, I noticed. Like a voice going over a hill.

Just talking about the city made me miss it before I'd even left it. I craned my neck to see if I could catch a quick glimpse of Aunt Odella through the window before the train pulled away. "You looking for someone you know?" Margie asked.

When I told her about my aunt being out there, Margie insisted on me taking her seat to get a better view. "I don't know a soul in Chicago," she said, sliding that cake box over. "So you take the window if you do."

Like I said, she was some kinda margarine-haired angel.

I gotta admit I was surprised to see Aunt Odella still waiting there in the crowds of people looking up at the train. You woulda thought she'd have been miles away by then, since she was the one who'd been so all-out determined to see me go. Squinting up at the windows, she stood on the platform looking somber as usual, wearing one of the plain dark-colored housedresses she always wore, with one of Granny's gold pins at the neck. Her sturdy brown legs were planted in an old pair of shoes that were almost completely run over on the sides, I noticed. All our shoes were falling to pieces because of the war shortages. It was a wonder we could walk in them.

Maybe it was the grimy dust on the window or the way the light was slanting, but as my aunt stood there so still and solemn—no-nonsense arms crossed over her chest, face serious—she reminded me of an old photograph. She looked like one of those faded snapshots we had of Granny, or some of the other long-dead relatives with their weary faces and simple work clothes.

Was she regretting sending me away? I pictured her running after the train, waving her arms, telling me to *come back, come back,* like the ending of one of those sad-sack movies. On Sundays after church, the two of us would always split a bottle of cream soda and listen to music on the radio station WIND outta Chicago. It was one of the few times you could count on Aunt Odella to be in a good mood.

Now she'd have to finish the whole sweet bottle herself. Who knows if she'd even bother to buy one. She always told me she didn't like cream soda before I came to live with her. "You got me started on this bad habit," she'd say in a half-joking voice—well, as joking as her voice ever got. "If it wasn't for these expensive cream sodas you always make me buy from Hixson's, I'd be a rich woman, you know. Probably have more money than Uncle Otis."

As the train whistle wailed and a cloud of smoke floated past the window, I tried waving, but Aunt Odella didn't move. Don't think she ever saw where I was sitting. With the train pulling away and my aunt fading into the wall of people, I had the feeling it would be a long time before I saw her again. After spending three years with her, day in and day out, she'd turned into a photograph, like my daddy and Granny and everybody else I knew had done.

8. So Long

I must've been clutching the armrests pretty hard as the train gathered speed because Margie looked over and asked me if I'd ever been on a train before.

"No ma'am," I admitted.

She laughed in her rolling Kansas way. "Well, it's nothing but dull. If I were you, I'd sit back and sleep for most of the ride. That's sure what I intend to do." Kicking off her shoes, she tucked her feet under her skirt. With a balled-up sweater behind her head, she leaned back on the faded seat cushions and closed her eyes. Her eyelids were pale pink and almost see-through, I noticed when I glanced over quick at her. Never knew white people had eyelids like seashells before.

There was no way I was closing my eyes, though. Not with all the things there were to see outside the window as we rolled out of the city. Criminy, Chicago was way bigger than I ever thought.

Sometimes we used to go up to the flat rooftop of Aunt Odella's building on hot summer evenings and sit up there cooling off with some of the neighbors. We'd chew on ice chips, play cards, and survey the neighborhood like proud kings. Like we owned it all. *Big Man, the king of south Chicago,* I used to think when I was looking down on everybody below.

Now I could see how we were kings of nothing but a street or two. Heck, there must've been thousands of families sitting on their rooftops just like us, chewing on ice chips and looking down at the exact same things. The crowded neighborhoods stretched for miles.

Once we left the city behind, the scenery outside the window changed fast. It turned from city blocks into flat scrubby fields crisscrossed by nothing but shimmery ribbons of railroad tracks—rows of them heading to the horizon. Hadn't gone too much farther when you could see what looked like smoke rising in the distance. Big clouds of thick smoke. Of course, my first thought was the war. You get jumpy like that if you watch too many war newsreels. Started worrying that maybe we'd been bombed by the Japs and nobody on the train knew it yet. A kamikaze attack on Chicago. Maybe we were heading to certain doom. I glanced over at Margie, wondering about waking her.

Then as we got closer, the outlines of factories and smokestacks began to appear outta the haze, and that sure was a relief. If you needed any proof that Uncle Sam was busy churning out things for the war effort, it was right here in front of your eyes. The whole smoky-yellow scene reminded me of the time Uncle Otis's barbecue got outta hand and set his yard on fire. That sent up a big cloud of smoke too. Brought half of the Chicago fire department.

Now, it woulda been nice to spot a few brand-new P-51 Mustangs from the factories, flying overhead with their wings glinting in the sun. Or a line of shiny tanks rolling by. But the tracks around us suddenly turned into Railroad D-Day. Heavy trains thundered past us from both directions. I'm telling you, when some of those big steam locomotives thump past your window, just missing your life by inches, it will stop your clock every time. Don't care how tough you are.

I think everybody was real grateful when things finally quieted down after an hour or two. The conductor came through the car, making jokes and sending paper bits flying as he punched tickets, but he was our only entertainment. People in the seats around me must've nodded off in the peacefulness because they hardly made a peep. I kept my eyes open as we rolled through miles and miles of empty farm fields. Never saw that much open space in all my life. Aunt Odella's kitchenette was so small, we had to move the table every time we opened her apartment door. Out here you coulda lined up a thousand kitchen tables end to end and never had to move a single one of them.

I wondered where we were—if we'd reached Indiana already. Or Ohio. On the old pull-down map in the social studies room at school, Ohio was a faded yellow that always reminded me of a lemon drop with the color sucked out of it. Indiana—an unfortunate shade of pink. Last year Archie stuck a wad of half-chewed gum on Indiana and it took the teacher weeks to notice it. Now I wished I'd paid more attention to that frayed relic of U.S. geography.

By late afternoon, the land around our train began to ripple with hills and valleys. Margie finally woke up when I unwrapped the wax paper from some of Aunt Odella's fried chicken to eat around suppertime. I'd tried saving it for as long as I could, but finally I couldn't stand it a minute longer. With the way Margie kept glancing sideways at my food, I could tell she was hoping I'd offer her a piece.

Well, it almost killed me to hand over one of my aunt's golden lovely creations to the lady, but I figured since Margie had given me a seat, it was the only decent thing to do. The sandwich vendor came around a little later, and the lady bought a Coca-Cola and a Milky Way bar for the rest of her supper. I tried not to mind when she ate every last piece of that beautiful candy bar herself. And licked the chocolate off her fingers too.

Not all angels are perfect, I guess.

Later on, Margie started telling me more about her fellow—what he was like and how much he loved her and how they planned to get married someday. Half of it I didn't even listen to because what did it have to do with me? The rocking of the train and the darkness were making me sleepy.

"How long's your father been in the war, Levi?"

"About three years, I guess." I leaned my head back on the seat and rested my eyeballs, which had seen more in one day than in the past thirteen years put together.

"You still remember what he's like after all this time?"

"Yes ma'am," I said, even though that was only partly true. What I mostly recalled was the photograph I had of him. His army uniform. Big shoulders. Small mustache. And I remembered pressing our arms side by side once, comparing them when I was real young—and his being a shade darker than mine. Picking up a buckeye from the sidewalk, my father had held it next to his skin and joked how he and the buckeye were a perfect match. "Doggone it," he said. "I believe I dropped right from this here tree." Then he'd looked up and pointed at the tree branches above us, trying to get me to believe the dumb story. I must've been about five or six at the time.

I'm sure that's where I got into the bad habit of picking up every buckeye I saw. Archie thought it was a plain crazy thing to do. I tried making up excuses about how they were for good luck, but I don't think he bought a word of it. "C'mon, how much luck does one person need?" he'd sigh as I'd hunt around for a few more and shove another handful into my pocket. Couldn't seem to help myself, no matter what I did. Leaving one sitting on the sidewalk felt like leaving part of my father behind somehow, you know what I mean?

Margie kept on with her dull story about her fellow, Jimmie, who was in the navy. I wondered if she'd ever find an ending. "When Jimmie left for the war, I was head over heels for him," she rattled on. "He was such a swell fellow and everybody in my family—I mean everybody—adored him. But it's been a couple of years since he left and things aren't the same as they used to be. Everything's changed now."

I figured she must not have been as used to change as I was. I'd have been more surprised if things stayed the way they were.

Her voice got softer, as if she didn't want the folks around us to hear what she said next. "You know, the war's changed a lot of people. Some of the boys who've come back haven't been the same people as they were before, because of the awful things they've been through. I'm going all this way to see Jimmie Ray, but I'm not sure I'll still love him like I did. Or that he'll still love me. Maybe I don't want to marry him now either. Maybe I've fallen for somebody else. That's what I keep worrying about."

Being only thirteen, I didn't know enough about love to be able to offer Margie much helpful advice. The Battles weren't a family who talked about love if they could avoid it. My father signed all his letters to me with *So long* in his scratchy pencil handwriting. And if Ella Fitzgerald or somebody else started crooning about love on the radio when me and Aunt Odella were listening, my aunt would roll her eyes and say she'd have time for love when chickens plucked their own feathers and pigs flew.

I tried telling Margie the cake was a good idea. "Bet your fellow will like that."

"More and more, I wish I hadn't made the cake or come here at all." The lady's voice got sadder and sadder, and I had the feeling she was close to turning on the big waterworks. No way I wanted to be around for that scene. I slouched down in my seat and pretended to be real exhausted. Rubbed my eyes and yawned.

"You tired, Levi?"

"Yes ma'am, a little tired."

"I'll be quiet then, so you can sleep."

She wasn't quiet, though. Once she turned toward her side, I could hear Margie snuffling back tears and breathing in hiccupping gulps of air. I guess I must've fallen asleep trying not to listen to her crying because the next thing I knew, it was early morning and our train was coming into the middle of a gray, foggy city that I figured must be Washington, D.C., because everybody was getting up and piling on coats and bags like they were leaving.

Margie had a new pink hat perched on her head and her lips were colored neatly with fresh lipstick, but her pretty seashell eyes were a mess. Looked like she'd been up all night. Holding that mashed cake box on her lap, she was a picture of sorrow. "Hope you get to North Carolina all right, Levi," she said, and then she pushed the cake box toward me. "I've decided I want you to have this for your trip."

"No, miss, you keep it," I tried to tell her.

"Nope." She set her lips in a firm red line. "I want you to have it. I've made up my mind about what I'm going to do, and I'm not changing it back."

I had the feeling her mind didn't include Jimmie Ray anymore and giving me the cake was a sign of that. Even though I didn't know her fellow at all, I felt sorry he probably didn't have any idea what was coming next. It'd be like one of those German V-1 rockets dropping outta the clear blue sky over London. He'd never know what hit him.

Uncle Otis believes my daddy still pines for my mother. Says his heart is probably still chasing after Queen Bee Walker, so that's why he's never married again or settled down for more than a minute. Aunt Odella thinks his theory is complete hogwash. She says Uncle Otis knows as much about love as flies know about horse droppings. He's already on his fourth wife.

"Take care, Levi."

With a small wave of her hand, Margie with the Margarine Hair moved into the packed line of people heading down the aisle. You could see her pink hat bobbing up and down like a tiny lifeboat in an ocean of dark hats. I waited until it disappeared before sneaking a peek inside the cake box. It was a sorry sight, like I expected. The perfectly swirled white frosting had hardened into something that reminded me of dried-up candle wax. When you touched it, little cracks broke across the top.

Tell you the truth, that cake was probably as good a picture of love as any. For most folks—except maybe Archie's parents, who still held hands when they were walking around together—it seemed as if love always started out looking sweet and perfect at first. But the longer you carried it around with you, the worse it became. And finally it got so bad, the whole thing crumbled into little bitty pieces, and you had to leave those dried-up crumbs behind for other people to clean up.

Even though I didn't want to keep the sad-looking cake from Margie, I didn't know what else to do with it. I considered leaving it on the seat for somebody else to find. But later on, I was glad I didn't. Margie's cake would turn out to be the last piece of sweet kindness I'd get for a while, once I headed south.

9. Southbound

After the car I was riding in emptied out, a colored porter came down the aisle with his shiny cap tucked under his arm and asked me why in the world I was still sitting there. The whole car was empty and silent. It was just me and my suitcase and Margie's cake box and a seat full of crumpled Milky Way wrappers. I was feeling like I'd been left on a desert island by the last ship.

I told the porter I was waiting to travel to Fayetteville, North Carolina, and I'd been told not to get off the train until we got there. Dug around in my pocket trying to find the mashed-up ticket.

The porter shook his head. "You been told wrong, son. This train ain't going anywhere near North Carolina. It's running back to Chicago. This is an east-west train. You wanna go south, you better find yourself a southbound one."

Heck, I didn't know what to do next. Felt like I was sunk.

"Lemme see your ticket." The porter sighed, as if I was

just one more fly in his soup. He glanced at my ticket and pointed through the window. "Over there and to the left is the place you need to be. That's the southbound train you want. You can see it on the tracks just past the end of our train."

I didn't see it, but I told him I did so I wouldn't look like any more of a complete fool. Lugging all my belongings down the aisle, bumping into everything, I stumbled in the direction he pointed. Outside, three more people had to tell me where to find the right train before I did.

It was a filthy-looking one called the Atlantic Coast Line. All the passenger cars were covered in a layer of yellow dust so thick you coulda written your name on them, and the biggest coal-burning locomotive I'd ever seen was at the front. With all its greasy iron and steel parts, it coulda been a dead ringer for one of Hitler's warships. I'm telling you, I wouldn't have been at all surprised to see some artillery come poking outta the mean sides of that thing and explosives start flying through the air.

Since there were no numbers on the passenger cars from what I could figure out, I picked one in the middle to climb on board. Only I didn't even get past the first metal step.

"You there, boy," a voice hollered behind me. "You got yourself a ticket?"

I headed backward like a fish drifting downstream, with people pushing and shoving past me. A white fellow from the railroad came closer, and you could see he was gonna be an old fussytail, just by the way he was acting. Big important ring of keys dangling from his belt. Chest puffed out as if he was something special.

"Give me that ticket you got and lemme make sure you're in the right place."

He took so long staring at my ticket that by the time he looked up again, I figured there probably wasn't a seat left in America. "Where you from?" he asked me, squinting.

"Chicago, sir." I kept my shoulders square and my voice steady, like I was older than thirteen. People often thought I was.

"Chicago. Only smart boys live there, I hear. You smart?"

I shifted uneasily from one foot to the other. How are you supposed to answer an ignorant question like that? Aunt Odella probably woulda called it rude and none of his darned business. The suitcase handle dug uncomfortably into my hand. Hefting it a little higher and shifting Margie's cake box to one side, I finally replied that some people might say I was smarter than others, but I didn't have any opinion on it myself.

The man chuckled to himself as if this was a funny answer to give. He ran his fingers through the few strands of greasy hair he had left on his head. "How'd you like to help me with an important job I got this morning?"

From the expression on his face, he seemed serious about wanting somebody to help—and what choice did I have, since he was still holding on to my lousy ticket? I asked him what needed to be done.

"Follow me." He took me along the entire length of the train until we got close to the first passenger car behind the locomotive and coal cars. It didn't have a lot of windows like the other ones did, only a few at the front, and the sides were covered in black soot so completely, they coulda been called painted. The man nodded in the direction of the odd-looking car. "That's one of our special baggage and mail coaches. You board at the front." He pointed toward a set of rusty steps. "You're gonna be one of the sets of eyes and ears guarding the real important baggage and mail we're carrying on this train today. You think you can do the job?"

Tell you the truth, I figured he was asking me for help because of the war. No other reason even tiptoed through my mind. Everybody had to do their part back then. In Chicago, even the youngest, droolingest kids who couldn't read a single word knew how to spot an enemy plane from the silhouettes they plastered all over our Wheaties boxes. Just because no enemy planes had flown over the city yet didn't matter. You had to be prepared for anything to happen.

So I shrugged as if it wasn't any big deal and told the man, sure, I'd help with keeping watch over the baggage, if he needed a spare hand.

"Good. Like Uncle Sam says, 'We need you.'" He handed me my ticket and waggled one of his fingers in my face, pretending he was some imitation of Uncle Sam, I guess, and then he walked a few steps away. Still keeping one sharp eye on what I was doing, I could tell.

Right then, I shoulda realized there was something strange about how the man was acting, even if I couldn't put a name on exactly what it was. Being smart, I shoulda asked what the important baggage was and why, outta all the civilians and soldiers crowding on that train, he'd picked me, a thirteen-year-old kid from Chicago with a smashed cake box and a shabby suitcase, to guard it.

Probably a second thought never crossed my mind because I often got picked for jobs at school. Teachers wouldn't trust Archie to walk from the front of the classroom to the back, but for some reason they trusted me. One time, a teacher sent me to the corner store to buy a sandwich and soda for her lunch—right in the middle of mathematics, I got to stroll outta my education. *Levi is one of the good boys,* my teachers liked to announce in a loud and embarrassing voice to any visitor who set foot in our classroom. *Big Man,* everyone would chant, thumping their fists on the desks. Which was why me and Archie stuck together—so he could be better and I could be worse sometimes.

Being a good kid, I headed toward the baggage car as if I'd been given a direct order by General MacArthur himself. But a worsening feeling came over me as I got closer and noticed how nobody else seemed to be sitting inside the car.

Which was strange, because you could look down the entire length of the train—must've been at least two dozen passenger coaches—and people were packed together everywhere else. GIs hung halfway out the windows waving and shouting, and families stood in little worried clumps waiting to see the train off. But outside the baggage car, only a couple of fat pigeons pecked at some bits of popcorn.

I was reaching for the railing to climb into the car when the whistle of that big locomotive let out a shriek and a hiss of white-hot steam shot out nearby. Scared the living daylights outta me. I cleared the last steps in a long jump that probably coulda won an Olympic medal and banged through the half-open door of the car with one shoulder and all my belongings.

First thing I noticed was the terrible sour smell inside. Second thing I noticed was how there wasn't a stick of baggage anywhere around. Third thing I noticed was the old Negro man slumped in the far corner seat like a bag of bones.

When I came falling through the door, his head jerked up suddenly from his chest and he grinned with a toothless, skeleton smile.

"Welcome," he said with a deathly kind of cackle, "to Jim Crow."

10. Jim Crow

My face must've looked as shell-shocked as I felt, because the old colored man kept asking me if I was all right. Still feeling shaky, I didn't answer. Instead, I slid onto a wooden bench in the farthest corner from where he sat and prayed hard that somebody else, anybody else, would come on board to keep me from being left alone to guard the baggage car with a crazy skeleton man.

"I says, you got a name, son?" the man hollered loudly from the corner. When I didn't reply, he still kept on trying. "Hey, up there. You, boy. You deef or did ol' Jim Crow scare off your voice?"

Finally, when the fellow wouldn't stop jabbering, I swiveled my head around and leveled a glare at him. "Never heard of Jim Crow. Now stop talking to me and mind your own business." Made sure every word was loud and clear. Turned my shoulders into a fortified wall that you'd better not cross if you had any smarts.

Guess the old man didn't get the clear message I was sending, because he smacked his hand on the back of the wooden seat in front of him and chuckled instead. "You a polite northern boy, ain't you? Setting there with your fancy starched shirt and store-bought pants and shoes. You never heard of Jim Crow before, has you? You is the very picture of innocence."

Outta the corner of my eye, I could see the stranger stand up, bones creaking, and stagger closer to me. He wasn't even wearing shoes, I noticed as he teetered down the aisle. Had raggedy trousers tied with a piece of twine. Good God. When he reached the seat next to me, he swung an unsteady arm through the air as if he was introducing himself. "Meet Jim Crow, son," he hollered.

Right then, the train whistle wailed for the final time. The front door of our car slammed shut, and the train jerked forward hard enough to send everything sliding. Jim Crow's hands grabbed for the back of my seat, trying to stay upright. "Hold on," he shouted over the earsplitting noise of the metal wheels shrieking to life. "We're on our way."

As the train gathered speed, the space around us suddenly began filling up with heavy smoke from the locomotive ahead of us. A choking cloud of cinders poured through the open windows like black snow. Above the thundering roar of the engine, I could hear Jim Crow shouting at me about closing the windows.

Well, I struggled like the dickens to shut the two open

ones on my side while the old man tried to slam down the others. Even with the windows finally shut, our whole car was still thick with ashes. A metallic taste filled my mouth.

Sagging into one of the nearby seats, Jim Crow spat loudly into a handkerchief and wiped off his mouth and nose. What was left behind on that handkerchief was the color of ink—I'm telling you the gospel truth, his spit was black. *Criminy.* I stared openmouthed at the sight. "That from the train?"

"Where you think it's from?" the old man snorted. "Few hours inside this car, you mark my words—you gonna be black on the outside and the inside too."

He wasn't lying. Glancing down, I saw how coal dust already covered everything I was wearing. My brown pants, my white shirt, my skin—all of it sparkled with glittering-sharp bits of black. There was no brushing them off either. They stuck to your palms and left them smelling like rust. Made me think of the times when me and Archie climbed the spiky iron fence around the South Side cemetery. How our hands would smell of metal and death for days, no matter how much we scrubbed them.

"Chains smell the same way, you know." The old man spoke up from where he was sitting across the aisle.

I'm telling you, that observation didn't ease my mind much about him.

"But up in the lily-white North where you come from,

they probably don't teach you nothing about our people being in chains, does they?"

I shot right back that I knew plenty about chains and our people and history and such. People in the North weren't fools. Take Aunt Odella's church in Chicago, for instance— it had a preacher who'd become well known for his habit of bringing a heavy ship's chain up to the pulpit for his sermons. Whenever he noticed the congregation drifting off, he'd drop the iron rope to the floor and give us all an instant heart attack. "Colored folks is still in chains!" he'd shout, and pound the pulpit with his fist. "Not real chains like the slavery ones from years ago. But chains nonetheless!"

Then he'd go on with his message about the dangers of dancing the jitterbug or drinking whiskey or not honoring the Sabbath or something like that. Lucky for us, he'd given up his church chain for the war effort—donated it to one of the scrap drives in Chicago to be made into hand grenades. I figure there was probably enough metal in that chain to blow up half of Berlin. But the preacher still made me jumpy whenever he stood up to give the sermon. Who knows what he'd find to drop from the pulpit next. Boulders maybe.

"They teach you about Jim Crow too, up there where you is from?" the old man said, coughing so hard I was afraid his lungs might come out on his hankie. "Or this the first you seen it with your own eyes?"

Now, up until that moment, I still thought the fellow was calling himself Jim Crow. The raggedy suit hanging loose on his narrow shoulders coulda easily passed for the tattered wings of a bird. His skin was a dark ink-black. The man waved his arm through the air again. "Jim Crow. That's where you setting. Real pretty, ain't it?"

His words weren't making a crumb of sense. Aunt Odella probably woulda called him a few cards short of a full house. Again I cast a look around, trying to come up with another place to go, but there was nowhere else in sight. Only the coal cars and the engine rumbled in front of us, and our car didn't have a back exit. There were just six rows of wooden seats and behind them was a solid wall with a locked door, where I figured the special baggage was being kept.

"The car's called Jim Crow," the old man repeated.

"What?"

"You see any white folks around this place?"

"No sir, just us." I tried real hard to keep my eyes from rolling at his questions.

The man snorted. "Us white?"

"No sir."

"Well, then welcome to your first ride on Jim Crow."

I told the old man he was wrong about why we were there. Told him how I'd been sent to guard the baggage and help out with the war effort. He just leaned his head back and howled, his toothless mouth wide open, showing nothing but pink gums. "Son, you wasn't sent to this baggage car to be a guard—you was sent here because of your brown skin." He wiped tears of laughter out of his eyes. "You ain't guarding nothing you wasn't born with."

Heck, that idea was pure absolute nonsense. Heat warmed up my ears as the old wreck of bones kept up his howling. Who ever heard of cars called Jim Crow for colored people? My daddy had never written a single word about riding in them. And nobody on the Chicago train put me in a separate car, did they? Look at Margie with the Margarine Hair—she was a white lady who'd shared her seat with me and she'd given me a cake to keep. Was the old man just trying to make a fool outta me? Razzing me because I was from somewhere else and on my own and all?

Well, it burned me up listening to him go on and on. Standing up, I headed toward the little washroom in the front corner of the car, figuring maybe I'd just slam the door and sit inside there for a while. Get some peace.

But I didn't even get one big toe through the doorway. The sour smell stopped me first. I pushed open the half-closed door and the odor that came pouring out was straight evil. There was no real toilet inside at all—only a wooden box with a hole in it and tracks flying right below that hole. Scores of flies covered the walls and ceiling. There was no washbasin. No water. No towel. The smell drifted up my nose. I backed out, feeling like I was gonna be sick.

"No use," the old man hollered when I tried pulling the door closed again. "I done tried all that before. You just gotta grit your teeth and live with what we got right here. No other choice. You gonna learn that lesson soon enough."

His words made me madder, as if somehow he was to blame for me being covered in coal dust and stuck in the worst car on the screwball train. Maybe he thought it was funny, but heck, nobody I knew would put up with this place. Not Aunt Odella. Not Uncle Otis. I didn't give a fly's behind what the car was called. I just wanted to be off it. Smacking into the corner seat again, I turned my face toward the window and let a bunch of curse words ricochet around in my brain for a while. Then I licked my dumb metallic-tasting lips and cussed inside my head some more.

For a long time, the only sound inside the car was the rhythmic clatter of the wheels below us as they rolled along the tracks. Then I heard some music start up in the far corner. Glancing back, I saw the old man sitting there, bent over a banged-up guitar. His eyes were closed, but he swayed back and forth in his seat, plucking the strings and singing a little sideways song I couldn't make out the words of.

"You like music, son?" He stopped in the middle of his tune, like he knew I was watching, and opened his eyes.

I didn't answer, but he swung the guitar over his shoulder anyhow and came swaying down the aisle to take the seat behind me. "Here, I'll play you a little something I made up," he said, sitting down and strumming again with his fingernails, which were the yellow color of beeswax.

"It's a tune about coming and going, living and dying," he said.

From what I could tell there was only one verse to his tune, so who knows if it counted as a real song or not.

Wish I was a little rock a-settin' on a hill,
Without another thing to do, but just a-settin' still.

He sang those same words over and over, plucking different strings and tapping on the front of the box with his fingers, making up the accompaniments straight out of his head as he went along, it seemed like.

In no time at all, of course, my mind started drifting to my mother—picturing her sashaying into a spotlight wearing a sparkly kinda dress with her hair done up in a shiny roll like a movie star. Music often afflicted me like that. Whenever somebody started singing, my mind went straight to thinking about Queen Bee Walker. Nobody in the family had a single snapshot of her, so who knows what she looked like in person. Aunt Odella always said the lady didn't stick around long enough for a flashbulb to pop. I wondered what tunes she sang at the jazz club the night she met my daddy. Must've been good if he fell crazy in love after only hearing a couple of them.

* * *

The old man brought me back to where I was. "You hear the coming and going in my song, son? How sometimes you gotta move and sometimes you gotta stay where you is?" He stopped strumming and waited on an answer.

Nope, I didn't hear any of those things, but I nodded politely anyhow.

"See, I sing what I'm feelin' right inside here." He tapped two shaky fingers on his chest. Looking at him closer, I wouldn't have been surprised if he was a hundred. His eyes made me think of the old river catfish Uncle Otis sometimes caught and brought home. He had those same muddy catfish eyes that had seen a lot.

"So where you coming from and going to, son?"

I told him I was going from Chicago to North Carolina to see my father in the army. He shook his head slowly as if that was a bad idea and absentmindedly plucked a few strings on the guitar.

"See, you just like that little ol' rock I been singing about. You been setting on top of the hill in Chicago, living up there in the North where everything is fine and dandy, and now you about to come down from that pretty mountaintop, getting smaller and smaller the farther south you go. Once you step off this train in North Carolina, only one piece of you'll be left. Know what that is?"

"No sir." I tried not to sigh, guessing another dried-up kernel of wisdom was about to drop off the cob.

The old man held up his hands. "Your color. That'll be

the only piece left. You can go ahead and forget your name and your fancy ed-u-cation and everything else you learned up there in the lily-white North, 'cause only one thing will matter once you get off this train . . . and that's what color skin you got." He gestured toward the window. "There's only two shades outside our train now. White and Colored. Every sign you see and every doorway you go through in the South is put there to remind you which color you are. And you better be sure you choose the right one every time. No tellin' what kinda trouble you get into if you go and forget who you are. No sir, no tellin' what big kinda trouble you'd get into . . ."

Picking up his guitar, the old man started plucking out his strange tune again.

Wish I was a little rock . . .

I had no idea whether to believe what the old man was telling me or not. I remembered Uncle Otis worrying how I wouldn't know the rules in the South. Had he meant the kinds of things the old man was warning me about? Or something else?

I kept my eyes open, but I didn't spot much in any of the ho-hum towns we passed through as the morning wore on, so maybe it was all made-up nonsense. The South sure had some odd names. One place was called Carmel Church, which Aunt Odella probably woulda called an outright insult to religion. I almost expected the next town to be called Milky Way Bar. Farther down the tracks was one called Skippers. Good God. It made me feel glad to be born in Chicago.

By the time the train finally arrived in Fayetteville, North Carolina, it was midafternoon and the heat shimmered in waves above the tracks. Only thing I wanted by then was a drink of water and a soft seat. Watching the train slow down, the old man fanned his face with a square of newspaper and said I was real lucky to be getting off. He was going all the way to Georgia. Who knows how much farther it was to Georgia, but seeing how tired the old man looked right then, I worried about him making it there alive. The front of his shirt was soaked with sweat, and his thin shoulders rose and fell with each gasp of air.

As our train pulled up to a low brick building with FAYETTEVILLE on the side, the old man reminded me again, "Only thing you gotta remember when you get off this train is your name is Colored down here. Don't you forget that, son. Always keep your eyes open and look for that word first, you hear?"

He picked up his guitar and started strumming again. "Gonna write me a song about meeting you . . . 'One day I met a little rock a-settin' on a Chicago hill . . .'"

His catfish eyes crinkled into a wistful smile. "You take care now."

* * *

I told the old man goodbye and left him the rest of Margie's cake to eat along the way. We'd already finished most of it anyhow, along with all the butter cookies Aunt Odella had tucked in the bottom of my paper sack. Never did find out what the man's real name was, and I don't think he ever asked mine either. Always thought of him as Jim Crow. Later on, there were times when I wondered if he'd been real or if I'd dreamed up the old man singing his songs and coughing up the color black.

Mostly I wished I'd listened to more of what he'd tried to tell me. Wished I'd asked more questions. As I stepped off the train that day, I had less sense about what I was doing than I coulda ever imagined. Because it turned out my next lesson about the South wouldn't come from an old colored man trying to keep me outta trouble—it would come from the end of a gun.

11. Signs

Stepping onto the steamy Fayetteville platform one slow foot at a time, I'd be lying if I didn't admit to hoping maybe—by some chance—my father would already be there waiting on me. Pictured myself coming off the train and spotting him standing by himself in his sharp army uniform and cap, looking around with a worried expression on his face. Then I'd stroll over to him, real nonchalantly, before he even noticed me, and say, "How ya doing, Daddy? It's your son, Levi, here." When he turned and saw who it was, he'd wrap me up in one of those strong, man-type hugs and tell me how long it had been since we'd seen each other and how much he'd missed me. Had the whole scene planned out like the end of a satisfying movie picture.

Nobody was waiting, of course.

Guess Aunt Odella was smart enough to figure out if she told my daddy I was coming, he woulda found a good reason why I shouldn't. Still, part of me had held out hope he might've had some sixth sense about me showing up on his doorstep.

Aunt Odella was big on signs and sixth senses. She used to tell me how she woke up with a real bad feeling on the day Pearl Harbor was bombed and put an extra spoonful of salt in her Coca-Cola that morning because she thought for sure the sick feeling was a bad headache coming on. Then the news about Pearl Harbor being attacked came over the radio. "See, I shoulda known that sick feeling was a sign," she'd say.

Lately she'd been going on and on about a cactus. She must've told the story to everybody we knew, a dozen times at least—how, at the beginning of April, a tiny bud had suddenly appeared on a half-dead cactus she'd had sitting on the windowsill for ages. Then, a week or two later, a big orange bloom the size of a half-dollar burst outta that bud like Lazarus himself coming back to life. My aunt was absolutely convinced it was a plant miracle. "Will you look at this, Levi?" She must've showed it to me *fifty* times. "Had this cactus my whole live-long life and never saw it bloom until now. It's a sign from above. No doubt about it. I'm telling you, Levi, it's a sign of change coming to this world. That's what it means. The war is gonna end real soon."

Now that I had the chance to think back and put two and two together, it wasn't impossible to see how the blooming cactus coulda been one of the main reasons my aunt sent me packing. It had convinced her the war was ending and our lives needed changing too. *A new day*, she'd said. Wasn't my life a crazy mess? I'd been left first on the front seat of a Ford by my mother—and now by an aunt and a cactus. Heck, it was a wonder I'd turned out okay so far.

As the last cinders from the disappearing train drifted around me like burnt snowflakes, I found myself thinking all these sorry thoughts and wishing Jim Crow had gotten off with me. At least he woulda been one person I knew. He coulda walked with me for a while carrying his guitar and singing one of his made-up tunes, and I swear I wouldn't have minded. Instead, I was standing on a train platform feeling almost more alone than I could stand. Even the air smelled different than Chicago. A humid soup of flowers, frying fish, coal smoke, horse manure, sweat—

All right, I'll admit the sweat mighta been mine.

Pushing up my damp sleeves, I picked up the suitcase and decided it was time to move on and find the bus to Camp Mackall, my father's army post, before I melted into a sorry pool of uselessness. But a small sign on the side of the train station caught my eye as I turned—a black hand pointed toward the back of the building. No other words. Just a pointing black finger.

Seeing that strange sign gave me a jolt, let me tell you. Right away, my mind jumped back to Jim Crow's warning. *Every sign you see and every doorway you go through in the South is put there to remind you which color you are. And you better be sure you choose the right one every time.* But I didn't know what the heck I was supposed to do. I didn't know what the sign meant. Were you supposed to follow it or not?

Feeling real jittery, I started around the side of the train station, not sure what kind of trouble would be waiting there. But there wasn't much to see behind the station. Only a few empty benches with another sign above them: COLORED. A water spigot nearby had the word scrawled on the bricks above it too: COLORED.

I let out a slow breath. So the old man hadn't been razzing me after all.

Wondering what else he'd said that might've been true, I stood there staring at the spigot for a few minutes, trying to make up my mind about using it. How dumb was it to have a faucet with your color written above it? Made me feel like I was a kid back in grammar school.

Still, I was so thirsty after the hot train ride and all, I finally decided it didn't matter to me what color was on the darn water. I leaned over to get a drink. Turned the squeaky spigot with my hands. Nothing happened. Put a little muscle behind it and yanked again. A trickle of rusty water splattered onto a slab of stone below my shoes and that was all.

I stood up feeling thirstier and angrier.

What kinda water did white people get outta their spigot? I wondered. *What would they think if I just strolled inside their train station and tried it out?*

Well, I'd almost made up my mind that's what I was

gonna do—water was water if you were desperate—when I spotted a Coca-Cola sign in the distance. It was hanging in the window of a grocer's store farther down the main street, maybe two blocks from where I was standing. It was like seeing Christmas, noticing that beautiful red and white sign waiting there for me.

At the exact same time, my fingers touched Uncle Otis's roll of dollars in my pocket—the ones he'd slipped into my hand when he'd dropped me off at Union Station the day before. Had it only been yesterday morning I'd last seen him?

It felt like a week.

Well, I decided the folks at the train station could keep their colored water and I'd have myself a nice cold Coca-Cola instead, courtesy of Uncle Otis's generosity. So, I drifted down the shimmering hot street toward the sign. Fayetteville was a nice-looking place, I gotta admit. Everything was neat and tidy as a movie set. There was a bench out front of the grocer's store with G. W. KEETON's & SONS painted on it and a bunch of faded war bond posters covering the windows. Pulling open the glass door, I stepped inside. The store was cool and dark after all the heat. A smell of flour and sawdust drifted up my nose. I stood there, blinking in the shadows, trying to see where the counter help was hiding, when a voice called out, "What d'you want, boy?"

You woulda thought the shadows were speaking.

"You got any Coca-Cola here?" I called out uncertainly. My words seemed to echo in the darkness, bouncing off the rows of metal shelves and disappearing into the depths. Something moved in the far corner and a man emerged outta the gloom. He had on a sloppy white shirt—collar hanging open, top button missing—and then the rest of him became clear. Aunt Odella woulda called him a big eater. His chin sloped into his chest, no neck to speak of. I couldn't tell if the man was G. W. Keeton or not, but I figured he worked there, by the look of the smudged-up canvas apron he was wearing. A can of apricots was in his left hand.

"Why you asking?"

The fleshy white face wasn't smiling in a friendly way at me. Maybe I'd interrupted his canned-fruit count, who knows.

I pointed at the windows behind me where thin stripes of sunlight were showing around the war bond posters and advertising signs. Tried making my best guess at where the Coca-Cola advertisement had been hanging. "Saw a sign up there in the corner."

"Did you now?" The man crossed his thick arms, staring at me with unblinking eyes.

Like an icebox opening, a chill swept over me even though it wasn't cold. I eased myself backward a little, leaning in the direction of the door, and glanced toward the windows again. "Yes sir. I believe so," I mumbled.

"You got any money to pay for your soda?"

I shoulda taken off then, feeling the icy dread that was getting stronger by the minute, as if the whole Antarctic continent was slowly freezing around me. But I was stuck. I'd asked for a soda pop and now I was caught by asking.

Trying not to seem any more jumpy than I already was, I dug around in my pocket for one of Uncle Otis's dollars and held it toward the man. Sodas were only a nickel, but I figured he'd give me back the change and all.

"Put it on the counter."

The counter wasn't far away. Now that my eyes had gotten used to the shadows, I could see the brass cash register nearby with some jars of gumdrops and licorice lined up next to it, just like Hixson's back in Chicago. There was a pyramid of dry-looking donuts stacked under a glass dome. And ads for Lucky Strike cigarettes. And Ivory soap. I stepped forward and slid my dollar onto the top of the counter, making sure the man could see I had plenty of money and wasn't trying to cause him any trouble.

He didn't take his eyes off me. Just walked over and snatched my dollar bill off the counter. "I'll get your soda from the back," he spat out, and I listened to his heavy footsteps thumping down the aisle as if he was the King Kong of the grocery business. Seemed like a long time before he returned holding a dusty bottle of grape soda.

"There's your Coca-Cola."

The bottle slammed down on the counter so hard, I swear you woulda thought it was a grenade exploding. How the glass didn't shatter to pieces I have no idea, but the noise shocked me so bad, everything from my feet to my head suddenly began prickling as if I was being stuck by a thousand ice-cold needles. Even my back teeth started rattling together on their own. Standing there in that dark, deserted store, I suddenly realized the trap I was in.

Crossing his arms over his chest, the fellow gave me a slow grin, as if daring me to reach for the bottle he'd thrown on the counter. He was looking to pick a fight, you could tell. Heck, I wasn't that stupid. I was tall, but it woulda taken two of me to equal his size. Archie woulda taken him on probably and popped him in the gut a few times, but not me. I wasn't a fool. My brain told me to leave the soda where it was and run. Forget the rest of Uncle Otis's dollar and bust outta that store in whatever way I could.

I tried turning.

But the man moved faster than I did. His hand snaked behind the counter and came up holding something small and metallic. "Don't you even think about moving, boy." My mouth went chalk dry.

Clenched in his hand was a gun.

Time seemed to stop.

Sounds seemed to stop.

The world outside the store shriveled up and disappeared.

The man shoved the bottle toward me with a lopsided grin. "Drink it."

There was no way I could drink anything in that bottle. I couldn't even swallow my own spit right then. My arms felt as heavy as hundred-pound rocks. I couldn't lift them.

The man stepped closer and rammed the glass bottle at my chest. Grape soda splattered all over my good shirt and pants. "I said, drink it."

My hands shook so bad, the glass clattered against my teeth and soda spilled outta the corners of my mouth and ran down my neck, until there were rivers of purple spreading across the front of my shirt. It was all I could do not to gag as the bottle emptied with sickening slowness. I don't know how old that soda was. The liquid at the bottom was thick and bitter-tasting.

After every last drop was gone, the man told me to put the bottle on the counter. Slowly. And then step away from it.

My right hand trembled as I set the bottle down and moved backward, willing it not to fall over.

The man stepped closer. "You come walking through the front door of my store and ask me for anything again—next time, I'll put a bullet in your head. You understand me?"

I whispered that I did.

"Didn't hear you."

"Yes sir."

"You got three seconds to get your tail out that door, boy." The gun waved sharply toward a propped-open back door. As I stumbled down the dark aisle, the man let loose a volley of words behind me. Words you use for dogs and inhuman things and anything worthless in the world—

Even years later, I could still remember every single word he said as clearly as if they'd been burned into who I was that day. Long after the storekeeper was probably dead and gone, those terrible words never left me, and that's the honest truth.

When I finally reached the back door, I slammed it open and half fell into the desperate heat and sunshine. Beyond the store stretched an empty lot full of weeds and bricks, and I crossed it at a flat-out run. Somewhere behind me, the empty bottle cut through the air and shattered against a pile of bricks nearby, sending up a sharp rain of glass shards. I kept going, my feet pounding through sand and dust and glass, as I ran faster than I'd ever run in my life. Faster than Jesse Owens in the Olympics. Faster than the wind in Chicago. Faster than the train that had brought me south.

I ran until the town disappeared, until the roads disappeared, until the people disappeared, and then I leaned over in somebody's overgrown field, holding my aching stomach, and got sick all over the ground.

12. Captain Midnight and His Secret Squadron

What I didn't understand was what I'd done wrong. Like I said, I'm not one who gets bothered over much of anything. Sock me in the stomach and I don't crack even a little. I was a good kid, most people said. Never tried to cause Aunt Odella or Granny or my daddy any trouble, although there were a few times I did. Stole a pickle from Hixson's Grocery once—but it was on a dare from Archie and he ate it, not me. Busted the school fence during a game of pie tag. But nothing big.

The storekeeper woulda killed me, given half the chance.

As I crouched in the field on my hands and knees, sick as a dog, ants crawling up my legs, flies buzzing around my face, hot sun beating down, that's the thought that kept pounding inside my head. *He woulda killed me for nothing.* That's the honest truth. Just for coming into his store and being the color I was.

There was death in the newspaper all the time, but

I'd never thought about one of those deaths being mine. I wasn't a German or a Jap. All I'd asked for was a soda pop. Never imagined I could lose my life as quick and heartless as one of our soldiers in battle. But the look in that man's eyes had been pure straight evil. Don't think Hitler himself coulda looked any worse.

With my head down and my elbows in the dirt, I felt like I'd been dropped straight into the middle of the war itself. It made me start thinking about Archie's poor brother and how helpless it must feel to be lost behind enemy lines—spending days and weeks running and crawling for your life, not knowing who was after you, or where to go, or if you'd live to see the next day or hour. On the *Captain Midnight* radio show that I listened to each and every week, the Secret Squadron would always dive in to rescue stranded soldiers at the last possible minute. *The roar of the airplane engine, at first in the distance . . . then stronger as it sounds in a dive . . . this was Captain Midnight!*

I knew the lines by heart.

But in the real war, maybe there was no Captain Midnight or his Secret Squadron coming to your rescue. In the real war, soldiers not much older than me were probably lying facedown in fields all over Europe. Lying there as hopeless as I was, with the smell of their own vomit and fear all around them, with no help ever coming. Maybe Archie's lost brother was one of them.

Uncle Otis had tried to warn me, hadn't he? He'd called

me a lamb going to the slaughter. But who woulda imagined you could become an enemy in your own country? Never thought I'd come south and feel afraid of my own skin. I'd never been in this kind of trouble before, and I'm ashamed to admit the tears started flowing and there was nothing I could do to stop them.

An hour passed, maybe more.

Wiping off my face with the edge of my shirt, I finally sat up and decided it was time to stop bawling and figure out what to do next. Our brave soldiers didn't lay down and die, so I wasn't gonna wave the white flag either. Levi Battle wasn't surrendering without a fight. The afternoon sun was sinking fast, and it seemed to me I had only two good choices left.

I could try getting back to the train station in Fayetteville and buy myself a ticket out of town. Use up all the money from Uncle Otis and Aunt Odella to ride as far north as I could go.

Or I could stay where I was and figure out how to get to my daddy and Camp Mackall—although I had no earthly idea where I'd ended up after all my running.

While I sat there, making up my mind, a glare of sunlight suddenly bounced off the windshield of a truck turning down the road and coming toward me. Sinking lower into the weeds, I started praying hard to God, Jesus, the Holy Spirit, Moses, Aunt Odella, and all the other righteous people I could name that the truck wasn't chasing after me. Finally it got near enough for me to see the color of the arm poking out of the open driver's window. Brown. Not white.

Heck, I just about melted into the ground with relief.

Standing up cautiously from where I'd been hidden, I waved one hand trying to flag down that rattletrap truck. I must've scared the driver pretty bad because he whipped his head around to stare wide-eyed at me as he passed. Wheels skidded to a sudden stop, dust and gravel spraying everywhere. "Sweet mother of Pete, you been shot?" he yelled, still staring.

I'm sure I must've looked like a terrible apparition rising up from that weedy field with my purple-stained shirt and ruined trousers. No doubt about it, Aunt Odella woulda been furious at the spectacle I made. The shirt had been one of my good Sunday ones, and it still had all its store buttons.

Taking a step or two toward the truck, I tried explaining how I was from Chicago and how I'd got lost while trying to reach my daddy at Camp Mackall. Didn't breathe a word about stumbling into that store in Fayetteville.

"You come all the way from Chicago?" The driver whistled through his teeth. He was wearing a straw hat with a raggedy white goose feather stuck in the brim. Looked like somebody who worked in the dirt all day. Soil still clung to his fingernails, and the truck's steering wheel was covered with dark palm prints of earth.

"Shoot, I never been outside North Carolina. I never

even seen a big city." The man pointed at my clothes. "See, I could tell by your clothes you wasn't from around here. When I first spotted you standing by the road, I figured you was a city fellow who got into some bad kind of trouble and got dragged out here and shot. I said to myself, 'Don't even stop, Amos Broadway. Don't you even think twice about stopping and getting stuck in somebody else's mess that don't concern you a-tall.' Good thing I did, right?"

He studied me for a minute. "How old's you?"

I lied. "Fifteen."

"Shoot." His head wagged back and forth. "I thought you looked real young. All the way from Chicago to here and not even being sixteen."

Not even being fifteen, I thought.

He waved his arm toward the back of the old farm truck, which was filled with a mound of potatoes. "Come around to the other side and I'll take you to Mackall. I got this load to deliver there anyhow. You'll wear out your feet trying to walk there from here. It's a good ways down the road."

Well, it wasn't Captain Midnight and his Secret Squadron, but I wasn't gonna complain.

I climbed onto the passenger seat, being careful to avoid some of the nasty-looking springs that were poking up through its torn cushions. Probably give you lockjaw or something worse if you sat on them. Easing down real gingerly, I slid my suitcase in front of my knees. A large scrap of cardboard covered the floor under my feet, and I could just make out the words HOL-RYE WAFERS printed on it. Right away, I thought of Aunt Odella, who always bought boxes and boxes of those bone-dry crackers, saying they were good for the digestion. Also they were cheap. I wondered if maybe that piece of cardboard was a sign she was worrying about me. Well, she needed to worry a lot harder, in my opinion.

The driver stuck out his hand. "I'm Amos Broadway, but almost everybody around here calls me Show."

Took my brain a minute to work out the connection: Show and Broadway, that is. To be honest, the driver looked like the last person on earth who'd use a nickname like Show. You'd expect somebody called Show to be strutting around a big city in one of those new baggy suits all the jazz cats were wearing. Not to be some skinny, plain-looking farmer with faded overalls and knots of hair springing out from under his hat.

Show studied me, still trying to figure out what was all over my clothes, I think. "You got a different shirt with you?" he said finally. "If the guards at the post get a glimpse of you riding with me, they gonna think the worst and prob'ly not let me in."

Opening up the suitcase, I pulled out a clean shirt from the ones Aunt Odella had carefully folded and packed, and stuck the other in a rolled-up ball on the top. Tried not to think about what had happened back at the store.

"All that other shirt needs is a good scrubbing," Show

offered, wanting to be helpful, I guess. When I didn't answer, he started up the motor, and after a few coughs the truck lurched down the road churning up big clouds of dust behind us. I watched the field where I'd been hiding disappear in those clouds, glad to see it go. Tell you the truth, the farther away we got from Fayetteville, the better I felt. I felt so good I ate half a pork sandwich from Show and drank the whole thermos of lemonade he offered me as we drove.

By the time we finally reached the army post, it was getting close to dusk. The truck was traveling through a shadowy woods and Show was yawning about every five minutes and picking boredly at the dirt under his fingernails when suddenly—outta absolute nowhere—an airplane the size of a city block sailed right above the pine trees. I nearly jumped out of my own skin, it startled me so bad. Just from pure instinct and all our air raid drills back in Chicago, I ducked.

Show glanced over at me and grinned. "That plane's on our side," he said, not even flinching. "We're comin' up on Mackall now."

After that, it was like we'd been dropped straight into a newsreel from the front lines. You could hear machine guns rattling louder and louder and the heavy thump of what sounded like artillery firing somewhere in the distance. More airplanes soared over the trees in front of us, heading toward their airstrips. One C-47 after another. Almost could have touched the warm bellies of some of them. It was something to see.

Next thing you know, Show was pulling up to a chain-link gate with a plain square sign announcing CAMP MACK-ALL in white letters. When I saw those words, my heart started hammering so loudly, I could hardly hear myself think. What was I gonna say to my father now that I was about to see him? Did I even remember what he looked like? Should I take out the snapshot of him and sneak a quick glance just to remind myself?

While Show was checking with the guard, I tried to get myself shaped up. Criminy, I was a mess. My hair stank of cinders and the Vaseline I'd worn on my head back in Chicago hadn't done any amount of good. Tried smoothing out my shirt so it would look more decent, and then one of the buttons on my sleeves popped off. *Heck.* Jammed the sleeves back up to my elbows again. My daddy would have to see me like the train wreck I was.

Coming around the truck, Show leaned in my open window and asked me if I recalled what part of the army my daddy was serving in. I knew his unit was called the 555th since I'd written those numbers on a lot of envelopes, let me tell you. Told Show their nickname was the Triple Nickles because of the fives. I probably shouldn't have added how they jumped outta airplanes because Show's eyebrows rose up doubtfully. "Never heard of any colored fellows in the paratroops before, but I'll go back again and check with the guard."

There was a lot of pointing and shrugging and head shaking before Show returned. I didn't have a good feeling watching the conversation. He slid back into his seat and started the truck before telling me, "Guard's new. But he says he don't know nothing about any Negroes at Mackall training with the airborne. Even if it were true—which he don't think it is—he says your daddy'd be bunked with the colored service troops just like everybody else. So that's where I'm gonna drop you off."

Once the gate swung open, Show pushed the pedal to the floor and headed down the road fast, as if he was anxious to get where he was going. Or maybe he was ready to be rid of me, who knows. You could hear the potatoes in the back tumbling together as we sailed around the curves. All they'd need was a little gravy and butter after he was done.

There were army buildings on both sides of the road. I caught glimpses of long rows of one-story sheds and barracks with large white letters and numbers painted on them. Passed a couple of airstrips stretching across the open fields, and all kinds of military buses and trucks roared past us as we drove, kicking up so much dust we had to stop and wipe off the windshield twice. Finally Show swung onto a narrow road among some trees and came to a halt in front of a group of barracks scattered in a gloomy pine woods.

I stared through the windshield at the collection of

dumpy buildings, trying not to seem too shocked. They were nothing but long sheds on concrete blocks. Walls covered in wrinkly black tar paper. Here and there, rusty stovepipes stuck up through the roofs, and there wasn't a pane of glass in any of the windows, only screens. Don't know what kinda place I expected to find my daddy living in, but I sure never pictured him being a U.S. Army soldier in a lonely tar-paper shack.

"Here we are," Show said, nodding at the barracks.

Still feeling kinda stunned, I eased open my door and jumped out. Big pinecones the size of mortar shells covered the ground everywhere you looked. As my feet landed on the soil, a smell like Christmas came drifting up, which made me start missing my good life back in Chicago. Started thinking about how me and Archie and the rest of the neighborhood gang would have snowball fights in the winter that could make your face sting for hours. How Uncle Otis would always bring us gifts on Christmas Day and Aunt Odella would always tell him he'd spent too much.

Swallowing that cold lump of memories right back down, I yanked my suitcase outta the truck. No time for feeling sorry. A bunch of bugs swarmed around my face like they were trying to cheer me up. Gave them a good hard swat.

Keeping the motor running, Show leaned across the seat to give me directions. "These are the colored barracks I was talking about. You just ask and I'm sure you'll find your daddy in one of them." He glanced around, probably noticing, like me, how silent everything seemed for a busy army post. "Looks like the fellows ain't back from chow yet. But they gonna be heading back soon. You just hang around for a few minutes and they'll be here before you know it." Giving me a wide, unconcerned smile, Show reached out his grimy hand to shake mine. "All right now, Amos Broadway's gotta be on his way. People's waiting. You take care now, y'hear?"

I closed the passenger door reluctantly. "Thanks for the ride."

"No trouble." The brown arm gave a friendly goodbye wave as Show's truck made a beeline down the road, potatoes rolling, and left me standing in the woods by myself.

I wasn't sure what time it was, but the sun had sunk behind the trees, and it seemed kinda late to be eating chow. Food was one of my father's favorite letter topics. He enjoyed giving us all the details of how the army could ruin any decent meal on earth. How they'd serve you a beautiful slice of meatloaf—and then dump a load of watery butterscotch pudding on top of it. Or you'd get a big spoonful of cold beets plopped in the middle of your warm applesauce. *"Bombs away" on our chow again tonight,* he'd write. A few times during field marches, the army even made the fellows eat horsemeat stew, which woulda turned me off the army, and eating, forever.

Another cloud of insects swarmed around my head, and

I grabbed my suitcase off the ground, figuring I had to make a decision. Couldn't stand around waiting for the bugs to turn me into an army meatloaf.

All the barracks nearby had numbers painted on them. One sounded more familiar than the others: 6301. I'd been reading one of my father's recent letters out loud to Aunt Odella over supper—a funny note where he'd been describing a bad snoring problem in the barracks. *The loudest snoring son of a guns sleep in Barracks 6301,* he'd written. However, I didn't get too far past "son of a guns"—which I'll admit I got a kick out of saying—before Aunt Odella had leaped up, yanked the letter from my hand, and tossed it into the trash in a big huff, saying how her home wasn't the army and we weren't a bunch of foul-mouthed men.

Still grinning about the scene with Aunt Odella, I headed toward the tar-paper shack with 6301 painted on the outside of it. Felt more reluctant as I got closer. Put up some barbed wire and a guard tower, and the whole place coulda passed for a prison camp. There was a pile of rusted coffee cans and other rubbish near the steps leading up to the screen door. A small brown lizard skittered under the cement blocks and disappeared. I kept glancing around, hoping the men would start coming back from chow. The silence filling the pine woods was getting more thick.

Easing open the screen door of 6301, I called out hello. At the same time, an angry wasp came shooting outta the shadows like a kamikaze pilot and just about took off the top of my head. That set me back on my heels, I'm telling you. Seeing that deadly aircraft coming at me. *Criminy.* Once my heart started beating again, I stuck my head carefully back inside the doorway for a quick look around. What I saw inside the barracks made any hope I had fizzle right out and disappear.

There were no blankets on the beds. No uniforms hanging on the hooks. The two rows of bunks in the room were cleared off and empty. Any soldiers who'd been there were long gone.

13. Missing

Feeling real lost, I started down the row of deserted bunks, my footsteps echoing in the emptiness. There weren't many clues about who'd been there—or where they might have gone to. Looked to me like no human being had been around the place in days. I lifted up the lids of the footlockers at the ends of the bunks, checking inside them, but all I found was a torn picture of the movie star Lena Horne and a couple of cigarette wrappers.

And a whole lot of dead wasps, if you want to count them.

At the back of the room were some chairs and a sorry-looking Ping-Pong table with two warped paddles sitting on the top. I sagged into one of the chairs not having a single idea floating around in my brain about what to do next. From the silence outside, you could tell all of the barracks nearby were as deserted as this one. Didn't need to bother looking.

Opening up my suitcase, I dug around until I found the

stack of letters I'd brought from Chicago. Hands shaking, I picked at the knot of red string around them and started shuffling through the pile, wondering if there was something I'd missed. Another name or address, maybe.

The one on top said *Camp Mackall* in the corner of the envelope, no question. The return address was scrawled in my father's familiar handwriting—so light you had to squint to read it—but it was there. Clumsily I sorted through the rest of the stack. Letters slid onto the floor in a mixed-up jumble of weeks and months that I'd never get straightened out again, most likely. All of the recent ones, at least a dozen of them, said Camp Mackall, North Carolina. Wasn't that proof enough I was in the right place?

Could the 555th be in a different part of Mackall? Show had said the guard was new, right? Had he sent us to the wrong barracks? The army post was huge. There were hundreds of buildings, from what I'd seen. Even a guard who'd been there awhile could probably get the directions wrong.

Darker thoughts crept in behind those—such as maybe my father had never been stationed at Camp Mackall in the first place, despite what his letters said. Maybe Archie had been right all along about him being a spy. It was hard to know what to believe in the war. You could listen to radio programs so real you'd swear they were being broadcast straight from the front lines. There'd be the *ack-ack* of machine guns and propellers whirring and all that. When the truth was, the whole show was being made up by actors sitting inside a radio station in Chicago or New York or who knows where. Aunt Odella always said not to put too much faith in what my father wrote, didn't she?

My eyes drifted toward my daddy's photograph sitting on top of the suitcase. Seeing him looking up at me from that frame, with his proud soldier smile and sharp uniform, made me feel like I was being a traitor for letting all the crazy doubts run through my head.

The door at the far end of the barracks suddenly creaked open, startling me.

"Hello?" I called out.

"Somebody in here?" a voice answered, sounding confused.

The rest of the letters slid onto the floor as I shot to my feet before the person in the doorway thought I was causing some kinda trouble by being there. Or in case they were toting a gun. Words fell over each other coming outta my mouth as I tried explaining how I was Levi Battle from south Chicago who'd come to Camp Mackall looking for my father, Lieutenant Charles Battle, and how he was in the paratroops, but nobody seemed real sure of where they were, and how the barracks were empty when I got there.

"I was only waiting to see if anybody came back from chow," I added in a rush. "But it doesn't look like the soldiers are around here since it's already getting dark, so I was just getting ready to leave."

Good grief, I sounded like a complete babbling fool.

"Holy mackerel." A colored soldier came hobbling through the doorway on a bum foot. He looked young—I woulda said maybe just twenty-two or twenty-three. He was thin and lanky, like a speedy length of rope. "You telling me, gospel truth, you are Charlie Battle's son?" he said.

The feeling of relief that the fellow knew who I was talking about—that he'd heard of my father—made my legs start to wobble. For a minute, I was afraid my whole body might slide right onto the floor with all the envelopes and letters. A big alphabetic pile of relief.

Leaning on a cane and walking faster than he probably should have, considering the plaster cast on his left foot, the soldier thumped down the aisle between the empty bunks. "Lemme get a good look at you." He was about as dark black as Uncle Otis, with a wide white smile. Picture a lot of shiny forehead and a friendly river of smiling teeth. That was him.

Throwing his cane down, the soldier reached out and squeezed the sides of my shoulders when he got to where I was standing. "Here I was just stopping by the barracks tonight to make sure the fellows didn't leave nothing important behind. Never thought I'd find a person here. So you're Lieutenant Battle's son?" He squinted at me, trying to look more serious, but the corners of his lips twitched upward. "You're being truthful with me, right?"

Told him I was.

"You just blew into town on the wind?"

"I came on the train. From Chicago."

The soldier couldn't keep his big smile down. It crept across his face. "You just packed up your bags and came down here all by yourself to find Boots?"

"Boots?"

The soldier grinned wider. "Lieutenant Battle—otherwise known as Boots."

I tried not to let on that everybody in the U.S. Army might've known my daddy as Boots, but it was news to me.

"So?" The soldier was still eyeballing me, like he was waiting to hear more details. "Did he know you were coming here?"

Although I was sure it would sound like a made-up piece of fiction, I told him my aunt was the one who had sent me for a visit.

"Uh-huh." He clasped his hands behind his back. "What did you say your first name was again?"

"It's Levi." Being polite, I tried asking him, "What's yours?"

"Ah . . ." He grinned and shook his head. "Legs don't get to ask questions around here. Not until you get yourself a pair of nice jump boots like these."

The brown leather boot the soldier was wearing on his good foot slid forward so I could examine it more closely, I guess, and be impressed. Tight laces crisscrossed each other at perfect angles all the way up and the soldier's trouser leg was bloused just as neatly over the top. Honestly, the boot's shiny round toe was so slick with polish you coulda used it as a mirror.

"How about it, Legs?" the soldier said. "Would you jump into the sky to get yourself a pair of these beauties?"

I remember thinking maybe I hadn't heard him right.

"What?" I said.

The soldier gave me an odd look. As if I was the next village idiot. "Don't tell me you never once thought about what it'd be like to follow in your daddy's footsteps and jump outta airplanes like we do. Get your wings and jump boots and all that. Heck, I was guessing you probably ran off from Chicago to come down here and join up with us, right?" He was razzing me now, but I was miles away by then, still trying to gather up the pieces of what I'd just heard.

My father jumps out of airplanes. Real airplanes. Into the sky.

I stared at the soldier's polished boot as if it might lift off and go soaring around the room on its own. *Son of a gun, the stories my father had told us were all true?* Aunt Odella would have a holy fit when she heard the news. She'd probably pray for a solid year without stopping. God would be sorry he ever started listening to her.

"Your daddy don't just *jump* outta airplanes either." The soldier got a sly look in his eyes, like he was having even more fun. "Sometimes, he's the one who closes the door, you know."

Closes the door? Good God. My father jumped out of airplanes—and then reached back and closed the door?

A slow-cooking smile spread across the soldier's face like he knew I was swallowing every word he said. He let me think for a while before he added, "Last one out. It means the last one to jump outta the plane. Nobody closes the door." He patted my shoulder. "Shoot, you got a lot to learn, Legs, if you wanna do this for a living someday."

"Levi," I said, thinking maybe he hadn't heard my name before.

"Naw, everybody who don't jump is called legs around here. You're Legs." Lifting his cane again, the soldier rapped it against his bum leg. "Me, I'm half legs right now. Landed on a tree stump in February when we were coming down in the dark and busted my doggone foot in two places. Haven't jumped since." He stuck out his warm hand to shake mine. "Anyhow, I'm Calvin Thomas, one of your daddy's outfit. The Nickles. The troopers. The jumpers. Whatever you want to call us. But everybody around here knows me as Cal."

His face grew serious as he glanced down at my suitcase, which was still open on the floor with my daddy's picture sitting right on top, letters scattered all over the place. There was an uncomfortable long silence before he said, "You traveled all this way hoping to see him, huh?"

Right then I knew it wasn't gonna happen. I been left

behind enough times to be able to tell bad news is coming before it does. Put on my silent movie face and waited for whatever I was gonna be told next. In the distance, a roll of thunder rumbled as if a storm was moving in from somewhere. Cal rubbed the handle of his cane with his thumb, making little circles. Cleared his throat.

"Well, knowing your daddy like I does, I'm sure he woulda given anything in the world to be here today to see you. Anything in the world. But the honest truth is, the men got orders from the army and had to ship out real sudden. The whole battalion left. You only missed them by a little." He paused as if he was weighing how much more to say. "They pulled outta here by train early yesterday morning."

Yesterday.

Now, I'll admit missing my father by one day stung a little. No doubt about it. Twenty-four hours was a hard fact to swallow. Tried not to let Cal hear the sigh slipping out of me as I put the blame square on Queen Bee Walker's curse again—for being the first to leave and causing all the rest.

Looking down, Cal kept rubbing his thumb on the cane. "I'm real sorry to be the one to give you that bad news. I'm sure it ain't easy to hear after all your trouble coming this far."

The rumbling outside grew louder.

"Their orders were top-secret—so even if your daddy wanted to, he wouldn't have been able to tell you much. None of them knew their destination. Probably still don't.

That's the army for you—you don't find out where you're going until you get there." He glanced toward the windows, where bright lightning was starting to flash. "My best guess is, they're heading to the Pacific to fight the Japs. Or they could be on their way to another U.S. Army post, who knows. Once my foot heals up, I'll probably get my orders to join them somewhere too. All I can tell you for certain is their train left Fayetteville yesterday going north. Probably heading north first, then west to the Pacific."

I kept acting like my Big Man self. Like it didn't much matter to me. It was nothing but a fist in the stomach that was supposed to hurt but didn't.

"He moves around a lot." I gave one of my careless shrugs. What I didn't say was how you couldn't catch up with my daddy before the war either. Back when I was in grammar school, he used to drive his old jalopy all over Illinois selling encyclopedias outta the backseat of it. Stuck me with Granny while he was gone. Just passing the time, I used to play with one of the sets he kept at home. Could still remember the shiny gold edges of those fancy encyclopedias and the snow-white pages that felt like cotton sheets. I used to mix up the volumes and then put them in order as fast as I could, A to Z. Maybe I couldn't make my daddy stick around, but I could put the whole world in order in ten seconds flat, let me tell you.

Later on, my daddy gave up selling books and joined one of the Negro League's baseball teams, so he was gone then too. I remember how I always tried hiding in his automobile before he left, hoping he'd forget and take me along with him.

It never worked.

"You in here, Levi?" he'd holler, and pretend to look everywhere. Tap on the hood loudly. Blow the horn. Look under the seats. Then, after he found me curled up in the back—where I always was—he'd pick me up and throw my puny self over his shoulder. I could still recall the minty aftershave scent of his neck as I bounced along, teeth rattling, miles above the ground. He'd carry me up to the front steps of Granny's apartment building, plop me next to her, and leave us sitting in a cloud of mint. Funny how I recalled that smell more strongly than anything. How my daddy had a mint-smelling neck and arms the color of buckeyes. What stupid things to remember.

"You all right, buddy?" Cal looked at me with real sympathy.

A strong gust of wind caught the screen door at the front of the barracks just then and slammed it back against the wall, making both of us jump. A real bright zap of lightning lit up the trees outside.

Wincing a little, Cal bent down on one knee and started clumsily trying to scoop up the letters and envelopes that had slid all over. "Let's get your things picked up and we'll bug outta here before the storm. You can come and stay with me and Peaches tonight until we figure out what to do."

I didn't even ask who Peaches was. Or where we were going. As Aunt Odella would say, sometimes you're too far past caring to care. By the time we got out of the barracks and squeezed into Cal's truck, it was pitch black and pouring rain. With all the lightning and thunder exploding above the trees, it coulda been the London blitz. Cal hunched over the steering wheel, nose to the windshield almost, and roared down the winding roads of Camp Mackall as if hell was on fire. He was a crazy driver. Way worse than Uncle Otis, and that's saying a lot.

"If me and your daddy were setting inside a C-47 right now, this is what we'd call flying into the soup." Cal grinned like a big kid, sending me careening into his shoulder as he swerved around a tree branch as big around as my leg. "Sorry about that." Popping a piece of red licorice in his mouth, he kept on flying through the storm and rain without stopping.

Even with all that danger, I couldn't keep my heavy eyes open.

I remember Cal offering me a stick of licorice. I don't remember eating it.

I remember a lady's voice, much later, saying something about boots.

I remember walking through a room full of webs. And that's all.

14. Room of Webs

Next morning, I woke up and thought I was floating through a sky full of parachutes. Thought my daddy and all the other soldiers were dropping down for a visit. Above my head, a sky full of white squares flapped gently in the breeze. It took me a minute to realize it was laundry I was looking at, not parachutes. I was lying on a lumpy mattress on the floor of a room full of clotheslines strung across the ceiling like webs.

A creaking sound near my feet made me realize I wasn't alone either. Hoisted myself up on one elbow to look at who was there. A woman sat in a rocking chair a few feet away. Eyes closed, she was easing the rocker back and forth with one bare toe on the linoleum. The lady coulda been an African queen with how regal and peaceful she looked. Long, straight nose. Shiny mahogany-colored cheekbones. Black hair swept up from her forehead. A faded green housedress the color of a summer garden.

As the lady rocked back and forth, you also couldn't help noticing the huge round stomach that swelled out in front of her, taking up most of her lap. Her hands rested across the top of it. I'm telling you, she looked like she'd gone and swallowed a pumpkin.

"You 'wake already?" The brown eyes flew open suddenly and glanced over at me. The woman's heels touched down quick on the floor and the rocking stopped. "Thought you were gonna sleep till next week with the way you were lying there so quiet-like on the floor. Not even MawMaw's crazy rooster woke you up." The lady's face eased slowly into a warm smile. Her voice had a soft drawl to it.

"You're probably just looking around this place, thinking to yourself, 'Where in the sweet and sugar world am I? All this laundry hanging up? And who's that fat dumpy lady sitting over there in that rockin' chair?'" The woman stood up slowly, big pumpkin belly leaving first, and came closer. "I'm Peaches. You met my husband, Cal, last night. He's the one who brung you here. I'm sorry you didn't get a good look at our pretty town of Southern Pines when you came in last night. Probably seemed liked forever driving in that bad storm." She glanced toward the one window in the small bedroom. "You ain't real far away from civilization here, though, even if it feels like it. Only about an hour's drive to the bright lights and big city of Fayetteville."

That news didn't bring me much comfort, but I didn't let on.

The lady smiled and patted her stomach. "Oh, and this here is baby-about-to-be-born."

I eyed the big stomach uneasily and hoped baby-about-to-be-born would stay where it was for a while. I wasn't a big fan of babies. Seemed like Archie's family always had one or two crawling around with nasty things coming outta their noses, you know what I mean? The lady must've noticed my uncomfortable look because she switched the subject fast. "So, I hear you're Charlie Battle's son, right?"

"Yes ma'am."

Maybe she was just being nice, but she said she remembered him talking about having a son back in Chicago and how there was a clear resemblance in our looks. That she coulda picked out our similarities anywhere. "You got his chin, no doubt about it. And you smile the same way. And your eyes are exactly alike," she said, studying my face for a minute. "They got the same serious look your daddy's eyes always does. Is he worrying about something—or just thinking? You never know for sure. A man of few words, that's him." Reaching upward, Peaches started plucking some of the laundry from the clotheslines above her head and kept on talking. "So, how about hitting a baseball? You as good as your daddy?"

I shook my head. "No ma'am."

Like I said, I didn't inherit much of the Battle talent for athletics. My batting was average and Archie, short as he was, had a better throwing arm than I did. I got the tall part of the Battle family and Queen Bee Walker's ear for being in tune when you sang—although I'm not sure how those two gifts were supposed to be useful to me.

Peaches laughed at my answers. "You as humble as your daddy is, I can tell already. He always insists he's nothing special and then he tears the leather off the ball with one swing. When Cal's on his team, they always win big against the other army boys. My Cal's a catcher."

With an impressive tower of laundry tucked under her chin, Peaches turned toward the door and I jumped up to open it, like the gentleman I been raised to be.

"I know how much you boys like to eat," she said over her shoulder. "So I got breakfast waiting in the kitchen whenever you're ready for something. Kitchen's down the hall on the left. Washroom's at the end. I'll leave you be for a while." As the pillar of laundry and stomach tottered through the doorway, I gotta admit I held my breath until it was safely down the hall.

Peaches and Cal's house was roomy but completely empty of people. I gathered that much information on my short stroll down the hallway. Like the barracks, everything had the air of being recently left—and I sure recognize that feeling when I come across it. There was a row of empty towel hooks nailed on the bathroom door with no towels on them, except for a frayed blue one with somebody's initials. A chipped ceramic bowl full of Ivory soap bits sat next to the sink. Used them to wash off the grime of the trip. As I wandered back down the hall, I could hear the cheerful din of cooking pouring out of the kitchen. Made me miss Aunt Odella's fried chicken already and I hadn't even been gone three days.

"Come on in and have a seat." Standing at a cast-iron range that looked like a relic from the Civil War, Peaches waved a spatula in my direction. The kitchen was small, but you could tell somebody had tried to fix it up nice. There was a red-checked tablecloth on the table and a jar of droopy flowers. Curtains on the window. And a calendar showing a tropical scene of palm trees and water. Which is something you'd never see on a wall in Chicago, that's for sure.

I pulled out one of the four kitchen chairs and sat down, feeling kinda uncomfortable sitting in a kitchen—in a house—that wasn't mine. My knees caught the bottom of the wobbly table and nearly pulled off the nice tablecloth by accident. Good grief, what a mess that woulda been.

Peaches chuckled at my choice of chairs. "You know that's the one your daddy always chose whenever he came over here for Sunday dinner with the other fellows from Mackall. Always that chair at the end of the table. Funny how you picked the same one."

I couldn't help casting my eyes around their kitchen as if some other sign of him might still be hanging around. Wondered what were the chances of traveling all the way to

North Carolina and ending up in the same spot where my father had eaten Sunday dinner? Half my brain insisted this coincidence must be a good sign. The other half said, *Who the heck cares?* because he still wasn't around.

Standing at the range, stirring a bubbling frypan of sausage gravy, Peaches started lobbing a bunch of questions at me. I had the feeling she and Cal must've come up with a whole list of them the night before, after he'd brought me here, and now she was sorting through the pile, one by one. "First thing I want to know"—she reached for some flour and dumped a powdery handful in the gravy—"did Boots know you was coming down here or not?"

See, there was the same tricky question Cal had asked me. No, my father didn't know I was coming—but it wasn't exactly his fault. Or mine. Not sure what made-up answer to give, I finally admitted he didn't have any idea.

Peaches frowned. "Cal told me your aunt was the one who sent you down here. She's one of your daddy's folks, then? His sister?"

I nodded, picturing Aunt Odella at the train station again—those sad old shoes she was wearing, and everything about her looking worn and tired.

"So she sent you here, not knowing your daddy had gone and shipped out. She thought because he was training down here, you could drop by and pay him a visit, right?"

I mumbled, "Yes ma'am."

Not saying the visit was supposed to be permanent, of course.

Peaches kept stirring and I cast a desperate glance toward the pan of sausage gravy, hoping it would cook faster. Peaches must've seen my look because she slid a steaming bowl of gravy and a plate of biscuits in front of me soon afterward.

Man oh man, it was like going straight to food heaven.

She wasn't giving up on the conversation, though. While I filled my plate, Peaches kept talking. "Well, we don't want your aunt worrying about you. Soon as we can, me and Cal will let her know what happened, and we'll get you back on a train to Chicago."

I tried to be as careful as a soft-boiled egg with what I said next. "Not meaning to be rude, ma'am," I mumbled between mouthfuls, "but I don't believe my aunt wants me back right now."

"What?" Peaches stopped what she was doing and gave me a hard stare. "You in some kinda trouble back home, Levi? That why she sent you here—for your daddy to straighten you out?" The lady looked like a symbol of female righteousness, standing there glaring at me with the crusty gravy spatula still in her hand. "You tell me the real story straight out. Right now. I got four younger brothers and I don't put up with no nonsense."

Heck, where was I supposed to begin? Way back with how my life was always about leaving? Or with Aunt Odella deciding my time was up? Mostly I just wanted to make it quick before my gravy got cold. So I started with how my aunt often got stuck taking care of everybody in our family and ended with how it wasn't my daddy's fault he had to make a living, and then the war had come along, and the army had shipped him from one place to the next.

I could see my story was having an effect on Peaches, but not the one I expected. As I talked, her whole face took on the appearance of a warrior queen. The spatula in her hand started to resemble a deadly weapon. "That ain't right," she said after I was done. "Your aunt sending you down here like a cast-off because she's tired of taking care of you. Who does that to a boy? Especially when your daddy's been sacrificing and serving his country these past three years."

I shrugged and told the lady how I was thirteen now and fine with taking care of myself. Hadn't learned to walk yesterday, you know.

"Thirteen ain't grown-up in my book." The cast-iron pan clanged heavily on the range as Peaches moved it from one side to the other. "Me and Cal will have ourselves a little talk. Your daddy wouldn't want us sending you back home if your people don't want you there."

Well, Aunt Odella wasn't that bad, I wanted to say. She wouldn't fry me for lunch if I came back, anyhow.

The lady eased into the chair across from me, her angry eyes still popping like sparkle-fire sticks. Next to the table was a shabby icebox, and Peaches reached over to open it.

Scooping out a handful of ice chips from the top, she offered me one and folded the rest into a dish towel to hold on her neck.

"It's gonna be a hot one today," she said after a long silence.

I was eyeing the gravy bowl left on the table, wondering about taking thirds, but she nodded toward the screen door that separated the kitchen from a little side porch. Flies were already collecting on it. "Why don't you go and do some exploring while Cal's away this morning? We got a real pretty creek running through our town. Called McDeeds. Maybe you could try some fishing or catch some crawdads or something like that. Cal's got a pole outside if you want one."

I'm sure Peaches was only trying to be helpful and make me feel at home, but I wasn't keen about exploring anywhere, not after all the things that had happened to me the day before. Honestly, I'd just as soon stay put and not set one foot in a world where people would shoot you over a soda pop. Took my time chewing on that ice chip and tried to change the conversation.

"This your own house?" I said, glancing around.

"Naw." Peaches smiled and shook her head. "We only rent one room. For a while there were eight of us army wives renting the house and sharing this tiny kitchen. Couple of children running around too, if you can believe that. We were like pickles in a jar." She looked around as if the people were still there. "With so many of the soldiers shipping out this spring, all of the families have been moving out and going home. Can't get used to the quiet these days. Guess it's just us until some new folks move in."

The other soldiers had their families with them? Hearing that news kinda set me back a little, and I think Peaches must've seen the look crossing my face as I put two and two together, because she hurried on to say, "It was just a few little ones here and there. Nobody as old as you."

Which just goes to show you—not all mothers take off and leave their children behind.

Peaches waved her hand toward the screen door again. "Go on and take a wander around outside this morning. You don't want to be cooped up with me all day." Putting the cold cloth against her pretty forehead, she closed her eyes as if she wanted some peace and quiet. Not wanting to wear out my welcome, I unfolded my legs reluctantly and stood up.

Beyond the kitchen door, you could see the yard already shimmering in the morning heat. It didn't look real friendly. An overgrown shrub crowded the porch steps. A few big pinecones lay scattered here and there on the open stretch of sandy dirt. I stood at the door for a good few minutes before getting up the nerve to ask how white folks in Southern Pines felt about colored folks.

Peaches laughed. "Ain't no white folks living around here," she said. "This is the west side of town. West Southern Pines. White folks live over on the east side, where the sun rises and sets on money. You'll know it if you happen to stumble over there. Golf courses. Big fancy houses with tile roofs and iron gates. Flowers like something outta a magazine. All you have to remember is the clay roads are always our roads. Paved roads are theirs. The creek's mostly ours too. You'll be fine. Around here, white and colored folks are polite enough to each other, not like some other places."

Paved roads for whites. Clay for coloreds. White water. Colored water. Criminy, who could keep it all straight? The South was a complete mystery.

Peaches told me it was simple to find the creek. She drew a map on the checkered tablecloth with her finger. Go down the road they lived on, which was called Stephens. Turn left at the house on the corner with the chinaberry tree. Walk down the hill toward the bridge and the railroad tracks, and there's the creek. Can't miss it.

Just being polite, I took Peaches's advice and headed for the creek later that morning. Wearing one of the school shirts Aunt Odella had packed, I swear I stood out like a target with my brown skin and my starched white shirt. Good God. I coulda been one of Jim Crow's signs, walking around. COLORED.

If it were up to me, I woulda rather stretched out on the shady porch that wrapped around Peaches and Cal's house and taken a snooze under the drying pillowcases flapping there. I didn't give a darn about exploring a creek. As I started down the dusty road, my body was a walking ball of knots.

On both sides of the street you could see small tin-roofed houses with wide porches and square dirt yards around them. Some of the houses sagged like tired grannies on their concrete blocks, but others had nice victory gardens and fresh-painted outsides. I could hear voices as I walked, but I didn't spot a living soul. Couldn't help gawking at some of the odd-looking pine trees growing in the yards around me, though. Never saw trees like them before. They reminded me of something from a cartoon, with their skinny trunks and hairbrush branches. Guess I was so caught up with staring at those crazy trees, I almost missed the sound of somebody calling my name.

"Levi?"

At first I thought it might've been a radio playing. Nobody knew me down there in Southern Pines, did they? I moved a little faster, my fists bumping like rocks against my sides.

But the voice came through loud and clear the second time.

"That you, Levi Battle? Don't you go passing by my house without saying a good morning. I been setting here all this time waiting to meet you."

Heck, I didn't know what to think.

15. Keeper of Secrets

I'm sure I must've looked like a complete fool, standing smack in the middle of the road, turning around as I tried to figure out where the voice was coming from. The closest house looked like a run-down shack. It didn't even appear lived-in. There wasn't a lick of paint on the place. A jungle of overgrown vines and big clumps of baskets swallowed up the front porch. Scruffy chickens pecked in the yard.

"Boy, up here." Among the vines and baskets, there was a sudden flash of color as something moved. Thought maybe I saw a hand waving. "I'm setting up on the porch," a voice called. "Gate's open."

Never noticed the gate until then. Right in front of me was a plain wooden gate with a faded sign hanging on it: OPEN. BASKETS FOR SALE. Still feeling cautious, I stepped carefully toward the porch, squinting into its green, dapply shadows. Somebody was sitting there, I could tell that. Only the person didn't seem to have much shape.

As I got closer, I could see the outlines of a lady who might've stepped straight outta slavery times from the way she looked. The woman was sitting in an old cane-backed rocker, and she wore a shapeless gown made of mismatched remnants—as if a bunch of cast-offs had been turned into somebody's idea of a dress. A red cloth turban was knotted around her head. As I reached the porch steps, the turban leaned forward and two eyes peered at me from a face so wrinkled, the eyes coulda been mistaken for knotholes in a tree. How those little bitty eyes could see, I don't know.

"You Levi?"

"Yes ma'am," I answered, wondering how in the world my name had already reached this lady. Word didn't even travel that fast in Aunt Odella's building, where the walls were paper.

"Heard about you already," the woman said, leaning back in her ancienty chair. "You come down here looking for your daddy, ain't that right?"

Her words ran together worse than slow syrup pouring. Wasn't sure I caught half of what she said, but I nodded anyhow.

"You been looking for him for a long while, I hear."

No, I'd only left Chicago on Saturday, I told the lady.

The old woman shook her head. "Way longer than that you been looking for your daddy. Way longer than that, I'd say."

I gotta admit, those words rattled me. Couldn't tell if

she was just an old lady babbling nonsense or if she knew about my life somehow, or if I was hearing every single word wrong. She reminded me of something you'd find in a museum—something that you'd stare at and wonder what the heck it was. She was an odd, talking artifact.

"Folks around here call me MawMaw Sands," the woman continued, picking up a half-finished basket near her feet and licking the end of her finger. Working on the top edge of her basket, she started pushing a flat, green reed through the woven coils using the sharpened handle of a spoon to make holes. Then she'd pull the reed through the holes and wrap it around the top. It was hard to tear your eyes away from watching the rhythmic pattern of her dark hands working.

"Almost nothing in this world I don't know about." The woman's eyes flashed up at me quickly, two tiny pinpricks of light. "You ask any folks around the Pines and they all know me. White, black, brown, purple. Don't care what color they is. I been here way longer than anybody else. I seen it all and then some." The old fingers kept working as the woman talked. "Heard you been searching for your daddy since you was a little child. Ain't that right?"

Now the real creepy-crawlies were popping out all over my arms. How did she know all these things about me? I eased up two of the sagging porch steps, trying not to look as all-out curious as I was, but I'm somebody who likes proof, you know what I mean? Had she met my father, maybe? And what other sorry stories about me had she been told?

There was a faint smell of vanilla as you got closer to the top of her steps, and I swear there must've been an entire squadron of fat bumblebees buzzing around the purple flowers dangling from her porch. Had to keep ducking out of the way because I did not want to get hit by any of that deadly yellow and black ammo, let me tell you.

When I reached the top step, the old woman put the basket in her lap and rested her elbows on the arms of her chair. "So, you come from Chicago," she said, closing her eyes for a minute. "Busy place, I hear. Lots of hustle and bustle going on."

"Yes ma'am." I nodded, still wondering how she knew.

"So that makes you a northern boy. A Yankee. A *brown* Yankee." Her eyes snapped open and she chuckled at her own joke. "Let's see—you're smart but quiet. Big and strong, but not as tough as your last name sounds. And you got a place in this world but no home."

Well, she might've been right about some things, but she was dead wrong about the rest. Gotta admit it burned me up a little to hear the old lady making judgments about how tough I was or wasn't when she didn't even know me. But the remark about me not having a home and all that— well, those words were tiptoeing close enough to the truth that it gave me more goosebumps on top of the ones I already had. I was convinced she'd talked to my daddy.

"You know Lieutenant Charles Battle?" I asked.

Couldn't tell if the lady missed hearing what I asked

or was flat-out ignoring it. Saying nothing, she picked up the basket from her lap and started working again, her thin lips staying as tight as the coils she was making. The rocker creaked back and forth in the silence.

Tell you what, the curiosity was killing me.

Aunt Odella probably woulda said it was impolite to keep on pestering—she was an old lady and the morning was warm—but I tried repeating my father's name, louder this time, and asked MawMaw Sands if she'd heard about him leaving town with the other soldiers.

This time the old lady nodded and glanced toward the side of the porch. "Go on over and get that basket for me." She pointed at one that looked more like a round cookie jar than a basket. It was made of coils of dark and light grass with small handles on each side and a woven lid covering the top. "That's a sweetgrass basket you're holding," the old woman said as I carried it to her. "All my baskets is made of sweetgrass. They all got names. That one's called Keeper of Secrets. Go ahead and open it. See what you find."

I lifted the woven lid reluctantly. Who knows what would be hiding inside, waiting to jump out and scare the daylights outta me, right?

But the basket was empty. Just some bits of grass and a vanilla smell, and that's it. "Nothing in there," I told her. Tried not to sound irritated at being taken for a big fool.

MawMaw Sands plunked her weaving spoon down in her lap and gave me a glinty stare. "Now, if there was to be something in there, it wouldn't be called Keeper of Secrets, would it?" She jabbed one finger in my direction. "That's what I'm trying to tell you. War is full of secrets. Some you can see and some you can't. That's the hard part—believing what you can see and trusting what you can't."

Right then, the only thing I believed was that Maw-Maw Sands was making up absolute jib-jabbering nonsense. Showing me an empty basket and telling me it was full of secrets—only you couldn't see them? Well, Archie mighta fallen for that trick, but not me. Half the time he believed everything he saw in the movies was real too. One time he dragged me around Chicago searching for a gangster's stash of gold. Nearly got both of us flattened by a train. Me, I was somebody who liked proof. Don't try and ask me to believe something dumb.

Still, I tried not to make it too obvious that I didn't buy one word of the story. She was an old lady, after all, and you don't want to be disrespectful. Setting the basket back down on the porch, I pretended to take a minute to study some of the other ones hanging there, like maybe I was interested in them too.

Brushing bits of grass off her lap, the old woman came shuffling over. "All these baskets here got names," she said. "This one's called Cat Chasing Tail." She reached for a basket with a thick coil twisted around the outside and showed me how you couldn't tell where the coil started and ended as it circled around and around the basket.

"And this one's Signs and Wonders." She held up a flat, star-shaped basket about the size of a dinner plate. "Made it after I saw a shooting star land in my garden one night and grow into a tree."

Didn't believe that story either.

Next to the star basket hung a heart-shaped one.

"Love," MawMaw Sands answered before I asked.

I gave a loud snort.

"Now, love ain't all bad, Levi Battle." The old woman's face crinkled into a papery smile. "You just wait and see."

Uh-huh. I hadn't forgotten about Margie with the Margarine Hair, and the crumbled cake that didn't even make it from Kansas to Washington, D.C. Or my daddy and Queen Bee Walker. Love was a mess. Nobody could convince me otherwise.

While we were standing there talking, a fancy Packard pulled up, all shiny and sparkling in the sunshine. A white lady stepped outta the passenger side and came up the dirt path to the porch. She was wearing a straw hat the size of a turkey platter and high-heeled shoes. They tottered sideways on the uneven ground. "You sell baskets?" she called out, as if she didn't have eyes and couldn't see them hanging everywhere.

"Yes ma'am, I does," MawMaw Sands answered back, real polite.

The lady sashayed up to the porch and took forever studying all the baskets, holding them up to the light and turning them back and forth in her hands like she was buying diamonds instead of dried-up weeds.

MawMaw Sands didn't say a word about the baskets' names while the lady looked, just eased back down in her chair and worked on one real intently, humming a little to herself to fill the silence. Finally the lady picked out one of the largest ones—a kettle-sized one with all kinds of braided loops and twists all over it.

"This one's my favorite," the lady said. "I'll take it."

"Six dollars," MawMaw Sands told her.

I'm telling you, my eyeballs just about fell out.

Six dollars woulda bought a big part of a war bond to help the troops. Or an entire afternoon and evening of tunes on the bubbling jukebox at Lennie's in Chicago. Or who knows how many half-price double features you could see at the Regal Movie Theater with that kind of money. And the lady was spending it all on a basket.

I watched the woman dig through her pocketbook and pull out six crisp ones from a coin purse full of them. She made Uncle Otis and all his money seem like nothing special. After the lady got back in her car and drove off, I asked MawMaw Sands what the basket she bought was called.

"A Rich Lady and Her Money Is Soon Parted," Maw-Maw Sands said loudly, licking her fingers and laying the dollar bills on her lap one at a time. "That's what I call it, anyhow."

A snort of laughter escaped outta me, and the old lady gave me a sly sideways look before she started chuckling too. Pretty soon we were carrying on so much that the striped cat who'd been sitting peacefully on the porch bolted right over the railing from the noise. "Even the Cat Was Scared Off basket." I waved an arm in the direction of the fleeing cat, and we just about fell over ourselves crying with laughter again. Never did hear the real name of the basket.

I think the laughter must've worn out MawMaw Sands, though, because she got quiet after we were done carrying on and didn't make a move to pick up the basket in her lap. Just flopped her hands over the rocking chair arms, looking suddenly weary. "Hear there's a nice ribbling crick waiting on you," she mumbled, eyes closed.

"What?" I said, not following a word.

Sighing loudly, the old woman opened her eyes and waved her weaving spoon in my direction. "I says, it's about time for you to go ahead and visit that nice cool crick you was on your way to see. McDeeds used to have crawdads the size of Maine lobsters. Probably don't have none of those no more. Been years since I been down there myself. Stop by some other time and visit again, you hear? Gotta get back to my work."

Hunching over her basket again, the lady turned me off

like a radio. Taking a few steps backward, I retreated down the porch steps silently, closing the gate quietly behind me and latching it. Straightened the crooked sign too. Just being polite. It wasn't until I got to the road and looked back at the porch that I realized I'd never told MawMaw Sands I was on my way to the creek.

16. Cool Ribbling Crick

The creek sure was pretty, I gotta admit. Having grown up in the city, maybe it looked better to me than it would have to other folks who were used to that kinda thing. The water was clear and sparkly and ran above a pale orangish sand. Silver minnows the size of Aunt Odella's sewing needles darted back and forth in the shallows.

I leaned over the bridge, looking down, and tried to come up with a sensible opinion about MawMaw Sands. No matter how hard I tried to convince myself otherwise, I had to admit that something about the vine-covered porch had felt strange. Couldn't figure out how the old lady had guessed some of those things about me either. And I swear my ears were still ringing with the hum of those nasty porch bees. *Levi Battle*, I told myself, *you're going completely crazy. Two days in the South and you've lost your ding-donged mind.*

I picked up a warm pebble from the road and tossed it over the side of the wooden bridge, just for something to do.

Listened to its lonely plop in the creek below and weighed how close a person could get to the tempting cool water. Tall weeds covered the sandy banks on either side of the creek, but the idea of jumping down into the tangle of brush made me real uneasy. The dark pistol sticking outta that store-keeper's palm wouldn't leave my mind, you know? Had the jittery feeling of eyes watching me and kept hearing rustling noises in the weeds and that kind of thing.

Staying where I was, I scooped up a handful of pebbles and dropped them one by one into the creek, seeing if I could scatter the minnows. Tried skipping a few of the flat stones, although the bridge was too high and they ended up hitting land instead. Wasted more time than I probably should have on a bunch of rocks before I decided I'd had all the fun I could manage to squeeze outta the morning. Never did find the guts to go any farther than the bridge.

Shoving my hands in my pockets, I ambled back toward Cal and Peaches's house the same way I'd come, kicking up puffs of dusty clay as my shoes plodded along. Aunt Odella woulda called the day hot enough to melt the stripes off a candy cane. MawMaw Sands's rocker was empty when I passed by her house, so maybe she'd been run inside by the heat too.

The sight of a big sedan with white sidewall tires rolling slowly down the street and coming to a sudden stop right in front of Cal and Peaches's rented house made my heart skip about two years, though. When the driver started sounding his horn, the first thought that went tearing through my mind was that the storekeeper from Fayetteville had found me. My second thought was where in the world to hide.

As the jarring blasts of noise filled the air, I leaped off the road where I'd been walking and crouched behind a half-dead bush in somebody's yard. Tried to camouflage myself as best I could behind that useless plant. God knows what anybody looking out their window might've thought. After a good five minutes, when the loud honking had finally stopped and nothing more had happened, I got up the courage to stick my neck out and have a careful look around. That's when I spotted Peaches coming around the side of her house holding a basket of laundry stuck out in front of her huge belly. Opening one of the passenger doors of the sedan, she shoved the basket into the back, and a white arm reached through an open window and dumped some money into her hands before the automobile drove off.

Laundry.

Nobody was coming after me. They were just picking up their darned *laundry*.

Feeling like the world's biggest fool, I crawled out from my hiding place, cursing at myself under my breath. Couldn't believe I'd gone diving for cover like I was under enemy attack, over nothing but a bunch of laundry. Big Man had become a sissy girl overnight. Punch me in the stomach now, and feathers would probably fly out. Disgusted, I smacked the dust off my pants and flicked away a stray beetle crawling on my shirt. You see how much a person can change in just a couple of days.

"Catch-up jobs," Peaches told me later, after I got back and found her sitting on the side-porch steps fanning herself with a magazine. "Most everybody around here does laundry for money." She nodded in the direction of the other houses. "We get laundry from all the rich resorts around the Pines, and some of the army officers bring us their wash jobs too."

Not long afterward, Cal came back with a laundry sack stuffed full of one resort's dinner napkins. "Peaches, the lip nappies is here," he joked as he came through the doorway. Which busted me up since nappies are what babies wear on their behinds, not something you wipe off your lips with.

However, it wasn't so funny when I had to help clean those things, let me tell you. Cal showed me how to shake them out over a trash bucket and how to stack them in piles by how dirty they were. Trust me, you don't wanna to know what came outta some of the real dirty ones. I figure the resort must've served almost nothing but fish because there were enough little bitty fish bones when I was done to assemble a whole school. Cal said it wasn't unusual to come across teeth too. Human teeth, that is. "Even found a gold one once," he told me. "Thought I'd hit the mother lode when that chunk of metal landed in the bottom of the pail. Until I saw it was a tooth."

"You give it back?"

"Yes sir." Cal grinned. "Gave it straight back. Didn't want the rest of them teeth to come looking for me." He'd found a couple of pairs of eyeglasses and a woman's watch too.

I didn't find anything that exciting. But I decided if I ever ate in a rich resort someday, I would never use a napkin to wipe my mouth. Not after seeing what people left on them. Think I'd rather wipe my mouth on a baby's behind.

Cal and Peaches didn't bring up the subject of sending me back to Chicago until after supper that night. Maybe they wanted to get some work outta me first, who knows. I could tell they'd been discussing what to do. Caught some of the looks flying back and forth behind me, and saw the two of them having a conversation in the yard, just outta earshot of the house—Peaches with her hands never stopping as she talked, and Cal standing at ease, doing nothing but listening.

Peaches had just finished clearing the plates after supper when Cal pushed his chair back from the table and said maybe we could talk about some important things now that our stomachs were full. You could see he wasn't used to being in charge much. He was trying to be serious and all, but underneath the acting, he seemed closer to being an older brother than an older person, if you know what I mean.

He started by saying, "Me and Peaches, we've been trying to come up with the best thing to do, seeing as how you've come all the way down here." You could tell he was tiptoeing around the subject of Aunt Odella not wanting me back. "We know it's a tough spot you're in." He let out a puff of air from his cheeks and shook his head. "No two ways about it. Me and Peaches are both from big families ourselves, and we feel real sorry for how your family's treating you."

Like I said, Aunt Odella wasn't all that bad, even if they seemed to think so. Probably sleeping on a fold-out cot for three years wasn't easy for her. And when she'd sent me to North Carolina, how could she have known my daddy wouldn't be there?

It was easy to see Peaches and Cal hadn't been able to come up with a better plan for me either. Cal folded his arms and gave me what I think was supposed to be a wise look, although it seemed more like a wide-eyed gaze of desperation. "If it was up to you, Legs, where would you go? Back to Chicago or somewhere else?"

Honestly, I was all out of good answers. If I went back to Chicago, I'd be dumping the same burdens on Aunt Odella's shoulders again, and what would be the sense of doing that? Or would it be smarter to stay where I was for a few weeks? I wondered. Maybe what Aunt Odella needed was a little time to start missing me. And Peaches and Cal seemed like nice enough people who wouldn't mind some company for a short time.

On the other hand, there was a lot about the South that scared the living daylights outta me, and I didn't want to come face to face with those scenes again.

Watching me, Peaches and Cal must've thought I was feeling all torn up inside, because Peaches eased her pumpkin-belly self into the kitchen chair next to me and tried giving me a tender look of sympathy underneath all her wincing.

"You don't have to decide anything now," she said, patting my arm. "You can take a couple of days if you need to, but me and Cal think you should write a few words to your aunt and tell her where you ended up at least, so she won't worry." Peaches reached into an apron pocket and pulled out a scrap of paper that mighta been wallpaper once, by the looks of it. Paper was often in short supply because of the war.

"This is the best I've got right now," she said, pushing it across the table. Cal pulled a nub of a pencil out of his shirt pocket and rolled it toward me. Then the two of them tried to pretend they were real busy with other things while I stayed at the kitchen table swatting flies and sweating over the bad cursive I was doing. I knew Aunt Odella would notice my handwriting before she even bothered to read the words.

What to say was harder.

It ended up being a short letter. Told her where I was and how my father had to leave on an army mission right before I got there. Couldn't help adding how I found out it was true about him being in the paratroops. I underlined the sentence, so she wouldn't miss it. *He jumps out of airplanes with a parachute.* Could picture Aunt Odella smacking my letter down on the kitchen table, making the salt shaker jump, and saying, "Nohow. That can't be true."

I'll admit, I still had a few doubts of my own. Needed more proof before I could convince myself one hundred percent.

Anyhow, I wrote that I was staying with two nice people who'd been good friends of my father, and we were waiting on word from him next. Didn't say we were waiting for her to start missing me too. Thought about scrawling a quick note to Archie, but I couldn't come up with what facts to tell him, so I gave up. He'd probably already decided I'd run off to be a secret spy with my father. And who wanted to ruin that good story?

Ended with *So long, Levi*—just like my daddy's familiar letters.

I decided to hang on to the words for a few days before I mailed them to Aunt Odella, just to see what happened. Turns out a lot of things would.

17. Like White on Rice

The next day was my third day in the South. A Tuesday. It started out as one of those days when nobody was in a hurry to get up because nobody had gotten much sleep. Cal had tossed and turned and snored the whole night. It was like listening to a B-17 bomber rumbling down the runway. All. Night. Long.

I don't think Peaches ever went to bed, because every time I checked, her shadowy shape was still sitting in the rocker by the bedroom window, softly moving back and forth. I was stuck on the same lumpy mattress on their bedroom floor. "We don't pay for those other rooms, so we can't go using them," Peaches insisted when I asked. She was as much a stickler for rules as Aunt Odella.

The air was so stifling that night, it was a wonder all of us didn't suffocate in our sleep, crowded together in that breathless space. Only when I slid halfway off the mattress in the middle of the night and rested my cheek against the cool linoleum, outta pure desperation, did I get any relief.

When I woke up the next morning, my whole body was sprawled across the floor as if it was some refreshing iceberg I had crawled onto in the night. Let myself stay that way for a minute, just enjoying the soft morning breezes that were sweeping in. It seemed well past sunrise, from the bright light that already filled the room. Rising carefully on one elbow, I looked in the direction of the rocker where Peaches was fast asleep with her chin slumped on one shoulder and her hands flopped over the top of her big stomach. Cal was a mound of mashed-potato silence in the bed by the wall.

Seeing as how nobody else was moving yet, I decided to ease back down to the floor and keep snoring too. I snagged my pillow off the mattress and folded it behind my head, just closing my eyes and letting my mind wander. Thought about my daddy drifting down from the sky with his parachute. What would jumping into the air feel like? I wondered. Was it like water? Did you dive into it? Or did you start running, legs spinning like propellers, and take a flying leap into the sky?

When we were real young, me and Archie used to jump off the lower part of an old brick wall behind his apartment building, daring each other to move higher and higher, until our feet stung like pins and needles when we landed.

Tried to picture what Aunt Odella would be doing on

that same Tuesday morning back in Chicago. She'd be getting ready for work, of course. There'd be the smoky smell of the hot irons transforming her hair into its stiff rolls, along with clouds of Snow White talcum powder drifting through the rooms. "Don't know why I go to all this bother," Aunt Odella would always huff as she snapped her old pocketbook shut. She'd been a cook at a city high school for years and took cleaning shifts sometimes too. Plus, all her funeral work. It was easy to see why she was so wore out.

I wondered what my teachers thought of my disappearing from school outta the blue. It happened a lot during the war. Families came and went, but I still liked to hope people would miss me being around. *Where's Big Man gone to?* I pictured the little kids at recess asking, lips quivering and all. Nobody left to be their tree.

There must've been a lot of little kids living next door to Peaches and Cal's house because you could hear their screechy voices in the yard that morning playing a game of tag, it sounded like. They were shouting, "Lo, tally lo"— which must've been the words they used in the South for taking off from home base. They seemed to be running circles around the houses, from the way their voices rose and fell.

Gotta admit it felt kinda peaceful lying there on the floor listening to all the soft sounds floating around me. In

Aunt Odella's neighborhood, the racket from the streets never stopped, day or night. Friday nights, when the jazz joints were hopping with people, being the worst.

Maybe that's why the shriek that happened next—outta the clear blue sky—nearly launched all of us through the roof. The three of us were drifting along, real peaceful in our sleepy little worlds, when a woman next door yelled, "Lord Jesus almighty, everybody, listen up, listen up," at the top of her live-long lungs.

I'm telling you, her voice coulda brought the dead back to life. As if her screams weren't jolting enough, she began beating on something metallic—a cooking pan maybe—as if the entire German army was coming down the street. *Clangclangclang.*

Peaches's head snapped up from her chest and her wild eyes started searching around for Cal, who was yanking on his pair of pants backward and hunting around for his boots.

"What in the world's happened?" Peaches's voice was breathless, and her hands pressed against both sides of her round stomach as if that baby might come flying out next.

"Don't know. Don't know." Cal kept on repeating those same two words as we followed him. Limping down the hallway, he headed out the kitchen door with his cane and his one good foot stuck in a jump boot with its laces loose and dangling. In the distance, you could hear more pots banging.

Seemed like folks up and down the street were picking up the warning.

Me and Peaches stood helpless by the door, knowing the flimsy screen full of holes couldn't protect us from anything when it didn't even keep out flies. I was afraid maybe the Japs had invaded the country. Or the Germans had planned one last surprise attack. Maybe the rumors of the war ending soon had been a trap and a secret air attack was on its way. What if Hitler wasn't dead? It was a crystal-clear day. You could almost picture dark waves of German bombers winging their way across the Atlantic right then, loaded with bombs, ready to level North Carolina. Or Chicago. Or who knows what.

Peaches reached over and squeezed my arm as if she was thinking the exact same things. But I don't think half a minute passed before Cal came hobbling toward the house, a huge grin running from ear to ear.

"The radio," he hollered at Peaches before he even hit the porch steps. Everybody in the neighborhood was hollering about something right then, it seemed like. He had to repeat "radio" twice before we understood what in the world he was shouting. Then the three of us nearly fell over one another as we reached for the little Emerson radio sitting in the middle of the kitchen table like an innocent box.

We got it warmed up and tuned in just as President Truman was speaking.

Now, this was the first time I'd heard President Truman

talk. He'd only been president for a few short weeks since our brave President Roosevelt had passed on so suddenly, after collapsing one afternoon and never waking up. It was a tragedy most people still couldn't bring themselves to talk about without fresh tears springing up in their eyes. I gotta confess, the new president's weak-sounding voice sure was a letdown. He seemed like somebody who could use a few lessons from Aunt Odella.

When he started out his radio speech by saying something about it being a solemn but glorious hour—heck, we didn't know what to think. How could something be solemn but glorious at the same time? Had some war miracle happened for the Allies? Had President Roosevelt somehow come back to life? You never knew what to believe during the war since things changed so fast. Peaches glanced over at Cal with a puzzled look and he held up one finger, still grinning from ear to ear.

When President Truman got to the next part about the German forces finally surrendering and the flags of freedom flying over Europe, a joyous whoop burst out from the whole neighborhood. I'm telling you, every person in town must've leaped up from their chairs at the exact same time and shouted with joy. You woulda thought Louis Armstrong had suddenly blasted the world's biggest trumpet into the sky. Even Peaches did a little hotfoot dance around the kitchen table.

Only thing was, it wasn't over.

That's what we found out next. Cal flapped his arms trying to silence us. "Hush up. He's still talking."

The three of us leaned closer to hear the next crackling words, almost nose to nose with the radio, and that's when we found out the Germans might've surrendered, but the Japanese didn't intend to budge an inch. They refused to lay down their arms and give up the fight. "Our victory is but half won," the president continued in his weakly way. "And every American must stick to his post and keep working to finish it . . . the whole world must be cleansed of evil—"

"Well, you shoulda just waited until *all* the evil was gone to tell us about it," Peaches interrupted, her dark eyes turning stony. "Why'd I get up from my nice sleep if that's all the president was gonna say? Don't need to hear no more of that nonsense." She reached out and switched off the radio right in the middle of the president's sentence. "Don't need to listen to another word," she said.

Pressing her fingertips against her closed eyelids, Peaches let out a slow breath of air. Sitting there so still, she reminded me of a flower that had suddenly gone all wilted and droopy in the sun. Outside, the whole neighborhood fell silent. Everybody else must've been as disappointed as us. Honestly, it kinda took the wind out of the celebration, hearing how the Japs weren't giving up yet.

But I don't think me or Cal was expecting Peaches to lay her head down on the table and start crying about the news we'd just heard. Without any warning at all, that's what she did. She leaned over and started sobbing as if her heart had shattered like a plate. It took me by surprise, that's for sure.

Cal leaped up. "Good gracious, sugar honey, what's wrong?" One arm swooped around her shoulders as his other hand waved me toward the door.

Let me tell you, I didn't waste any time getting myself out of there.

Even sitting at the far end of the porch, I could still hear a good bit of what was being said. It was impossible not to. From what I could put together, Peaches was scared to death about Cal getting called up to fight next. "I thought everything would be over by now and you and me could stay right here together." Her voice rose to a wail. "I don't want you leaving to fight in the war, Cal. What if something happens to you over there in the Pacific? Why couldn't the Japs have surrendered, same as the Germans? Who's gonna help me with the baby coming and all?" Her voice went on and on, rising and falling, repeating the same things over and over.

It started to make my stomach ache, listening to how sad she was. Probably this is wrong to admit, but I hadn't been too worried about my father being sent to the war until that very moment. Guess I figured him being in the army wasn't much different than when he was away selling encyclopedias, or hitting baseballs, or what have you. Yet hearing the president talk about all the evil that still lurked around us and seeing how afraid Peaches was about being left alone in the world had turned on the worry spigot in my brain. All kinds of dire thoughts were pouring out.

Not much later, Cal came out and slouched down on the porch steps next to me. I could hear Peaches scorching up a late breakfast in the kitchen, pans clanging around, bacon crackling in the fat.

"Holy smokes," he said, rubbing his hand over his close-shaved head and giving me a sideways look of frustration. "She's in a mood this morning." He leaned back, elbows resting on the top step, staring silently at the yard.

"So you think the Japs will keep on fighting?"

Cal's voice was flat. "Like white on rice. They're never gonna give up."

"Is that where everybody'll be going now?" Meaning my father, of course.

Cal shrugged. "Hard to say. Most likely." He reached for a stem of dry grass next to the porch, broke off a piece, and stuck the end in his mouth. It was quiet for a while and the air felt heavy with all these things not being said. Finally I got up the nerve to ask Cal what he'd do if he got ordered to the front lines.

He pretended to give me a deadly serious look. "Well, Legs, I didn't practice jumping outta airplanes to spend the whole war sitting here, shaking gold teeth outta rich folks' lip nappies." Then he busted up laughing. "Me and your daddy and the other fellows, we got more training than the entire U.S. Army put together. The Japs won't stand a chance when we hit the ground. They'll see our brown faces coming down under those chutes, and they'll wish they'd surrendered when they had the chance."

You couldn't help feeling better about the whole sorry world when you were around Cal, even if there wasn't much in life he took seriously. Wished I'd grown up around somebody like him. Not being disrespectful of my own father, of course—but it woulda been nice to have a brother or an uncle like Cal to talk to once in a while. Archie had two older brothers. The one who was missing in action had been his favorite.

"Son of a darned gun," Cal sighed, turning back to glance through the screen door at Peaches, who was making an awful loud racket with her cooking. "I hope that baby's born soon."

Turns out we didn't have too long to wait.

18. Victory

Peaches's baby came into the world a few days later, right in the middle of the Lord's Prayer at Our Lady of Victory Church. Even though Peaches had been feeling sharper pains in her stomach and was sweating so much she looked like a glazed donut, she still insisted on going to church for Sunday services because President Truman had declared Sunday to be a day of prayer for the war.

Me and Cal told her she should stay home. We told her we'd go in her place and promised to pray extra hard, but she wouldn't listen. I think she felt not going woulda meant bad luck for Cal. Maybe the Lord wouldn't watch over him in the war if she didn't show up to pray.

So we got ourselves all shined up for Jesus, as Aunt Odella would say.

I pulled on a pair of my miserable school pants and the only starched shirt I had left that was still clean. Cal loaned me one of the civilian ties he hadn't worn since joining up.

It was striped, blue and green, and about four inches short of my belt. Good thing I didn't know many people down there because I looked like some kinda comedy act.

Both me and Cal got a little carried away with the aftershave too. I'd never worn it before, but Cal slapped a cool palmful on my neck from a bottle he had on the bathroom shelf, and then I couldn't help sneaking more when he wasn't looking and patting it all over the front of my shirt because I smelled like the inside of Aunt Odella's musty suitcase walking around. Wasn't long before all the wasps in the neighborhood were after me, I stank so bad.

Peaches took the longest getting ready, but you couldn't miss her when she finally made her way gingerly down the front steps toward the gate where me and Cal had been waiting on her for about an hour, it seemed like, swatting at the dive-bombing wasps.

She was wearing a yellow dress and looked like a drunken sun as she came toward us, swaying heavily from side to side. A wide-brimmed straw hat was balanced unevenly on her head, with a loose ribbon dangling off of it, and her fingers were stuffed into a pair of white gloves like a set of sausages. Don't think she could bend a single one of them. Even her red lipstick was too bright and had smeared a little on her teeth. She was a mess, although I knew how hard she'd tried to look pretty that morning.

"Y'all waiting on me?" she said, flashing a droopy smile.

Cal reached out to give her his arm. "I been waiting for

you my whole life, sugar pie," he said. With the wasps trailing us like a choir procession, we joined the rest of the world heading to church that Sunday. You could hear church bells jangling all over town. I walked alongside Peaches and Cal, keeping a wide berth between them and me—as if I knew the two of them but wasn't close family. Couldn't keep my eyes from drifting over their way every once in a while, though. Like I said, love ain't something I been around much, so I was curious. But not too curious.

I wondered if Queen Bee Walker and my daddy ever strolled to church arm in arm like Peaches and Cal. Likely not. Aunt Odella always said they argued worse than two alley tomcats. Fur would fly, she said, whenever they were together. Still, it surprised me that Cal didn't fix the loose ribbon on Peaches's hat or tell her she had lipstick smeared on her teeth before we got to the church and everybody saw her. I know Aunt Odella woulda said something. When Uncle Otis's third wife wore a moth-eaten wool jacket to Granny's funeral, my aunt asked her, right to her face, if she lived in a house without mirrors. "Or did the moths eat up your jacket on the way here?"

Trouble was, everybody else heard Aunt Odella too. That chewed-up jacket was the talk of the funeral. Which was part of the reason why Uncle Otis eventually had to marry again, I think.

Maybe love was keeping your mouth shut.

* * *

We passed by MawMaw Sands's house and the BASKETS FOR SALE sign was off the gate. "Looks like she's got the place all closed up this morning," Cal said to Peaches, nodding in the direction of the overgrown house.

I hadn't dug up much useful information about MawMaw Sands. When I'd told Cal and Peaches about meeting her on my way to the creek and how she seemed to know an awful lot about me for being a complete stranger, Peaches had just smiled and nodded, saying, "She always knows everybody's business around here."

Cal told me there were rumors the lady was the straight bloodline descendent of an old African healer who'd lived in the Georgia swamps for years after jumping off a slave ship. "You can believe what you want," he'd said, grinning. "But I'm always real careful to say good morning to her. Don't want her putting the voodoo eye on me."

Tell you the truth, MawMaw Sands's house didn't look like anything out of the ordinary that morning. You wouldn't have guessed anyone special lived there, just by seeing the outside of it. The baskets seemed as if they were part of the scenery, as if they'd grown from the porch vines by them-selves. I thought about the Keeper of Secrets basket sitting up there. Guess it wasn't much of a secret anymore where all our country's soldiers would be heading next.

As we got closer to the church, we joined a lively parade of colors. Big hats and flowered dresses trailed into the building from all directions. The ladies outnumbered the men by a long shot, but it seemed as if every man who wasn't in uniform had on those fancy two-tone shoes you see a lot of the jazz cats wearing, and neckties in patterns that woulda made a blind man dizzy. I saw one fellow strutting up the church steps in lime-green shoes—swear to you, I did.

Our Lady of Victory Church wasn't what I was expecting for a house of worship either. The building was made of wood shingles instead of brick like Aunt Odella's church, and it was painted barn red. White steps led up to the door and two long white crosses hung on either side of the entrance. It seemed kinda strange to me that a house of worship would be painted red, but you know, the South was different.

Our Lady of Victory Church was Catholic, Peaches told me. I didn't know a thing about Catholics. We were Baptists going way back. Maybe being Catholic was the reason the church had a big statue outside it of a white lady holding a baby. Honestly, you couldn't help gawking at the sculpture because it looked like a woman who'd been turned to stone as she was running barefoot with a small child. I mean, it was that real-looking. You could almost hear her saying "I Am Levin" as she took off. Later on, somebody told me the statue was supposed to be Mary and baby Jesus. Still don't know what she was running from, though.

Inside the church, there were more white statues—smaller ones—and rows of lit candles, their smoke curling into the stifling air. With no warning at all, Peaches and

Cal both kneeled down one knee as we were heading toward some open seats. It startled me so bad, I jumped toward Peaches to help out, like the gentleman I been raised to be, until I saw everyone else kneeling down and pointing to their foreheads too. Feeling real uneasy, I began to regret coming along. I'd figured every church was the same as Aunt Odella's in Chicago. But it was clear they weren't.

Once we got to our seats, I kept my hands shoved in my pockets and my eyes glued on the brown neck of the middle-aged man in front of me. It was covered in shaving bumps, so I could tell he didn't go to a barber as good as Uncle Otis. After a while I began to nod off, what with the heat and the smell from the candles. The prayers for the war and our soldiers seemed to go on forever. Up front, the white minister who they called Father John—even though it was pretty clear he was nobody's father in that congregation—had just started the Lord's Prayer and everybody had finished repeating "Thy kingdom come" when Peaches let out an unearthly shriek next to me and sank down on her chair as if she'd fainted.

The whole kingdom came to us right after that, I'm telling you.

Cal started hollering something about the baby and all the women standing nearby pushed toward Peaches, some of them scrambling over the rows in their Sunday dresses, Bibles still in their hands, purses hooked over their arms, hats tumbling off—while the men and children fled in the opposite direction, toward the double doors at the entrance, like sailors jumping off the decks of a torpedoed ship. It was pure pandemonium, let me tell you.

I was caught up in the crowd heading out. Somebody put their hand on my shoulder and pushed me forward into the aisle with everybody else. In no time at all I was outside, blinking in the painful sunshine. Around me, the hum of excited voices sounded like an Allied radio broadcast.

Nobody seemed to be paying much attention to me, so I eased myself over to the statue of the white woman and leaned in the small slice of shade in front of her. Pretended to be studying something on the sandy ground by my shoes. Heck, I didn't know what else to do. Should I be fetching a doctor? Seeing if Cal needed help? Sending up a quick prayer for Peaches and the baby? Nobody else around me seemed to be fretting one little bit. A few were even taking bets. Nearby, a group of men collected money on the sly, keeping their voices low.

"Fifty cents says baby girl," I heard one of them say.

"Seventy-five says baby boy."

"Dollar says twins."

"I ain't betting on no twins."

A sharp female voice cut in loudly. "Y'all oughta be ashamed of yourselves, this being Sunday and a churchyard and all. Can't believe y'all are taking bets on Peaches's baby. Shame on y'all."

From what I could tell, the only thing they did was slide

a little farther away. You could see dollar bills and change gliding smoothly from one pocket to the next around the whole yard. Good thing nobody asked me what I'd bet on, because I woulda told them how Peaches and Cal were one hundred percent sure it was gonna be a boy since Peaches was from a family of four brothers. They'd already picked out the name: Calvin junior, of course. No question about it, the two of them insisted the baby was gonna be a boy and a star athlete because of how strong he'd been kicking Peaches in the ribs for weeks.

After maybe an hour or so had passed, the church door opened and a hush fell over the entire churchyard. The crowd was wilting in the heat and if it had been much longer we woulda been puddles of Crayola. But Cal came outta the church just in time holding a little bundle in his arms and everybody leaped up to see what it was. Cal was smiling as wide as the Mississippi River.

"It's a girl!" he hollered.

Which just goes to show you that girls can kick as hard as boys, I guess.

A whoop went up from the crowd, and Cal looked around. "Where's Levi standing?" he said, acting like I was part of his family or something.

I lifted up my big arm reluctantly, feeling all those strangers staring.

"Come on up here!" He waved.

Man oh man, I did not want to go up there, but I did. Aunt Odella woulda been real proud of my manners because I did not make a rude face while leaning down and looking at that baby, even though it was hard not to. Never saw anything so ugly in my whole life. The baby's face was a wrinkled shade of purplish brown and she had a huge puff of soft black hair on her head. I'm telling you, she looked like a shrunk-up prune lady wearing a black feather hat.

"Ain't she the most beautiful thing?" Cal breathed.

I nodded solemnly, saying yes she was, and hoped God would not strike me dead for telling an outright lie on the front steps of his church.

Somebody in the crowd called out, "What's her name?"

Heck, now that was a problem. I could see Cal's eyes roll wildly and I could tell he was panicking because he was still thinking Calvin junior. No other possibilities had even floated through his mind yet. Trying to help, I glanced around, as if a good name might be hiding somewhere nearby. My eyes fell on the church sign: Our Lady of Victory.

Well, she was a lady. Ugly, but a lady.

"Victory," I offered, and Cal grabbed hold of that name like I'd just lobbed him a football in the last minute of a championship game.

"She's Victory," he shouted to the crowd.

I gotta admit I was kinda pleased with myself for coming up with that name outta thin air and all. Queen Bee Walker, who named me by accident too, woulda been proud.

19. Love Conquers All

Now, it didn't take long for that prune-faced baby to become the center of her own tiny universe. Me and Peaches and Cal were the only planets in her universe and our sole purpose was to revolve around her, day and night. It was a good thing people brought us food during the first week after she was born because we woulda starved to death if they hadn't. The pots of chicken and rice they left on the porch saved our lives. If nothing showed up by suppertime, me and Cal would cook frankfurters and open a can of Heinz baked beans outta pure desperation. After a couple of days, I never wanted to see another plate of franks and beans as long as I lived. Got pretty tired of warmed-over chicken and rice too.

Far as I could tell, that baby never slept one minute of its life. It did two things. Cried at the top of its puny lungs. And shot things outta both ends, if you know what I mean. Nothing else. You couldn't get a wink of sleep if you were in the same room with her, so me and Cal had started dragging two army cots onto the wide porch and sleeping outside, with who knows what crawling over us in the middle of the night. We were peppered with bug bites. Peaches swore we'd probably caught fleas from being out there in the dark like two strays. Every night she'd start crying, watching us leave.

I figured something in Peaches's mind must've dissolved after having the baby. She cried almost as much as Victory and lost her temper over the smallest things. It was as if that strong pumpkin lady had suddenly turned all mushy and soft. One morning, when she burned off a little clump of hair on the back of her head while putting in a curl, you woulda thought she'd whacked off her own arm with a butcher knife. Hearing her screams, one of the neighbors came running over to check she wasn't dying.

Another morning, she found the note I hadn't sent to Aunt Odella yet. "You mean you never mailed this letter to your auntie?" she said, waving the wallpaper scrap in the air. With all the things that had happened, I hadn't found the post office or stamps or an envelope yet. Plus, like I said, all of us had been too busy to think. "You march it to the post office this minute and mail it," she said, her eyes popping mad. "Your people are probably worried sick."

I kept a careful eye on Cal's truck, figuring it was only a matter of time before Peaches ran off from us and left Victory on the passenger seat with a note written on a napkin.

* * *

"Naw," Cal said when I told him one night what I was worrying about. "No chance." We were stretched out on the porch, barefoot, eating a bowl of peanuts in the dark. I gotta admit, I never had much of a taste for peanuts before, but now I couldn't get enough of them. Me and Cal would put a big bowl between us and spend the evening sitting on the porch, just outta range of Peaches's wrath, cracking the shells and flicking the pieces into the shadows.

"Women, all of them, go a little crazy after having a baby," Cal said, splitting a shell between his teeth. "She'll be fine in no time. I ain't worried one little bit about Peaches."

I tried explaining about Queen Bee Walker leaving me and how you couldn't be sure. How my daddy was taken by complete surprise, people said.

"Shoot, I can't picture anybody going and leaving you and Boots in the dust like that lady did. She musta been just plain nuts. That's the only explanation," Cal answered. "Plus, if Peaches was gonna leave me, I'd be the first to know." He grinned, his teeth flashing white in the shadows. "The whole town of Southern Pines would know. Shucks, McDeeds Creek would shrivel up in its banks. Birds would fall outta the air—"

I gave Cal a soft punch in the arm. "Stop. I ain't joking."

"All right, Legs." Cal tried to look serious. "I'll keep an eye on my old gal in case she gets the crazy idea to steal the truck and take off without me."

It was silent for a few minutes. The crickets were making a whirring racket in the darkness. Something was scratching under the porch. A woodstove was going in somebody's kitchen, for no good reason that I could think of, since it must've been ninety-eight degrees that May night. A haze of smoke hung over the whole neighborhood.

Cal swatted at a bug and leaned back against the house. "So you wanna hear how I met Peaches? It's a good story—might give you some ideas of how to meet a pretty gal someday."

I said no thanks, but Cal ignored me.

"About two years ago, me and a few of the other fellows were coming back from a training exercise in one of those six-by-sixes, army trucks, down there in Georgia. It was hotter than a firecracker that day. I was driving the truck, which was a heap of junk, going down a winding country road faster than I should have, when all of a sudden this tall gal with thready braids flopping all over her head—I'm telling you she looked like a wild woman—leaped in front of my truck, holding a sign. It was a wonder I didn't run her over because that truck had prayers for brakes." He glanced over at me. "Guess what the sign said."

I cracked a dusty peanut with my thumbs and pretended not to be too interested.

"It said—right there in black and white—*Peaches and Cal*. And I thought to myself, 'Holy smokes—this must be the woman I'm meant to marry. A lady named Peaches.'"

I snorted loudly and brushed peanut shells off my shirt. I wasn't stupid enough to fall for this crazy tale.

"I ain't finished yet, Legs—keep on listening. See, then the crazy-looking gal got a little closer to my truck and I saw how there was another word, real teeny-tiny, squeezed sideways into the corner of the sign, because it didn't fit. The word was *Lemonade*. That's when it hit me—*Peaches and Cool Lemonade*. That's what the sign was advertising. *Cool*, not Cal. Shucks, it didn't have nothing to do with me. Nothing at all.

"Still, I wasn't ready to bug out right then. I looked back at the rickety stand where the lady had been sitting. There were way too many baskets of peaches still waiting to be bought and a jug of lemonade getting warm in the sun. So I asked her, 'How much for two baskets of peaches and a drink?' 'Fifteen cents,' she told me. 'And what's your name?' I asked her as she handed me my change. She gave me this prickly old glare and told me it was none of my darned business, so I said all right, I'd just call her Peaches."

Cal chuckled. "Every week, whenever I passed through town or something, I'd stop by that rattletrap stand, wave, and holler, 'Hey, Peaches. How ya doing today?' Then I'd buy a basket or two of peaches and some lemonade from her, so she'd have to talk to me. It took a whole month before she finally agreed to go to church with me one Sunday. Rest is history. Her real name's Pauline. Don't that sound like an uptight, schoolteachery name?" Cal rolled his eyes.

I had to admit I couldn't picture Peaches as Pauline.

"So, of course, I kept on calling her Peaches, even after we got married. Let's see, counting today"—Cal held up his fingers—"we been married almost a year and six months. A Georgia country gal and a city boy from Richmond, Virginia. See, that's how you know it's real love."

"How?" I said, in spite of myself.

"Because I can't stand peaches. Haven't eaten a thing with peaches in it since I was a baby. Worst fruit ever. But love conquers all. If it's real love, you'll do anything for it, even buying twenty-two baskets of peaches you can't much stand to look at, let alone eat. Just to get a date with a pretty girl."

Now, I didn't want to argue with Cal, but it seemed to me that love and a few baskets of peaches might conquer some people, but it didn't conquer everybody. Love didn't keep me from being left on the passenger seat of a Ford, with a goodbye note, for instance. It didn't keep Margie, who I'd met on the train, from giving away the special cake she'd made for her fellow before it even got to Washington, D.C. And love had probably given up on the likes of Aunt Odella.

Anyhow, the whole subject was starting to get old fast.

"You see that lightning bug?" I pointed in the direction of a flicker that had glowed by the bushes near the gate. "It's not even the end of May and I swear that was a lightning bug."

Cal pelted me with a handful of peanut shells. "You don't like my love stories?"

I shrugged, hoping he'd get the message that I didn't.

Inside the house, Victory let out one of her earsplitting howls, and Cal gave a weary sigh. "You ever hear the story about the cat who swallowed a whole ball of yarn?" A small grin tugged at the corner of Cal's mouth, so you knew his sad idea of a joke was coming next, but I went along with it anyhow.

"Well, there was this cat, see, who got real hungry one night. And there was no food at all to be found in her house, so she went and gobbled up a ball of yarn instead. Right after that, guess what happened?"

"I don't want to know."

"Well, she had a half-dozen kittens," Cal kept on. "But there was something very strange about those kittens. You wanna know what it was?"

I shook my head. "Nope."

Being Cal, he started hooting and falling over, even before getting to the punch line. "They were all born with knitted sweaters!"

I busted up too, even though it wasn't all that funny. It was stupid funny, you know what I mean? Kinda like love.

"Y'all stop making that racket," Peaches shouted, and rapped on the window above our heads. "The baby's sleeping."

Cal grinned and closed his eyes. "See, that's pure love right there. You heard it."

Sure it was. I was still gonna keep an eye on the truck.

20. Telegram

Being stuck on the porch every night gives you a lot of time to think. I swear some nights my brain was like the jazz clubs back in Chicago. It didn't open until after dark. I'd be lying there, trying to snooze, but my brain would be wide awake and kicking. If one of MawMaw Sands's imaginary shooting stars had sailed over the house and landed in the garden late one night, I can promise you I woulda been the person to see it.

Sometimes I tried to pass the time by dreaming up things my father might be doing at that moment. Was he sitting on a dark train somewhere in the United States, waiting on orders? Or standing on the deck of a troopship steaming across the Pacific? Or jumping outta an airplane over enemy territory? He often looked more like a superhero than a human being in my imagination. As if a parachuting Captain Marvel had become my father overnight.

* * *

When I heard back from Aunt Odella, her words didn't ease my mind much either. After getting my note in the mail, my aunt sent a speedy reply by telegram saying I should let her know as soon as I got any news from my father—or if I didn't hear from him soon, she'd send money for a ticket home. The telegram ended with the words *God bless folks keeping you,* meaning Cal and Peaches, I guess. Even being as short on words as it was, the note must've cost a lot to send, Peaches said—maybe thinking a little better of my aunt after we got it.

Trouble was, there'd been no word from my father or the other paratroopers since they'd left town. It had been almost four weeks. We weren't getting much war news either because Peaches had traded away the radio, not long after the president's speech. In fact, I'd been standing in the kitchen on the day Cal came home to find the radio missing and the worst piece of art you ever saw sitting in its place. A peacock. Painted metallic silver and gold, with wilted feathers for its tail and chips of red glass for its eyes.

Cal asked, "Where's the radio gone to?"

"Thought something else looked better sitting there instead," Peaches answered, smooth as meringue on a pie, not letting a hint of shame at what she'd done slip into her voice. I stayed quiet and kept drying dishes, not letting on what I already knew, of course. Figured Cal was smart enough to find out the truth himself. He didn't need me.

"So you moved the radio somewhere else?" He stepped into the bedroom to look for it.

"Miz Mayberry down the street needed a radio," Peaches said, still sounding innocent.

Cal's head poked out through the bedroom doorway, eyebrows rising. "You gave her ours?"

"You can't put a price on art," Peaches answered, pulling herself up to her full noble queen height. "Miz Mayberry bought the peacock from a real famous artist in Florida. I told her how I wouldn't mind having something to brighten up the kitchen, and she gave it to me in exchange for that old worthless radio. Thought it was a fair trade because when all is said and done, art's gonna be around long after this miserable war ends. Nobody'll need their radios then."

We hadn't had much news since.

Only reminder of us still being at war was the sharp smell of the boot polish Cal used every night. After supper, he'd sit in the kitchen for an hour at least, hunched over the table, shining the brass on his uniform with Blitz cloth and polishing the same jump boots he'd polished the night before.

The cast had finally been taken off his foot, so he was wearing both boots, but he still walked with a slight limp. According to Cal—who could rarely be believed—the army docs had advised him to jump out of a plane and land on a tree stump with his good foot next just to even things out. And if that didn't work, he was supposed to allow himself a few days of walking practice, and pretty soon everything would be good as new.

All of us were too busy to realize what that verdict would mean.

On the morning the letter arrived from the army, me and Cal were doing laundry in the kitchen. We'd been trying to keep up with Peaches's laundry jobs so there'd be extra money still coming in. With our elbows deep in Rinso suds, we probably looked like a couple of girls as we washed dinner napkins from the resorts and starched officers' dress shirts from Camp Mackall—leaving Peaches to worry about taking care of baby Victory, who was still a wailing handful of trouble.

Coming up the steps, the postman ducked around a row of freshly washed sheets me and Cal had just strung across the porch, still dripping gently. "Mail for Sergeant Calvin R. Thomas," he announced through the screen door.

Even though the words weren't spoken that loudly, I'm telling you they silenced the whole house faster than a preacher standing up to talk at a funeral. In the bedroom, Victory stopped in mid-howl. Cal's hands, in the middle of wringing out a shirt, stopped and sagged into the washtub we were using. I worried about his whole body tumbling into the suds next, from the way he looked.

"You want me to get it?" I asked, not knowing what to think. Had Aunt Odella sent us another message?

"Naw." He stood up and walked slowly toward the door. "It's for me."

As the screen door squeaked open and Cal reached for the envelope, the entire neighborhood suddenly got dead quiet as well. No birds making a sound for a hundred miles. Not a whisper of air moving.

The postman kept his expression carefully blank as he handed over the mail. You could tell he'd practiced giving the right look—keeping his eyes fixed only on the envelope and not on the person getting it. I'm sure he had to play the part a lot with all the bad news he had to deliver in the war.

After the fellow left, Cal kept staring at the letter too. Not reading it yet. Just looking at it. In the bedroom, there was the muffled sound of Peaches crying. My feet began to move on their own, doing a nervous bounce on the black and white linoleum. When Archie's brother went missing in action in Germany, the news came in a War Department telegram and Archie's momma collapsed into a heap when she got it. They had to fetch a doctor to revive her.

"Is it bad news?" I ventured to ask.

Cal sighed and put the letter on the table without even reading it. "It's my new orders from the army, telling me where I'm going next."

When he said those words, I knew I was sunk too. No doubt about it. Cal and Peaches would be moving out of the house and I'd be on my way back to Chicago in no time.

Cal stood next to the table with his hands clasped behind his back, staring silently at the calendar on the kitchen wall. Hard to tell what he was thinking, but the month of May coulda caught fire by how hard he was looking at it. A steady *drip-drip* sound from the leaky kitchen faucet seemed to get louder the longer the silence went on.

"How about if I go down the road and talk to MawMaw Sands for a while? I'll come back later on," I mumbled, pushing open the screen door and letting it ease shut behind me. Wanted my own peace and quiet to come up with what to do next.

Nobody answered me.

I'll admit it was a relief to see MawMaw Sands sitting on her porch as I came slouching down the road like a sad sack. Even from a distance, you could spot her red turban and patchworky dress. Looked as if she was working on baskets like it was an ordinary day.

"How you, Levi?" she called out, without glancing up.

"Fine, ma'am," I mumbled.

She didn't seem to notice my down look. Or she was pretending not to. As I came up the steps, she kept on studying the basket she was working on, her face set in a look of concentration. "You know anything about basket making, boy?" she said, her lips pressed together like a tight twist of rope.

"No ma'am, I don't."

"Well, come over here and pull up a seat. I'll show you some things."

Now, learning how to make baskets wasn't the kind of help I was hoping for, but I plunked myself down on an old crate sitting in the porch corner and tried to look interested. MawMaw Sands turned over the one in her lap to show me the bottom of it, her fingers tapping on a small brown knot at the center. "Starting a basket, see, that's the hardest part. Every basket—don't matter what kind you make—always starts with a knot at its center. Myself, I like to use pine needles for the knot. You twist the needles together, and then you wind your coils around the knot, see?" Her fingers followed the spirals. "Every part leads to the next."

She reached into a rusty pail of dry stalks next to her feet and handed me a bunch of them. A faint vanilla smell wafted upward. "That's the smell of sweetgrass," she said, as if reading my mind. "It comes from the dunes and salt marshes miles from here. Twice a year, I go there and gather it myself because you can't give the job of pulling sweetgrass to somebody else. You send somebody ignorant out to do it for you, and they'll bring you back seaweed instead. Best thing to do is collect your own. Put some turpentine on your shoes to scare off all them poisonous snakes hanging around there, find a good spot, and start pulling sweetgrass. None of those snakes will bother you one bit. Nohow. Just dip your shoes in turpentine and you'll be all right." A sly smile spread across the old woman's face, as if she truly loved facing down poisonous snakes.

Tell you what, I was starting to believe the stories about her ancestors living in the Georgia swamps.

"Now, before you can work on a basket, you gotta make the knot first." She dropped a bunch of long pine needles into my hands and I did my best to knot them together, but it was way harder than you'd think. If you were lucky enough to get something that looked like it might hold for half a minute, then you had to start winding the sweetgrass coils fast around your little bitty knot before it all fell apart.

No matter what I did, I couldn't get anything close to the start of a basket. Sweetgrass stems sprang outta my hands. The knots came untied. Poked my thumb with one sharp stem and drew blood, for Pete's sake. Finally I tossed the whole mess back into the bucket and gave up with an aggravated sigh. Good grief. I wasn't God's gift to basket making, that's for sure. I think the orange-striped cat on the porch must've felt sorry for me because he came over and rubbed his ears against my knees.

MawMaw Sands jabbed her weaving spoon in my direction. "There now—you see how hard it is to make one of these baskets. Folks always think it looks real easy, that anybody can make a basket, but no sir, it sure ain't simple. Far from simple."

Her eyes peered at me from the wrinkled depths of her

brown face, two chips of white china staring. "Don't you forget what a struggle every basket in this life is to make, and how at the center of every single one, there's a knot of pain. You can't have one without the other. Pain gets woven right along with the beautiful parts, just like everything else in this world. Sweetness and pain. Same as life."

Since my right thumb was still throbbing like the devil, I didn't figure I'd be forgetting about pain or pine needles or her darned baskets anytime soon. Me and the cat were quiet. I think we'd both had enough of MawMaw Sands's too-deep wisdom for the time being. I'd been hoping for some useful advice, and she'd just given me another big dose of doom and gloom. Standing up, I cast an uneasy glance in the direction of Peaches and Cal's house. "Guess I better head on back and see what's happening there."

MawMaw Sands nodded. "Yes, already heard about you and them leaving."

Those words stopped me in my tracks.

The old woman studied her basket, still talking. "Now, it might seem far away where they're being sent to, but nothing's as far off as it looks on a map, you remember that. People's the same everywhere, no matter where you go. And someday, mark my words, Levi Battle, you gonna come back here to see me again." Her foot tapped on the porch planks. "I'm gonna hear your feet comin' up these steps again loud and clear."

Her predictions made me so jittery, I know I careened

like a row of dominoes down her steps and through her gate without saying so much as a polite goodbye. Probably forgot to latch the gate too. As I was heading back to Peaches and Cal's house to find out what was true or not, the old woman called out a few final words from the porch. "You stop by before you leave, you hear? I got something to give you."

21. Blackout Jump

If I wasn't a believer in MawMaw Sands's peculiar gifts before that day, I was after it. Because unless she read the official orders of the U.S. Army before they were sent, there was no way she woulda known about Cal being shipped so far away. Not when he hadn't even read the news himself. And, believe me, if you were asked to draw a diagonal line from one end of the United States to the other, you couldn't get a line much longer than one going from North Carolina to the place where the army was sending Cal.

Pendleton, Oregon. That's what the orders said. Cal showed me the letter when I got back. It said Sergeant Calvin R. Thomas was ordered to duty with the 555th Parachute Infantry Battalion at Pendleton Air Base in Oregon under the control of the U.S. Ninth Army Service Command.

Now, if I'd been asked to guess the location where my father and the other troopers might be, Oregon was a place that never woulda crossed my mind in a million years, that's for sure.

"Why there?" I asked Cal, rereading the official words again as if there might be some clue we missed.

He shrugged. "It's the army. Who knows."

Later that morning, we walked to the little Southern Pines post office to look up Oregon on the old U.S. map they got hanging on the wall. Probably made people wonder what the heck was going on when they saw the strange parade of me and Cal and Peaches and Victory—with a nappy over her head to keep off the hot sun—coming down the street. Had a couple of neighborhood kids trailing after us too. I remember how all of us crowded into the musty-smelling mail room and squinted at the yellowed map on the wall, which had probably been up there since the Civil War ended, by the looks of it.

Peaches pointed at Oregon. "All the way up there, Cal? That's where the army is sending you?" The words came out as a quivery whisper. Like a tiny crack opening in a flood-wall, you could tell it wouldn't be long before everything busted to pieces and a terrible torrent came pouring out. "How could they send you *all the way up there?*"

Cal tried joking. "Well, it ain't Japan at least."

"It's close enough." Peaches stabbed a finger toward the map. "Look there. The Pacific Ocean is right next to Oregon. From there, the only place you'd go to is Japan. Cal, they're sending you to the Pacific to fight, I know it. Cal, you can't go and leave me. You can't—"

And then the whole floodwall came crashing down. Peaches and Victory began wailing like a funeral chorus, and the postmaster—who was a nervous-looking fellow— came scurrying from the back, where he'd been eating his lunch, I guess. Sandwich still in his hand and crumbs all over his shirt, he shooed us straight out into the street. "What's the matter with you folks? Take your arguing outside." His sandwich-free hand propelled Peaches out the door.

By the time we got home, Peaches's pretty face was a crying mess and the white collar of her dress was damp with her tears and Victory's drool. "How can you go so far away from me?" she wailed. The whole neighborhood was taking note of the noise, I'm sure, and wondering what was up.

Trying to soothe Peaches's nerves, Cal said he'd do some checking around Camp Mackall to see what he could find out about the mission. "Maybe a couple of the fellows have sent back some news by now. I'll see what the scuttlebutt is around camp."

Scuttlebutt being gossip. You can see I was getting a good education from the army, even if I was missing school.

Cal was gone the rest of the afternoon, but he didn't find out much. I wouldn't be surprised if he just motored around the army post real slowly to get away from Peaches and Victory for a while. When he got back, he told us nobody at Mackall had heard a word from the paratroopers since they'd left, or knew much about Pendleton Air Base and what the army would be doing there.

Not wanting to be one more problem sitting at Peaches and Cal's table, I stayed outta sight once Cal got home. I stretched out on the porch and read some old *Sky Aces* magazines from Cal's collection. Aunt Odella never woulda approved of all the smash-ups and death in those stories, but after reading a bunch of them cover to cover, I decided I could become a big fan.

Inside the house, Cal and Peaches talked for what seemed like hours. Through the kitchen door, I could see the two of them facing each other across the table with Cal's strong hands reaching across the middle and holding tight to one of Peaches's hands, as if he was the lifeboat and she was the capsizing ship. The peacock sculpture drooped forlornly on top of the icebox. Victory slept in her crib, being quiet for once.

I caught bits and pieces of the conversation, although I swear I was trying hard not to. Couldn't help it if some of the words floated out to me, right? Heard my name mentioned a few times. And there were a lot of waterworks, of course—plenty of boo-hooing and *don't leave me.* Peaches and Cal talked so long, it got dark and the crickets came out.

When they finally asked me to come inside, I figured the news wasn't gonna be good. I'd already got myself prepared to head back to Chicago and Aunt Odella again. Slouching into the kitchen, I made sure my face was set in the expression of no emotion it wore most of the time. Nothing they could say would shake me at all.

"Sit down," Cal said, nodding toward one of the empty chairs.

Peaches pressed her fingers against her temples like she had a bad headache. "I haven't made us a thing to eat today. It's way past suppertime and we haven't had a good meal all day. What's wrong with me, Cal? I'm just falling to bits and pieces, aren't I?"

Cal shook his head like he'd had enough of being a lifeboat. Leaning back in his chair, he slowly unwrapped the foil wrapper from a roll of Charms candies. Passed one to Peaches, then me. Tucked the rest back in his pocket and turned to face me. "All right, Legs—"

"Levi," Peaches insisted in one of her extra-righteous tones.

Now, I'll admit I kinda liked the name Legs. It had grown on me. But I wasn't gonna jump in and correct anything between the two of them right then. Just kept myself as tough as a tree and tried to ignore how my heart was starting to slam against my ribs, knowing what words were coming next.

"All right, *Levi*," Cal said. "Me and Peaches have done a lot of talking tonight, looking at things from all directions.

Thinking about all the possibilities. And what we've decided is that we don't have no choice in these circumstances but to do a blackout jump. You know what that is?"

"No sir." My heart was knocking even harder. A blackout jump? I pictured them teetering on the edge of a cliff, hand in hand, like two star-crossed lovers in a movie picture. Good grief almighty, they wouldn't do something dumb like that, would they?

Peaches gave an exasperated sigh. "Just tell it to him straight, Cal. Stop dragging on like you do. Good Lord."

Cal wasn't gonna be moved from his storytelling, though. "See, a blackout jump is when a trooper closes his eyes as he jumps outta the airplane. Of course, nobody's *supposed* to jump that way, but sometimes, when you're first training, you can't help it. You close your eyes outta plain instinct because you're too darned afraid to look at where your backside is gonna end up. And that's what they call doing a blackout jump."

I could absolutely understand that reaction. Not only would I squeeze my eyes shut, I'd stay inside the plane too.

"Anyhow," Cal continued, "me and Peaches have decided to try something like a blackout jump. Instead of Peaches wandering around Southern Pines by herself after I leave, or going back to live with her folks in Georgia, we've decided it's better to stick together. So we're gonna close our eyes, jump on a train together, and head out to Oregon.

Never been there before, so who knows what we'll find—but we've made up our minds to load up baby Victory and all our belongings and see what happens."

His next sentence turned my strong tree self into a wobbly stick.

"And we'd like to ask you to come along with us."

I'm telling you, his words caught me by surprise and almost made me start bawling like a baby. Big tears began burning up my eyes, and my throat felt like I'd got something stuck in it. I started coughing and wiping my eyes, and Cal leaped up, thinking I was choking on the Charms candy, of course. He thumped me on the back while Peaches spilled water all over the checkered tablecloth, hurrying to give a glass to me.

Wherever she was, I hoped Queen Bee Walker was watching and taking careful notes. See, even with all their troubles, Peaches and Cal weren't taking off and leaving me with a goodbye note. They were inviting me to go along with them. All the way to Oregon.

Cal kept talking while I gulped water. "Now, if you don't want to come to Oregon, that's all right with us. We're leaving it up to you. We can get you squared away and sent back to Chicago if you want. Your choice," he said. "Shoot, we may get all the way out there to Oregon and have to turn around and come right back if the Japs surrender quick." Cal gave Peaches a reassuring grin. "But seeing how long it's been since you've spent time with Boots, and how many bad twists and turns this war's taken, we thought you oughta have the chance to at least see your daddy in person if he's out there. Maybe he can come up with a good place for you."

Cal reached for Peaches's hand across the table. "And me and Peaches want you to know you been a real big help to us ever since you got here. You're a good kid, Legs, even if some people in your family act like fools. We'd be real grateful to have you along for the trip, especially if I have to ship out once we get to Oregon."

His last words threatened to start Peaches crying all over again, so Cal finished quickly, before she could get any worse. "So what do you think, Legs? You want to come along with us?"

I nodded, not taking the chance of saying anything dumb.

"Good." Cal smacked his hands together and jumped up. Tying one of Peaches's ruffly aprons around his army fatigues, he stood next to the range. "Now how about if we have ourselves some delicious franks and baked beans for supper? After all this talking, I am starved."

You could tell Cal was already taking off with the whole idea of the trip. As he opened a can of beans and dumped them in a saucepan, he made it sound as if crossing the entire United States would be as simple as making supper from a can. We'd pack a couple of suitcases and some food, and take the train to St. Louis and then another one west. It might take three or four days, he thought.

Mostly I was gung-ho too. Although I'll admit to worrying about the fact I was leaving the South in the same speedy way I'd left Chicago—without knowing enough about what I was doing or what dangers might lie ahead. Most of what I knew about the West came from the movies—and that knowledge pretty much boiled down to cowboys, Indians, and the movie star John Wayne. Now, I wasn't dumb enough to think we'd run into John Wayne in Oregon. Or Indians either. Of course, the scorpion of death had come from the West too. Who knows if we'd find any of them scurrying around the state, but I decided this possibility wasn't something to bring up with Peaches sitting there.

Of course, she perked up once she started making lists of what she'd pack and what outfits she'd take with her. You know how women are about clothes. They start thinking about what they're gonna wear someplace and their tears dry up faster than a rainstorm in the desert.

22. Ain't Easy Being the Basket

We had two days to get ready to leave, and those two days were a whirlwind. The U.S. Army wasn't big on waiting around, I guess—kinda like Aunt Odella—so they didn't give Cal much time. Mostly it was just me and Peaches doing the packing up in the house, since Cal had his own gear to get squared away at Camp Mackall. To add to our troubles, the weather in North Carolina had suddenly taken a turn for the worse. Clouds had moved in and a steady rain fell from the gloomy skies, making it feel more like April than the beginning of June.

Maybe the rain was reminding me of Chicago, because Aunt Odella crossed my mind a lot as I packed for the trip. Kept remembering how she'd packed the same suitcase the month before—how she'd folded all the pants and rolled all the socks and how neat and precise her work had been.

Mine was a suitcase casserole.

Wondered what she'd think about me taking off for

Oregon. Peaches and Cal couldn't make up their minds about whether or not I should write to her about what we were doing. Cal thought if she'd sent me all the way to North Carolina to find my father, she probably wouldn't care if I went to Oregon to keep looking for him. On the other hand, Peaches said if something happened to us on the trip, nobody would know where I was. "Think how his family would feel if Levi up and disappeared."

I didn't say, *Well, it has happened in the Battle family before*.

Finally, I ended up sending a short letter to my aunt that probably wouldn't arrive in her apartment mailbox until we'd reached Oregon anyhow. Hoped the news wouldn't upset her too much when she got it. She didn't seem like the kind of person who'd ever go and topple over, but people can surprise you. All they need is one loose brick somewhere. Tried to add a little humor at the end by telling my aunt I'd let her know if I happened to meet John Wayne. She liked Westerns a lot.

Before we left North Carolina, I splashed through the downpour to say goodbye to MawMaw Sands, like I'd promised. Despite the rain, she was sitting in her usual chair, wrapped in a ratty blue blanket against the chill. With only her eyes showing mostly, she coulda been a war refugee in a newspaper picture.

"You feeling all right, ma'am?" My feet hesitated halfway up the steps.

"I'd be feeling better if you remembered your manners and took off your hat when talking to me, seeing as how I'm old enough to be your great-great-granny," she snapped.

Ducking under the porch roof, I swiped off the cap I was wearing against the rain. Still casting an irritated glance in my direction, she tugged the blanket tighter around her shoulders. "So, you must be here because you're leaving town."

"Yes ma'am. Tomorrow." I nodded uncomfortably, fiddling with the hat in my hand. The whole porch felt different. No fat bumblebees buzzing. Or cats lazying around. Just drippy vines and baskets hanging heavily from the roof. Felt as if the whole scene might tumble down into ruins at any moment.

"Get me that basket from over there." One skinny arm poked out of the blankets and gestured sharply at the Keeper of Secrets basket. "I want you to have that one," the woman said, pointing at the same basket she'd shown me before.

Heck, I didn't know what to do. I didn't want to take one of the old lady's nice baskets as a gift. Not when I knew how much they cost and how much hard work they took to make. Plus, what would I do with a basket in Oregon? Tried to tell MawMaw Sands to keep it.

"Now, who else am I gonna give it to?" she retorted. "You take that basket like I says, Levi Battle. Don't give me none of that sass."

You can see I didn't have much choice. So, I picked up

the basket from the porch corner and tucked it under my elbow. Mumbled a polite thank-you.

"You remember what it's called?"

"Yes ma'am." I nodded. "Keeper of Secrets."

"You gonna take good care of it, right?"

"Yes ma'am."

"Whenever you meet up with your daddy, don't you forget what I've told you about how hard it is to be the keeper of secrets, especially when everybody else around you has their doubts. It ain't easy being the basket, no sir, it ain't."

Good grief, the old lady was talking in circles. I wasn't following much of anything she was saying.

"And you remember how every basket in this world is made of sweetness and pain. You can't have one without the other. They all get woven together, light and dark, smooth and sharp, bad things and good." MawMaw Sands paused and gave me a hard stare. "You listenin' to me, boy?"

Told her I was—although, to be honest, my mind had been wandering back to Aunt Odella and thinking about how she was fond of giving out presents with important reasons attached to them too. It almost made you regret opening them. For instance, she once gave a neighbor lady some Odorono deodorant for Christmas. Lady never spoke to us again.

"Well, I sure hope you remember what I said, Levi Battle, and I didn't waste my last breaths telling you everything I know." MawMaw Sands rose slowly from her chair. "Now I'm getting chilled from all this rain, so I'm going in. But let me shake your hand first, since it'll probably be a while before I see you again." Her old hand reached out for mine, and it felt strange to touch her sandpapery fingers for the first time. I shook them carefully and said goodbye.

"Take good care now, you hear? Don't you grow up to be too tall for your boots," she said. Then the old woman turned and shuffled slowly into the house, leaving the porch cold and empty.

Tell you the truth, I felt a big lump of sadness rise in my throat when I closed the gate behind me for the last time. BASKETS FOR SALE. Read the words once more and patted the cat who was sitting next to the gate like a sorry mop of orangeade fur. Glancing back, I could see the curtains of the house move a little as MawMaw Sands watched me leave from behind them—probably making sure I was being careful enough with her gift.

Early the next morning, we rolled past MawMaw Sands's house and out of Southern Pines for good. Everybody was feeling blue. The rain was still coming down in a slow drizzle and we were squeezed together in the front seat of the truck, sticking to each other worse than paste on stamps. Cal kept peeling his arm from the side of mine to wipe circles in the steamed-up windshield, just trying to see where he was going. Victory whimpered and cried in Peaches's lap. It was pure misery.

Between being late getting started and getting wet as we loaded the truck, nobody was in the mood to give the town a fond backward look as we drove off. Big ruts of muddy water filled the clay streets of Southern Pines, and Cal seemed to nail each one. Hard.

"Sweet and sugar, can't you take it any easier, Cal?" Peaches said in a tight voice, shifting Victory onto her shoulder as we bounced along. "You gonna ruin all our things."

What she meant was our food. Stuffed into our suitcases and bags was enough chow to feed an army because Cal and Peaches said we couldn't count on buying anything good on the trains, being the color we were. "Me and Peaches, we lived in the South all our lives, so we know all the tricks," Cal told me. "Trust me, our food tastes better than whatever stale sandwiches they'd try to sell us. And who knows, maybe things will be different in the West. Maybe we'll get to eat our meals in the dining car at tables with white linen tablecloths."

In case that didn't happen, we were carrying two loaves of bread, along with four cans of Spam and tuna fish for sandwiches. Plus a few pickles and apples. We'd brought two thermoses full of sweet tea and one of lemonade. A pound cake wrapped in wax paper. One bag of fried fish and another one of fried chicken nowhere near as good as

Aunt Odella's. Cal had thrown in a pound of peanuts too, when Peaches wasn't looking. "In case we get captured by the Japs," he'd whispered to me. There wasn't much chance of that, of course, unless our train grew wings and took off across the Pacific on its own.

Maybe it was the bumpy roads or how we were packed together like sardines in a can, but the closer we got to the town of Fayetteville, the more dread I felt. Seemed as if the air inside the stuffy truck was slowly disappearing, and it wouldn't be long before it was all used up. "Could you open your window some?" I mumbled to Cal when I couldn't stand it a minute longer. By then, I was sucking eggs and my stomach was in knots, let me tell you.

Peaches cast a worried glance toward me and cranked down her window fast. "You feeling sick, Levi?" She tugged a blanket farther over Victory's head to keep her dry as rain splattered through the open windows on us all.

"How's that?" Cal shouted over the rushing noise. "You doing any better, Legs?"

But the feeling of doom only got worse. Heck, I didn't know what was going on. There was no reason why I shoulda been feeling as bad as I was. I told Cal maybe it would be a good idea if he stopped the truck. The wheels skidded on the gravel as he turned onto the roadside and swung open his door. "Come on, I'll give you a hand," he said, as he helped to pull me out of the truck.

Now, I thought being on the good solid ground would help, but the feeling didn't go away one bit. The world seemed to be closing in on me. Clouds were falling on my head.

"What's going on, Legs?" Cal leaned closer, squinting at my face. Raindrops speckled the shoulders of his olive-green army jacket. "You worried about something?"

That's when the reason came crystal clear to me. Fear—that's what was eating me up. Like I said, fear isn't something I'm used to feeling too often. But it had grabbed hold of me now and was shaking me hard. I was afraid. Gut-bellied afraid. Afraid of going back to the town where I'd nearly been killed over nothing. Afraid of seeing the store. The storekeeper. Who knows what else.

Before I could stop myself, I was pouring out the whole crazy story, telling Cal everything. How it had been a blazing hot day. How all I wanted was a soda pop. How I'd never seen a real gun before in my life. The story tumbled out in random pieces, probably not making any clear sense. "Thought the fellow was gonna shoot me then and there," I said. "Right in the middle of his store. Nobody woulda known a thing." I barely got through the part about hiding in the field and getting as sick as a dog—before my teeth were clattering together so bad, I couldn't keep going with the story.

But I guess Cal had heard enough.

He didn't say a word at first, just pulled off his army cap and smacked the rainwater off it. "That ain't right," he replied finally, his voice low and angry. "You being put through all that shameful stuff when you first got here. You were just a kid from up north. How was you supposed to know right and wrong?"

"Well, I learned my lesson anyhow," I said, and tried giving a shrug like it didn't much matter now. "Never gonna make that stupid mistake again."

"It still ain't right." Cal jammed his army cap back on his head. "Me and Peaches, we'll keep watch over you in town. You gotta trust us. We know where to go and where not." Cal draped an arm over my shoulders. "Just remember, Legs—you and me, we're on the same side in this war. We got your behind covered, if something ever happens again. You just remember that." He broke into a grin. "Shucks, I got so much rifle range training, I could blow the cap off any soda bottle you wanted." He pretended to blast away at a row of bottles. "Blam. Blam. Blam."

"What in the world are you both doing out there?" Peaches leaned out the open truck window, glaring. "Victory's fussing and we gonna be late."

Me and Cal headed back around the truck. All Cal said when we got inside was how the fresh air had done wonders for me. And I gotta admit, I did feel better after spilling out my soul on the side of the road.

It's probably still there today, who knows.

It wasn't until much later—long after we'd left Fayetteville and North Carolina in the dust—that Cal told me how lucky I was. How it coulda been way worse. There could have been anything in that soda I drank, he said. Spit. Laundry soap. Even rat poison. He knew of colored folks who'd found themselves in places they shouldn't be, where they weren't welcome, and they'd been poisoned and almost died. "Not trying to scare you," he'd said. "But it's something you oughta know, Legs. Evil's everywhere in this world, same as good. You just gotta be careful."

Tell you the truth, I wished he hadn't told me. There are times in life when being ignorant is a whole lot easier.

23. The World as a Colored Person

With all my carrying on, we got to the train station in Fayetteville way later than we were supposed to. I didn't even glance in the direction of G. W. Keeton's store in the distance. Didn't want to see one worthless corner of that place. Me and Peaches sat on the colored benches behind the station, while Cal hurried to drop off his truck with an army lieutenant in town who'd agreed to buy it. The money he was getting for the truck would pay for the civilian train tickets we needed. I tried paying for part of mine with the leftover money from Aunt Odella, but Cal wouldn't take one cent. "I still owe your daddy for half the poker games I lost to him," he joked.

Seemed strange to see Cal returning on his own two feet. You had the feeling we'd really gone and done it now—our wheels were gone. There was no turning back. I think all of us breathed a little easier when our train rumbled into the station and we could stop worrying about what would happen if it didn't. As the drizzly rain fell on our shoulders while we waited to board, I thought about the old man who'd ridden with me before. Could still picture him hunched over his worn-out guitar, strumming the strings and singing his made-up tune to me:

> Wish I was a little rock a-settin' on a hill,
> Without another thing to do, but just a-settin' still.

It woulda been nice to see him again, you know what I mean? Maybe apologize for being as green as I was back then and ask him for some good advice about Oregon.

But this time, the conductor waved us to the end of the train instead of the first car. You could hear him call out, "Negroes to the last car. Negroes to the last car."

We shuffled toward a wood-sided caboose that looked as if it was a leftover from the last century. Inside, there were rows of seats with shabby cushions that seemed to be missing most of their stuffing. As if the accommodations weren't already bad enough, people started shutting all the windows and yanking down their window shades. The whole inside of the car plunged into a damp, yellowish gloom.

Peaches, who was sitting in front of me and Cal, turned around and pointed at the shade on mine. "Why don't you pull it down before we leave the station, Levi?"

I shrugged and told her I was fine. Figured we didn't need

to worry about any coal dust getting in, since we were about as far as you could get from the locomotive and still be on the train. Plus, I liked seeing the world as it passed by.

Peaches's eyes darted nervously toward Cal. "You tell him to pull his shade closed a little," she insisted loudly, like that dumb window was a matter of life or death.

I looked to Cal for some explanation of why she was suddenly acting so nuts. He shifted uncomfortably in his seat. "It's a good idea to close the shades, Legs." His voice dropped to a quieter mumble. "Down here, some people who don't know any better throw rocks at the windows of the last car."

"What?" Wasn't sure I'd heard him right.

"Boys. Mostly just ignorant boys with nothing better to do. If they see a car full of colored folks, they toss a few rocks at it, just being kids, you know." Cal's expression was embarrassed. "Always better to keep the shades closed until we get farther outta the South, just to be safe."

You had to wonder where our mixed-up world was heading. That's what I thought as I yanked down my shade like everybody else. Counting Cal, there were five colored servicemen in the caboose—soldiers who were going off to defend our country, and yet they had to hide their faces behind paper shades so they wouldn't get hit by rocks? We had a few mothers like Peaches, with babies in their arms too. What kind of people would throw rocks at helpless babies and their mommas? Or U.S. soldiers?

I have no idea how long we sat inside the stuffy, clattering caboose as it rumbled northward. Seemed like an hour or two at least before folks finally started lifting up the shades and peeking out. Cal nodded at ours and said, "Think we've gone far enough to open up the windows. Why don't you give us a little air now, Legs, and we'll have some of our special war rations."

I wasn't feeling real cheerful or hungry, but I followed orders.

Cal dug around the food basket until he found our stash of peanuts. Opening up the paper bag, he stuck his nose inside and took a big snort of the dusty, peanutty smell. "Mmm-hmmm." Scooping up a handful in his palm, he started eating them like there was no tomorrow, leaning over every once in a while to fling the shells out the open window next to me.

Watching those little bitty pieces fly away got me thinking about how nice it would be if your color was something you could take off whenever you felt like it. What if you could crack open your skin like a peanut shell and toss it away whenever you needed to be free of it? Order whatever soda you wanted in the store. Ride in the nice comfortable train cars with upholstered seats. Then put your brown shell back on again. Don't get me wrong, I didn't want to be white. Just thought it would be nice to have the chance to be free of who I was every once in a while.

When I told Cal what I was thinking about, he shook his head and gave me an odd look. "Holy smokes, they must teach you some strange things in those schools up north." He balanced a peanut between his thumb and forefinger. "See, I think you got it all backward. You're looking at being brown as a bad thing. But you aren't considering all the *good* things in this world that got brown shells. Take peanuts, for instance. They're brown-skinned."

He dug around in his front pockets until he found a half-eaten candy bar. "Chocolate. That's a sweet brown shade. Trees . . ." He pointed out the window. "They got brown bark. And where would this world be without trees?"

"Buckeyes." I remembered the hundreds stuffed under my bed back in Chicago. "They got brown shells."

"That's getting kinda tricky." Cal dug out another handful of peanuts from the bag and started cracking shells. "But okay, Legs, I'll give you buckeyes as a possibility." He nodded at the farm fields alongside the tracks. "Dirt. Almost all of it is a shade of brown. In fact"—a triumphant smile flashed across his face—"since dirt covers the whole world, you could say the earth itself has brown skin." He stuck one finger in the air like he'd just hit upon his best idea. "So, that must mean the whole world is a colored person!"

"What in the sweet name of Georgia are y'all talking about, Calvin Thomas?" Peaches turned around to stare at us as if she couldn't quite believe what she was hearing. "The whole world is a *colored* person?"

"Me and Legs are just having ourselves a little philosophical discussion, that's all." Cal ducked his head and changed the subject to what we were gonna eat for our noonday meal. But the idea of the whole world being a colored person somehow made me feel better.

24. Six Days

Over the next couple of days, we rode on so many differ-ent trains and traveled through so many states, I gave up keeping track after a while. Cal had figured it would take us three or four days to get West.

It took six.

And let me tell you, when you are traveling on one train after another, day in and day out, for six straight days, pretty soon you lose interest in almost everything except the in-side of your own eyelids. Your brain gives up caring about the landscape and spends most of its time wondering when the next stop is coming up. Every now and then, you glance out the window and notice: *Oh, more trees, more grass, more cows.* And then you go right back to staring at nothing.

Heading west, we crossed the Mississippi River—and I'll admit the Mississippi was an impressive spectacle. We reached it in the late afternoon on our second day of traveling. Now, I was expecting it to look something like

Chicago's familiar blue-green waterway where Uncle Otis used to fish for monster catfish. But the Mississippi wasn't like any river I'd ever seen. It didn't even look like water—more like coffee with cream. Picture a smooth, wide, coffee-colored river.

Peaches held Victory up to the window to see the sight. "Look at that big ol' river, Miss Victory," she said. "That's the Mississippi. A lot of terrible things happened on that river a long time ago to people who were your ancestors. They got shipped down the river in chains and never came back. But ain't it a peaceful-looking picture today? M-i-ss-i-ss-i-pp-i . . ." She spelled out the name slowly, as if Victory was gonna remember eleven letters in a row, when she wasn't a month old.

Got my first taste of coffee after we crossed the Mississippi too. On the other side of the river, the train stopped at a station in St. Louis that was a river all by itself. Soldiers everywhere. Torrents of tan and khaki, moving in all directions. I saw fellows tucked in places you wouldn't think human beings could sleep. Me and Cal spotted one soldier stretched out on his army duffel under the men's washroom sinks. Swear to God, he was fast asleep under the water pipes with men shaving their whiskers and brushing their teeth right above his head.

While Peaches was cleaning up Victory in the ladies' washroom, Cal and me wandered over to a place called a canteen where they serve free refreshments to weary soldiers traveling through. Cal was a big friend of anything free. Being in uniform, he got one of the ladies to give him two steamy paper cups of coffee, and brought them over to me, balancing them in each hand. "How do you drink your coffee, Legs?"

See, this was a tricky question to answer, because the truth was, I wasn't allowed coffee. Aunt Odella woulda had a flying fit seeing me with a cup, because she believed it could turn you even darker than you already were if you drank it too young. She still fixed hers with extra cream, and she was no spring chicken. Trying to be cautious, I told Cal I drank mine with some cream added.

"Really?" Cal looked surprised. "No sugar at all?"

Heck, did you put sugar in coffee?

"Maybe a spoonful," I replied, hoping that was the right amount.

"Coming right up." Still carrying the cups in his wobbling way, Cal headed back to the table where they had cream and sugar for the soldiers to use, and he slopped some into each cup. When he returned, he handed over my portion of river-colored liquid—only a shade or two lighter than the Mississippi itself—saying how me and my daddy were nothing alike when it came to coffee.

"Your daddy, he uses half a family's sugar ration in his. I've seen him put four heaping spoonfuls into one darn cup. Then he sits there stirring and stirring his coffee, trying to get all the sugar to melt." Cal grinned and shook his head. "No fooling."

I tried to act like this was a habit of his that I already knew about. Took a confident swallow of my own coffee and almost spit the whole mouthful on my shoes. Even with the sugar and cream, it tasted darned awful. Chunks of curdled cream floated on the top. I blew puffs of air across my cup, pretending it was too hot to drink. Good God, it was no wonder my daddy put so much sugar in the stuff.

"You remember anything else about him?" I managed to choke out between swallows.

"Okay . . . what can I tell you about Boots?" Cal squinted upward like he was trying to pluck some possibilities out of the air. "Well, he got his nickname from always having the best-looking pair of jump boots in the whole battalion. Swear they could be a picture postcard for the army paratroops when he's done polishing them. Always makes the rest of us look like slackers." Cal grinned and there was a pause as he tried to come up with more. "Let's see . . . he's a heck of a hip shot with the Browning. You want him on your side if you ever end up in a battle. And like I've said before, he's real sharp at cards—poker especially. His eyes don't miss a trick. Now, that's kinda like you, Legs." Cal gave me a soft jab in the ribs. "You got his same poker face sometimes."

Cal drained the last drops of his coffee and smacked his lips together. "Sometimes he can be a man of few words, but mostly he's easy to talk to. Still, he don't tell jokes anywhere near as good as me." Cal tossed his paper cup into a nearby trash can as we headed back to the platforms. "You and me are gonna work with him on that weakness, once we get back together with him."

Once we get back together with him. No idea why those words stuck with me for the next couple of days, but they did. Maybe because Cal was so sure we'd meet up with the men, and I wasn't at all convinced it was gonna happen. Let's put it this way, if we were playing poker, I wouldn't have bet a dime on it. Cal didn't know my daddy's habit of leaving like I did.

Beyond St. Louis, the land outside our train turned into a pie crust. Aunt Odella used to flatten dough on our kitchen table using the side of a water glass as a rolling pin, but I don't think her pie crusts were as flat as the land we passed through heading west. Missouri and Nebraska coulda won a contest, hands down.

We watched a big full moon come up from the horizon outside St. Louis. From our train windows, the ghost-white orb didn't even look real as it rose into the sky. Guess it must've made an impression on me, because I dreamed about it later—and I don't dream much. Even more surprising was the fact my father was there in the dream with me. I remember how we were bundled up in heavy coats and gloves and all, like it was a freezing cold Chicago night. But we weren't stomping around Chicago—we were trying to climb a snow-covered mountain. Only it wasn't snow, I realized after a while. It was sugar. We were climbing mountains of white sugar trying to touch the big moon that was hanging just above them.

Each time we got to the top of a peak, the moon kept slipping farther away. It would look like it was right in front of us—just within reach, a few more steps—and then we'd get to the spot, and the moon would be farther off than we thought. Each time my daddy would say, "Well, let's keep on going and we'll try the next mountain." And so we'd keep climbing.

When I finally woke up from that crazy dream, I felt like I'd climbed the darned Himalayas. Peaches said it was probably the full moon giving me bad dreams. I figured maybe it was my punishment for trying out that nasty coffee, who knows.

By the time we'd spent another two days on trains, I don't think the sight of a rainbow-colored moon coming up from the horizon woulda impressed any of us. Only good thing I can say is that at least we didn't have to keep riding in the colored cars once we left the South. We could sit wherever we wanted to, but the better seats didn't change the fact we were still stuck on a train.

To pass the time, Peaches had taken to walking up and down the swaying aisles with Victory on her shoulder, hypnotizing all the passengers as she went back and forth, back and forth, stepping over people and all kinds of riff-raff, until somebody complained to the conductor, and they made her stop.

One afternoon, Cal decided to give me some paratrooper lessons. "So you can impress your daddy with how much you know," he said, but I think it was just something to keep us from going nuts.

He taught me the commands—Get ready, Stand up, Hook up, Check equipment, Sound off—and how you Stand in the Door and jump with your chin down, elbows tight to your sides, and your feet together. He had me practice it, right where we were sitting. In the middle of a Union Pacific train car. I'm sure the people around us wondered if I was having some kinda nervous attack.

When I asked what door the jumpers stood in, Cal looked at me as if I had way less sense than he thought. "The open one."

"While the plane is flying?" My voice was shocked.

Cal rolled his eyes. "How else do you think you get out of an airplane? The wings? You stand there in the open door until they say 'Go' and you feel a smack"—he reached out and gave the side of my leg a slap. "And then you jump out."

Holy creeping criminy.

Cal went on, "You count to yourself on the way down—one thousand, two thousand, three thousand, waiting on your main chute to open. If you get to three thousand and it doesn't look like it's gonna happen, you pull your reserve chute and float down to earth, no big deal."

Don't know about you, but it didn't bring me much comfort to find out you had two chances for complete failure before you slammed into the earth face-first.

"Now, assuming everything goes well and your main chute does what it's supposed to, you'll hear a snap as it pops open and you'll get yanked upward by the force. I mean, *everything* gets yanked up. Your eyeballs, your toenails, your teeth, your privates . . . everything." Cal gave me a wide grin. "We call it the shock." He said it was like being a stretched-out rubber band that suddenly flies backward.

"Know what you do after your chute pops open?"

I thought about saying I'd thank the Lord Jesus and promise never to be so dumb as to jump out of a plane again.

"You check for blowouts."

"What?"

"Parachutes get holes in them, just like anything else. They're nothing but nylon and thread. Anyhow, if a tear opens up, trust me, it's only gonna get bigger on the way down. Pretty soon you're holding on to Swiss cheese." I could see Cal's eyes dancing behind his serious expression, so who knows if he was razzing me or not.

"But if everything looks fine and dandy, no blowouts, then you just hang on and float down to earth, looking at the pretty world stretched out below you—the trees, the hills, the rivers—getting closer. I'm telling you, it looks like one big picture painting from up there, Legs." Cal pointed upward. "It's like being a giant butterfly or a bird or something. Everything's so quiet and peaceful as you float down. We call it enjoying the ride."

Okay, he made that part sound almost good. You could tell from the expression on his face, he lived for that moment. For the ride. It took me a minute to realize all the important details he was leaving out. Such as the fact that paratroopers didn't usually jump into peaceful places like the ones he was describing. In a battle, they'd float down into fields studded with artillery and tanks and enemies trying to kill them.

Since Peaches was sitting in front of us, flipping through a magazine, maybe that's why Cal was being careful with how much he said. I asked him if he ever got scared when he was jumping.

Cal tugged an apple out of the bag below our seats and took a loud bite before answering. "Maybe when I was first training. Not much now." He shrugged. "You're either somebody who can trust things or somebody who can't. Or you can trust certain things but not others. Emerald Jones, our battalion cook, washed outta the paratroops because he couldn't jump out of a plane. He doesn't worry one bit about cooking over crackling hot flames where he could set himself on fire any day of the week—but he can't trust plain old air enough to jump into it. That's why trust is a funny thing."

I wasn't a big fan of trusting things either. Whenever Archie was trying to get me to do something stupid, he used to tell me, "You gotta trust me." The few times I believed him, I paid the price. Still had the scar on my forehead from when we turned a packing crate into a toboggan and rode it down a flight of stairs in his apartment building.

And I'll be honest—when you get left by your own mother before your life is hardly started, it doesn't give you much faith in the rest of the world sticking by you either.

Cal wiped his hand across his mouth. Our end of the train car smelled like an orchard. "Golly, that was a good apple." He was done talking about the army, you could tell. "Look at all that nice scenery out there." He pointed toward the window.

Stretching as far as you could see, the land was covered with wavy grasslands. Oval-shaped clouds drifted neatly across the sky in patterns large and small. Looked as if they were making up their own Morse code. Who knows where we were by then. Idaho? Wyoming?

Peaches whipped around in her seat and added her two cents, as if she'd been listening the whole time. "I'm sick of scenery. Don't want to see no more scenery as long as I live. I want to get off this darned train. Get me off the train, Sergeant Thomas, before I go stark raving crazy." She thumped her hand on the top of the seat.

Cal wagged his head, pretending to be sorry. "Can't do that, ma'am. We got our orders. Nobody's allowed to leave while we're still in enemy territory. Sorry."

Peaches lifted up one of Victory's spit-up cloths, waving it in the air like a white flag. "Then I surrender. Just let me surrender and go home, Sergeant, puh-leeze."

Cal told her nobody could surrender until we reached Oregon.

25. Jump Outta the Bird

We were on our sixth morning and our last dried-up, crusty drop of hope when we finally reached Pendleton, Oregon. After going uphill for most of the night, it seemed like, our train arrived in a town that looked no different from a hundred other towns we'd passed through already. "Approaching Pendleton station," the conductor announced in a bored voice as he came through the cars. "Everybody off who's getting off."

Now, I'd been picturing a Wild West kinda place, with swinging-door saloons and fake storefronts, but all I spotted from the train windows as we slowed down was an ordinary Main Street of redbrick buildings, striped awnings, and stee-pled churches. Not a tumbleweed or cowboy in sight. Low rolling hillsides without much green on them surrounded the town. In the far distance, there seemed to be a bigger line of purplish hills against the sky.

You shoulda seen us shoving comics and magazines and

Victory's things into our suitcases and bags at the last minute as the train slowed to a stop. With six days to get ready, you'd think we woulda been better prepared to arrive, right?

We weren't.

Cal's uniform had lost all its sharp creases somewhere back in Nebraska probably. He tried to spit and polish what he could, tucking his tie inside his jacket like all the GIs did and setting his army cap precisely on his head. Edge above the eyebrow, that was the rule, he told me, pulling it forward carefully with both hands until it balanced on the tip-top of his eyebrow, but its peaks were crushed from being in his duffel too long. Peaches pinned a wilted hat on her head. I had an armload of suitcases.

What was surprising to me was how nobody else got off the train at Pendleton except us. We stepped into the warm June morning by ourselves and glanced around looking for where to go next. No signs seemed to be pointing their accusing fingers at us, so that was a good thing. Maybe Oregon would be more like Chicago after all.

There was a small group of white GIs waiting on the platform, lounging on a pile of army duffels and gear. Cal strolled over to them to get some directions, but a white wall probably woulda been friendlier. I heard him ask where Pendleton Air Field was, and one of the fellows pointed to the far left, in the direction of a hill you could see on the edge of town. When Cal asked them for a lift up there, the request went nowhere until he handed over some dough.

Then one of the soldiers reluctantly got up and flagged down an army truck nearby.

As we walked over to the truck, it was clear Peaches wasn't crazy about the whole plan of riding in the back, especially when she saw how the only seats were benches and there was a strong odor of musty socks under the truck's canvas top. Me and Cal got a good whiff as we jumped inside.

Reluctantly, Peaches handed baby Victory to us and then she stood there, hands on her hips, sweat dotting her mahogany forehead. "How'm I gonna crawl up there, Cal?"

"Give Levi your hand." Cal nodded at me. "He can help you climb in."

"I'm not running my good stockings," she insisted, not moving. She was wearing a dress with faded green stripes that had seen better days and a pair of scuffed white pumps.

The army driver revved the motor like he was running outta patience, and the smoky cloud of exhaust just about extinguished us.

"Sweet and sugar, almighty Jesus—" Peaches reached for my hand and yanked so hard I nearly ended up face-first on the Pendleton dirt like an outlaw in a Western movie.

"Don't you let go of me, Levi!" Peaches hollered as she scrambled the rest of the way inside, all arms and legs, showing who knows what-all to the world. We were hardly seated on the benches before the truck blasted off down the road and sent us sliding.

"Holy mackerel, the driver must do takeoffs and landings in his spare time," Cal joked, trying to hang on to Victory with one arm and save some of our belongings with the other. Still trying to straighten out her dress, Peaches shot a look at Cal that wasn't a smile of amusement, let me tell you.

We were dumped farther away from the airfield than we wanted to be. Who knows why the driver didn't take us the whole way—Cal said it didn't matter, we needed the fresh air anyhow. As we trudged up the hill to Pendleton Air Base, you could see it wasn't gonna be a real beautiful place. Mostly hard-packed dirt and white two-story buildings scattered here and there.

"So this is my new post," Cal said when we reached the top. He handed Victory back to his wife and turned around slowly, studying everything. About halfway through his turn he stopped and pointed at some far-off specks in the sky. "Will you look at that, Peach—the boys are jumping today."

Right away, Peaches smacked her hands over her eyes and plopped down on one of the suitcases, saying she wasn't looking at the men jumping, nohow. "It scares me half to death. Don't even like imagining what you do, Cal, let alone seeing it for real."

If you squinted hard, you could just make out a bunch of tiny gray dots in the far distance. "You sure those are parachutes?" I said doubtfully, because it looked like nothing but a faraway flock of birds.

"Yep." Cal nodded, shading his eyes. "And right now their chutes are drifting on the smooth morning air and they're just sitting back and enjoying the ride." His voice sounded wistful. "Boots and the boys are probably floating along, wondering what in the world those three sorry specks are doing at the gates of Pendleton. They people? Or ants?" He pretended to wave, although the specks woulda needed the vision powers of Superman to notice us from that far away.

"See, you can tell it's our boys by the way the chutes look," Cal said. "Everything's in a perfect pattern like one big connect-the-dots in the sky. They must've jumped outta the bird without missing a beat." He draped an arm over my shoulders. "I'm telling you, we are perfection in the air, Legs. You'll see—the 555th is sweet perfection."

Even with Cal pointing out every little detail, I had my doubts about what we were looking at. Like I said, the far-off dots didn't look much like parachutes, and you couldn't see any human beings holding on to them. I may not have had Aunt Odella's sixth sense for things, but whatever sense I did have was telling me there was no way my father was up there in the wide blue sky. No chance at all.

A white army guard interrupted our gawking. He came ambling toward us on the other side of the gate, toothpick dangling from his lip. His smooth young face didn't even look old enough to grow whiskers yet and his arms were a bright sunburned pink. "You folks want something?"

I think the twangy western sound of his voice impressed us all—it was kinda like being in a Western movie and a war newsreel at the same time. Tugging the official army letter out of his pocket, Cal showed it to the young soldier and told him how we'd come from Camp Mackall in North Carolina to join the 555th in Oregon. "And I'm hoping to find some off-post housing for my family," Cal said, nodding at us.

The young soldier's eyes rested on my face for a minute or two, as if he was trying to figure out how I belonged with the rest of them. We must've looked like a real mismatched set of silverware—Cal, Peaches, baby Victory, and then me, a thirteen-year-old kid standing next to them.

"I'll check with the commander." The soldier ambled slowly back to his small guard shack and disappeared inside. Meanwhile, we waited in the flies and hot sun, without a stick of shade anywhere. Peaches flapped a towel over Victory's face, trying to keep her cool. The sky was empty, and Cal said the paratroopers were probably on the ground rolling up their chutes at that very moment.

I thought it was more likely the birds we'd been looking at had flown away.

Finally the guard came back and swung open the gate without saying a word to us. Guess that was his idea of a warm welcome. After we got inside, he closed the gate again and took off in the direction of a white building nearby that had a round garden in front of it. A ring of desperate-looking red flowers was planted inside the circle of white bricks, with a flagpole stuck in the middle.

I figure the commander must've had radar for eyes because the guard hardly got past the garden before a uniform loaded with all kinds of badges and pins and patches came barreling out of the building. Cal snapped to attention as the white commander headed stiffly toward us. Me and Peaches stood up a little straighter too.

"At ease, soldier," the commander said, more to the flagpole than to Cal, it seemed like. Cal slid his arms behind his back, and Victory started making burping noises and waving her little fists as if she was free to move now too. The man's steely eyes slid in her direction. "Your family?" he asked Cal, not even trying to hide his disapproval.

"Yes sir. That's my wife and baby daughter. And the older boy is the son of Second Lieutenant Battle, sir. He's been staying with us for the duration."

The officer's eyes swept over me and I felt the same kinda chill I'd got from the storekeeper in Fayetteville. Antarctica in a uniform, that's what the commander reminded me of. The ground began to sway and wobble beneath me as I tried not to breathe too loudly. Or at all.

"And your mother is where?" the commander snapped.

Heck, I had no idea what to reply. You don't go around telling somebody who has more stripes on his uniform than a U.S. flag how your mother was a Chicago jazz singer who took off when you were a baby.

Cal jumped in to save me. "His mother is gone—deceased," he added, with only the smallest trace of a fib in his voice.

The commander's face grew more displeased, if that was possible. "Well, I don't like Negroes being here on this post—or in the town either, let me be perfectly straight about that, soldier." His eyes nailed Cal to the dirt. "If it were up to me, none of you would be in this war. You'd know your place and stay in it. And our GIs would be out fighting the Japs where we belong. We have a tough enough war to wage in this world without playing around with the color lines and wasting our damned time training Negroes to jump out of airplanes."

Let me tell you, I couldn't believe what I was hearing. *Could not believe it.* Had to practically glue my own lips together to keep my mouth from dropping clear open. A commander of the U.S. Army talking to Cal in that uppity way? Trust me, if Aunt Odella had been listening, there wouldn't have been a barbed wire pie big enough to serve the man. Couldn't see Cal's face from where I was standing, but his body didn't move an inch during the whole speech. He was a statue.

The commander continued his talking without letup. "But since I have my orders and you have yours, soldier, it seems there is nothing we can do about the problem of you being here at Pendleton, is there?" He glanced at his watch and gestured at the buildings around us. "Except for some of my officers and pilots, your battalion is the only one here. Their barracks are at the end of this road. I expect they should be back from their practice jump within the hour." His eyes swept over us again, a dark cloud cutting out the sun. "Good luck finding a place for your family to live. Negro soldiers aren't welcome in too many places around this town, and their families—even less."

Victory picked this moment to let out a sudden, earsplitting screech as if she'd just been stuck by the world's biggest pin. From the look the commander gave her, I was afraid he might take her outta this world right then and there. Peaches must've feared the same thing, because she pushed Victory's howling face into her shoulder and began rocking her worse than a ship. Thankfully, the commander turned and headed back to his headquarters, leaving us all in one piece.

Once the officer's door slammed shut, Peaches hollered at the top of her lungs, "You hush up," as if she was talking to Victory, but I don't think she was. Her words echoed in the stillness around us. *Hush up. Hush up. Hush up.* Cal rubbed his eyes and shook his head ever so slightly. Under his breath, he ran through a whole list of cuss words that woulda made Aunt Odella turn a new shade, let me tell you.

Then, just as fast, the storm cleared and he broke

into a wide smile. "Well, now that we got that pleasant conversation with the colonel squared away, I think it's time to find my buddy Emerald in this friendly place and get ourselves some chow."

We were walking in the direction of a building Cal thought was the mess hall when a collection of trucks and jeeps pulled up at the same gates we'd come through. Time seemed to slow to a crawl as we stopped and looked back, watching the gates swing open and the trucks start motoring through them, one by one. Next to me, I heard Cal shout to Peaches that it looked like Tiger Ted driving the first truck. With the sunlight glaring off the windshield, I couldn't see a soul sitting inside, but Cal waved his arms at the driver. I remember the trucks stopping all of a sudden and doors flying open as colored soldiers piled out of them, sweeping up Cal as if he was their long-lost brother. Me and Peaches had to step back before we got swallowed up in the fray. And somewhere in all that noise and confusion, I heard Cal shout, "Hey, Boots, you recognize that boy standing over there?"

26. The Shock

'll be honest—I don't think either of us recognized the other at first.

Once Cal pointed me out, I remember how all the soldiers suddenly moved backward like the Mississippi drying up—and how there seemed to be only one man left standing nearby, just a step or two away from where I was.

Now, I'd always pictured my father being way bigger than me, almost Superman in size—maybe because I was a lot smaller when he left. But I was almost eye to eye with the soldier across from me now. Same face as mine, with the jaw jutting out a little. Same nose. Same mouth. The look in his dark brown eyes was shock, I remember that clearly. I'm sure my eyes looked the same way. And in that split second as we stood there, staring at each other for the first time in three years, I knew exactly what Cal meant about the feeling you get when a parachute opens. How your eyeballs, your teeth, your toenails, everything gets snapped upward by the force of the parachute catching you. Because that's how I felt—as if my whole body had suddenly been yanked upward. Everything was a blur of air, sky, skin.

I remember how my father's big arms suddenly wrapped around my shoulders, and the loud clang as his helmet hit the ground. Heck, it felt like being clutched by an army tent, with all the canvas he was wearing. My worn-out Chicago shoes came real close to being pancakes too. Didn't need to wonder where my big feet came from, after seeing the size of his jump boots.

What got to me the most, though, was realizing how I was dead right about the buckeyes. My father was the color of buckeyes. *I'll be darned,* I remember thinking when I stepped back. Guess I'd always doubted that memory a little. Had my daddy really held a buckeye next to his arm and said he'd fallen from the same tree? But I would have known that familiar red-brown shade of his arms anywhere. Probably coulda made a whole father—a whole family—outta all the buckeyes I'd stuffed in my pockets over the years.

My daddy spoke first. His voice was softer than you'd expect from a big man, although I guess mine wasn't real booming either.

"How you doing, Levi?" he said, taking an embarrassed swipe at the glistening corners of his eyes. Then he glanced around at all the soldiers standing there gawking at us like we were humanity on parade. You could tell he was real uncomfortable, and I was feeling warm under the spotlight too. He cleared his throat once, and then again. Rubbed the back of his neck in a way that reminded me exactly of Aunt Odella. "Well, this sure is some kinda surprise I wasn't expecting today," he said finally.

I know people were waiting on me to say something warm and heart-tugging next, but every line of the English language seemed to have left my head. Instead, I stood there with my hands stuffed in my pockets and my feet shifting uneasily on the dirt. Felt the same as when we'd arrived in Pendleton earlier that morning—how even though we'd had six days to be prepared, we weren't ready. I'd had three years to plan what to say to my daddy when I saw him again, and now I couldn't come up with one useful word.

Peaches and Cal swooped in to save the day. "Holy mackerel, we been traveling across the country forever," Cal announced in an extra-cheerful voice. "We're ready for some eats. How about if we double-time it over to the mess hall and leave Boots and his son alone, so they can have themselves a little peace-and-quiet time?"

I don't think those soldiers coulda jumped outta a C-47 any faster than they took off after Cal said those words. Me and my daddy were left standing with nothing but our own shadows for company as they piled into the trucks— squeezing Peaches and Victory and all our gear inside with them—and zoomed off.

* * *

Now, you'd think we could have let down our guard after that and picked up the pieces where we'd left off as father and son. But, after three years of being apart, what do you talk about first? In the movies, it always seems perfect when two lost people find each other. Some sad-sack music starts playing and a sunset rolls across the screen and then the movie's over.

Heck, that woulda been nice, but it doesn't happen that way in real life, I guess. The sun wasn't anywhere close to setting and there was no orchestra in sight. Honestly, it felt like we were two strangers—as if we were two people meeting on a bus. Sure, we'd sent all those letters back and forth to each other, but letters aren't the same as a conversation, you know what I mean? By the time you get a reply to something you've written in a letter, you've half forgotten what you said.

Searching around for something to talk about, my daddy brought up Aunt Odella.

"How's Odella doing? She all right?" he asked hesitantly. You could tell he was wondering if something might've happened to her and maybe that's why I'd shown up on his doorstep all of a sudden.

When I told him she was the same as always, you could see the confusion deepen.

"How about Uncle Otis—he still cutting heads?"

I nodded.

"Huh." My daddy hooked his fingers behind his back and studied the cloudless Oregon sky. "So you came all the way out here with Peaches and Cal to find me?"

It was easy to see he was jumping to the conclusion that I'd run away from Aunt Odella. That somehow I'd ended up with Peaches and Cal while searching the country high and low for him. Well, the last thing I wanted to do was go into the long story after I'd just arrived. Sometimes, in life, the imagination is way better than the reality anyhow, you know what I mean?

So all I said was yes, I'd come along with the two of them. Then I veered down a new conversational road and asked my daddy if he'd been one of the paratroopers we thought we spotted in the sky that morning.

A big smile finally eased across my father's face. "Did you see us up there before?" He pointed at the sky. "Man, it was a heck of a beautiful jump this morning. Perfect weather. Warm and sunny, no wind. Couldn't have been better. Just perfect."

Even with the proof standing right next to me, I was still having a hard time picturing my father being up there in the wide-open sky. Kept glancing over at him like there oughta be part of a cloud stuck to him or something, you know?

Acting like he was eager to show me more, my daddy started in the direction of the mess hall, saying he'd give me a quick tour of the air base on the way to chow. I swear he walked at a speed most normal people would run. As I tried hard to keep up, he pointed out the different buildings on each side of the dusty road as if he was the official army tour guide and I was a fresh-off-the-farm GI.

Barracks. Officers' Quarters. Post Exchange. Dispensary. Operations Shed.

None of the buildings were real special-looking. Most of them were painted white and didn't appear to be used much. The whole place felt kind of deserted. As my daddy reached the screen door of the mess hall and pulled it open, I was glad to see people again.

"No officers' mess hall here," my daddy shouted over the clamor of a roomful of servicemen. "We all eat together, officers and enlisted."

Second Lieutenant Charles Battle. Heck, I'd forgotten all about him being an officer. Watching some of the soldiers jump up to clear spaces for us at the tables and seeing them plunk water glasses and silverware in front of us, I felt kinda proud all of a sudden, you know? Pulled my shoulders back a little as we strolled into the big room. I was an officer's kid, how about that? The Battle family. Kings of the mess hall.

Forgot my daddy was a lefty too until we banged elbows taking our first mouthfuls of the turkey and green beans piled on our trays. Guess he forgot I was a righty from the surprised look that passed across his face and how he said in an embarrassed voice, "Long time since we sat down to eat a meal together, I guess."

No two ways about it, we didn't remember the smallest things about each other. Even our elbows weren't very familiar.

After chow, the cook I'd heard about from Cal—the one called Emerald Jones—came out of the kitchen carrying a big batch of peanut butter cookies. My daddy might've complained about the army food a lot in his letters, but Emerald's golden-brown creations were the size of saucers. You could hear the cook's friendly laughter bouncing all over the mess hall. "For our guests," he announced, sliding the whole mouthwatering tray in front of our group. "You can share with some of the other fellows if you'd like, but only if they promise to do their fair share of KP." There was a loud groan. "Pans don't wash themselves," Emerald tossed out as he headed back to the kitchen.

Me and Cal had a good time passing around the cookie tray until it was empty. There were at least a hundred paratroopers packed in the room, and I swear Cal introduced me to all of them. Twice. "These fellows are the greatest troopers in the airborne," he repeated at each table.

Archie woulda been real impressed by all the muscle. I met the soldier called Tiger Ted who looked like he could beat the peanut butter cookies outta anybody. He'd fought Joe Louis once, according to Cal. Next to Tiger, there was a skinny soldier with light brown skin and a wide, goofy smile.

Swear he didn't look much older than I was. "He's a good kid," Cal said. "Everybody calls him Mickey." Opposite him, a scowling fellow known as Ace barely glanced up when we passed by, just kept shoveling food in.

"He'll warm up," Cal whispered.

One trooper even challenged me to an arm-wrestling match for a cookie. Seeing as how his arms were the size of most people's legs and his nickname was Killer, I gave him any cookie he wanted and got the heck outta there.

While most of the fellows were friendly, you got the strange sense that beneath the smiles and joking, there was something else brewing in the room. Seemed like the soldiers were trying to be polite to us and all, but it was a lot of hard work to do. And once you turned around, the sunny conversation slipped back into a black cloud. Cal noticed it too. "Guys don't seem real gung-ho today. Maybe they're all tired-out from the jump this morning, who knows."

While me and Cal were taking the peanut butter cookies around the mess hall, Peaches gave my father the scoop on Aunt Odella and how she'd sent me packing. Guess the truth woulda come out eventually, but it was too bad my daddy had to find out so soon that I wasn't the desperate runaway he thought I was. It woulda been nice to hang on to that piece of fiction for a while, you know?

What seemed to puzzle him the most was why Aunt

Odella decided to give me the heave-ho in the first place. "Doesn't sound like her at all," he kept insisting as the four of us talked after the meal.

I gotta admit I sweated over how much more to say, especially after what Peaches had already told him. Knew I had to walk a narrow tightrope with my facts. Couldn't exactly tell him how Aunt Odella thought he needed to take responsibility and be a father to his son. So, I tried to pin the blame on the cactus instead. I described how Aunt Odella had been convinced her old cactus blooming was a sure sign the war was ending and that's why she'd sent me to find him.

"Let me get this straight." My daddy plucked out the lollipop he was chewing on and gave me his best lieutenant stare. "Odella sent you away because a cactus told her the war was ending?"

All right, so it wasn't completely, one hundred percent true, but I nodded.

My daddy let out a long sigh. "Holy smokes." He shook his head slowly. "This war has turned everybody's minds a little crazy, even Odella's. Never woulda expected it of her, of all people. She was always a hard nut to crack, I thought, but maybe the war caught up with her too after all this time." He brushed off his canvas trousers and stood up like he'd heard enough.

Tried not to let him see my big sigh of relief.

"Well, we better get busy finding you and Cal's family a place to live. Can't have you bunking in the barracks, right?"

He cracked a smile. "Let's head out back and I'll introduce you to Graphite, our official army heap."

The four of us wandered outside, with Peaches holding baby Victory, who was fast asleep for once. Behind the mess hall, there was a well-worn Ford the soldiers had bought for themselves. It reminded me of the old jalopy my daddy used to drive.

"Only a 1937," my father said, "and it runs great." The vehicle had one door painted army green while the rest of the car was black, and there was a piece of plywood for a front bumper. Uncle Otis woulda called it a disgrace on wheels.

My daddy said, "Get in and I'll take you for a ride."

Now, you'd expect after three years of being away from my father, I'd get to enjoy a few minutes sitting next to him as we rolled down the road. But I guess some things never change, no matter how old you are. Cal took the front seat and I had to squeeze into the back along with Peaches and Victory and all our things, as if I was being returned straight to age nine. I'll admit it stung a little.

"Ain't it wonderful seeing your own daddy again?" Peaches whispered as we started toward town. "Can't imagine how you must be feeling after all this time."

I kept my feelings to myself and didn't point out how all I was looking at was the back of his head, which was a familiar memory of mine. Already knew the razor-sharp line his hair made just above his collar and the creases of his wide red-brown neck.

Once we got to the town, my father turned onto Main Street, showing us some of the local places: Rexall Drugs, the Hotel Pendleton, the Cherry Fried Chicken Shack, F. W. Woolworth's, Chinese groceries, and churches on every corner almost. The town reminded me a lot of Southern Pines—only without the bushy green pine trees and bright flowers. Low brown hills surrounded Pendleton and everything looked a little faded, as if it had been in the sun too long.

"They friendly around here or not?" Peaches leaned forward to ask my father. I knew she was wondering about all the flak that white commander had given to us.

"Not real friendly, no," my father shouted over the rushing noise of the open windows. "Most places you won't find signs like you'd see in the South. Out here, they'll just pretend they don't see you. You go into a restaurant and try to order something, and nobody will come to your table. The sun could rise and set for a week, and they'd let you sit there, waiting."

Well, how dumb was that? That's what I was thinking in the backseat. What was the point of spending six days sitting on our behinds and sleeping on trains to come to a place where people would pretend we weren't there? We'd gone from being colored to being invisible, which couldn't be considered any big improvement in my opinion.

"So we can't go in any of the places you showed us?" Peaches said, her voice rising.

"You can go in a few of them—Rexall's is fine. And the banks will take anybody's money, of course. And you can order whatever you want from the Chinese," my father said as we rolled past two tiny restaurants that didn't seem to have one word of English on their signs. Just a bunch of squiggles and shapes. My daddy insisted the Chinese were friendly and we'd learn to fall in love with rice and noodles.

Shaking her head, Peaches slumped into her seat and began patting Victory's back as if she was going for the land-speed record in burping. Don't think she was real happy with the idea of eating Chinese people's food. Franks and beans were beginning to sound good again.

Up front, the conversation switched over to the war itself. And things didn't get a whole lot better. I heard Cal ask my daddy if he knew when they'd be heading to the Pacific and what their mission might be.

There was a strange silence.

You could see Cal turn his head and glance curiously at my father. After another minute or two had gone by, I heard him toss out the same question again. "So what's the word on our mission?" he asked, being more casual. "Didn't hear nothing back at Mackall before we left. When we shipping out?"

Another long silence. My daddy's eyes didn't stray from

the road as far as I could tell. Finally I heard him say quietly, "We aren't shipping out to the Pacific, Cal."

I swear Peaches must've been hanging on to every syllable being uttered up front, because her happy voice suddenly shot out from the backseat, "Hallelujah, Lord Jesus, my prayers have been answered!"

Only thing was, Cal didn't seem to share Peaches's same hallelujah spirit. He jutted one elbow out the open window and gave a sigh of frustration you could hear in the backseat, loud and clear. "So we're not shipping out?" he repeated.

"That's right," my daddy answered.

"When are we gonna stand up and say we've had enough of this nonsense, Boots?" Cal's suddenly loud voice startled both me and Peaches. Didn't sound like Cal at all. "I'm done with coming to these places." His hand jabbed furiously at the scenery going past. "Nobody wants us here. Nobody wants us in this war. Uncle Sam sends us chasing all over the damn country from one hick army post to the next like a bunch of fools, telling us we're training for missions we never get sent to do." His voice rose. "They send half the airborne to invade Normandy. Never send us. Tell us we're gonna be the ones to go after Hitler and mop up in Germany. Never send us. Tell us we're training for Italy. Never send us. When are we gonna say we've had enough of being lied to?"

As Cal talked, my mind circled back to the train ride south where I'd been asked to do my part for the war and help guard the baggage—only there was no baggage to guard. Could still picture Jim Crow howling with laughter when I didn't know the real reason I'd been sent to the baggage car was the color of my skin. Cal's story had some of the same echoes of mine, you know?

In the front seat, Cal's voice rolled on, getting even louder. "We got the best damn jumpers in the army, Boots. We've done everything—every screwball stunt the army's asked us to do. Jumped out of gliders. Tried out parachutes nobody else would try. This time I thought for sure we'd be going to the Pacific. Thought there was no question at all." He shook his head. "Can't believe we've come all the way out here—to who the hell knows where—and the army's changed its mind again. It ain't right, Boots. You know it as well as I do. This whole war, we've been risking our necks day after day, trying to prove we can do things better than everybody else. And for what?" Cal swiped his army cap off his head and flung it angrily out the open window. "For a hell of a lot of nothing if you ask me."

That was a surprise, let me tell you—seeing Cal's good army cap go sailing into the weeds. A sweaty silence filled the automobile, as if everybody was waiting on everybody else to say something next. You could hear Victory's hiccupping breaths and the sound of Peaches mumbling "Sweet and sugar, sweet and sugar," under her breath like a piece of scripture. My father's shoulders didn't budge from their stiff place against the front seat. Don't know what I thought finding my daddy would be like, but I never imagined this crazy scene.

Finally my father broke the silence.

His voice was dead calm, like Aunt Odella's when she's in a fury. "You asked me about shipping out, and I said we weren't going to the Pacific," he answered evenly. "But you didn't ask me if we have a mission here." He paused, making sure he had everybody's attention, I guess. "If you had asked me that particular question, Sergeant Thomas, I would have told you yes, as a matter of fact, this time we do."

27. Secrets

Prying the details outta my father wasn't easy, though. Guess MawMaw Sands knew what she was doing when she gave me the Keeper of Secrets basket, because my father was one big keeper of secrets up there in the front seat, saying nothing more as he drove down the road.

Retrieving Cal's cap wasn't a piece of cake either. Me and Cal had to wade through a battalion of grasshoppers to get it. When we got back to the car, Cal kept apologizing for losing his cool and asking if it was a big mission or a small one. Was it gonna be in Oregon or somewhere else? Had training already started or not? But he coulda been talking to the scenery, because my daddy wouldn't answer one question until he was good and ready. Even Peaches couldn't get him to talk. She poked my father's shoulder with one of her fingers. "Puh-leeze, why won't you tell us more? I'm an army wife. And Levi's your son. And we don't know a blessed soul out here. Who we gonna blab secrets to?"

My father kept his mouth shut until we were well outside of town and all signs of civilization had disappeared. We were rolling through an empty landscape straight out of a Western movie, where you almost expected to see Indians coming over the grassy hilltops on horseback, when he finally stopped and took a left down another road. It turned out to be even more deserted than the one we'd been on. The road started out as gravel and ended up being nothing but two wagon ruts.

Peaches complained loudly, "Sweet and sugar, you trying to turn us all into powder in the backseat?"

The wagon trail ended in a grassy spot overlooking a shallow river. In the far distance, you could see the tip-tops of a few church steeples in Pendleton sticking up, and beyond that, the purplish-blue hills we'd noticed from the train.

"Wanted you to see the Blue Mountains," my daddy said, pointing at them through the windshield, "and the Umatilla River." It was a real pretty place, we had to agree. But I think even baby Victory—who didn't recognize the difference between food and her fingers yet—coulda guessed he hadn't brought us all the way out to the deserted spot to admire the landscape.

Sure enough, after we'd spent a few minutes gazing at the view, my father cranked up his window like we were in a spy movie. Without even being told, Cal rolled up the one on his side until we were sealed inside that Ford, tighter than a canned ham. "We're under orders to tell the civilians around here nothing," my father began in a low voice. "So you can't go and repeat—"

"We promise our lips are sealed," Peaches interrupted.

Cal turned around and gave her a glare. "Hush up. Let him talk."

What my father said next shocked us all. I don't think any of us were expecting to hear we were under attack. But that's exactly what he said. Clearing his throat, my father told us that we were under attack by the Japs.

"What?" Peaches shouted, bolting upright in her seat. "The Japs are here?"

All of us glanced nervously toward the closed-up car windows, as if the enemy might be lurking outside at that very moment. As if Japan was just over the next hill.

My daddy continued without a pause, telling us how the Japs had invented a new secret weapon and they'd already started using it to attack the West. Only the new weapon wasn't like the kamikaze planes they'd been unleashing on our ships in the Pacific, or the deadly bombing of Pearl Harbor, or anything like that. "The truth is," he said, "the Japs are attacking us from across the ocean using secret exploding balloons."

What?

I'll be honest, if I'd heard this story line from my friend Archie, I woulda called him flat-out nuts and asked for some proof. How could the Japs be attacking our country with balloons sent *all the way* across the Pacific Ocean? And if it was true, why hadn't we heard a single warning about it on the radio? Or read something about it in the newspapers?

But my father didn't seem to have any doubts about the story he was giving us. He went on describing how the enemy's new weapons looked exactly like giant hot-air balloons, only they were filled with hydrogen gas instead, and they floated across the ocean on the air currents carrying clusters of bombs beneath them.

"Bombs?" Peaches's voice trembled.

"Picture a huge white balloon, maybe three stories high, carrying a ring of explosives and fire bombs beneath it," my father said, sketching an invisible circle in the air.

I sincerely hoped Peaches didn't picture it.

"Once the balloons get here, they start drifting down and exploding. It's been so dry this spring, the West is a matchstick. Wouldn't take much for this whole part of the country to go up in flames. The army's put us in charge of fighting fires out here this summer and finding whatever balloon bombs we can track down. We've already started training." My father glanced toward Cal. "Army's calling it Operation Firefly."

Operation Firefly?

Honestly, even the name sounded made-up. A mission to fight forest fires and find balloons?

Guess Cal must've had a few of his own doubts because

he asked, "How many enemy balloons have you seen since you've been out here?"

And here's where the whole story began to deflate, because my father had to admit none of the paratroopers had spotted any yet. Not a single one. The army had given them drawings of what the balloons looked like, and a couple of photographs, and a small square of cream-colored paper the army claimed came from a Jap balloon, but none of the men had come across a real one.

Which might've explained the dark feeling me and Cal had noticed in the mess hall.

"We've only been out here a month," my father tried to say. "I keep telling the men it's only a matter of time."

Inside the automobile, the doubts and questions grew along with the temperature. Cal sighed and rubbed his forehead as if it was all too much to take in. Next to me, Peaches chewed on her lips nervously and stared out the window. It felt like the times when Uncle Otis told a wild story at the Sunday dinner table—something about ladies usually—and how nobody at the table would know what to say next and everybody would suddenly get interested in picking up their peas, one by one, with their forks. It was the same kind of embarrassed silence.

I didn't know what to think. The idea of big balloons floating all the way across the Pacific Ocean with bombs attached to them seemed nuts. On the other hand, it didn't seem likely that the U.S. Army would go around inventing stories either.

Up front, my daddy must have decided he'd spilled enough secrets for one day, because he cranked open his window to let in some fresh air and started up the motor. The sun was already low on the hills in front of us, casting shadows. "We better head back to town before it gets too late."

In no time at all, the conversation switched from balloon bombs to where we were gonna rest our weary heads that night. Guess the uppity army commander knew what he was talking about after all, because we stopped at two or three places in town with ROOMS FOR RENT signs, but I don't think they woulda opened their arms to Mary and Joseph if they'd been our color.

Finally we ended up at a house belonging to one of the few colored families in town. My daddy said some of the other troopers knew the Delaneys from church and they were real nice people—if you didn't mind the crazy shade they'd used to paint their house. When he pulled up to the front of it, all we could do was stare.

The place was yellow. Bright corncob yellow.

As if the eye-peeling paint color wasn't bad enough, the back of the house was next to the railroad tracks. Honest to goodness, if the place was moved a couple feet farther, locomotives coulda barreled right through it.

The landlady, Mrs. Delaney, told us her husband worked

on the Union Pacific Railroad as a porter and that was the reason for the color and the closeness to the tracks. "So whenever he's passing through town, day or night, he can always spot our house like a beacon among all the others."

I didn't say anything, but I thought, *Good God, why not switch on a lamp instead?*

"Least you can't see the glow from the inside," Cal whispered.

Easy for him to say since he and my daddy wouldn't be staying there.

As we wandered through the house, trying not to seem nosy, Mrs. Delaney told us chapter and verse about her family. She was a short, busybody lady who seemed to like talking more than listening. Her two grown sons, George and Robert, were serving in the navy, and she had a fourteen-year-old daughter named Willajean who was starting high school that fall. I didn't spot her daughter anywhere around, but you couldn't miss her sons because there were framed pictures of them everywhere you looked. It was like being in a George and Robert museum. Photographs of them in uniform. Pictures of them at graduation. A row of grade-school photographs. When she showed us the two tiny bedrooms she had for rent, it was no big mystery who the rooms belonged to. "These are my boys' rooms," Mrs. Delaney said. "What do you think?"

No matter what anybody thought, you could see we had to take what was being offered. It was like being the last one in the serving line at school, when all the choices are gone. My daddy and Cal shelled out a month's rent, plus a little extra for food. "No reason why we shouldn't share meals," Mrs. Delaney insisted.

I hoped the lady was better at cooking than she was at keeping house because the whole place was like Fibber McGee's closet—so crowded with furniture and all kinds of whatnot, you could hardly find a clear place to sit down. The four of us stood uncomfortably in the middle of the front room making last-minute conversation before my daddy and Cal left for the barracks.

Cal kissed the top of baby Victory's head and gave Peaches a quick goodbye peck on the cheek, telling them he'd be back soon. Of course, Peaches didn't want to let him go. You could see she was real close to coming apart at the seams.

"I'm not going to Japan, sugar pie. I'll be at the top of the hill," Cal tried to say, pointing at the windows. "If you look, you can probably see the airfield from here."

Doing his best to steer clear of the discussion between the two of them, my daddy told me he'd send Aunt Odella a telegram to let her know I'd got to Oregon safe and sound. He looked as if he still couldn't quite believe I was there. "Be a big help to the Delaneys, all right? Me and Cal will stop back again as soon as we can."

From the doorway, Mrs. Delaney jumped in to add how

I reminded her exactly of her younger boy, Robert. "He's the spitting image. It'll be like having him back home again. I'll spoil him like I did Robert."

Already I could tell she was gonna be a pain.

Then my father and Cal headed for the door and I'll admit it was harder than I woulda expected to watch them leave. The scene took me right back to the days I used to get left with Granny—the way my father always pulled the door shut softly behind him and the extra skip you could hear his feet make on the last step. I swear the only thing missing was the disappearing smell of mint.

For a minute or two I was afraid I was gonna have to embarrass myself by reaching up to wipe my darned eyes, but then Mrs. Delaney came barreling into the rooms and started switching on every lamp until the place was blazing. She insisted we sit down for a getting-to-know-you chat. Meaning me and Peaches, of course.

"Won't take no for an answer," she said. "And I'll introduce you to my daughter, Willajean." She hollered for the girl to come downstairs. "Willajean!"

Now, I don't think her daughter was real gung-ho to meet us, because there was a long wait before the girl finally slouched down the stairs. Honestly, she was about as unattractive as her name sounded—long-legged and skinny, with a pair of black-framed eyeglasses and a scorched hair-do that didn't add much to her looks. Her skin was a nice shade of almond brown, I'll give you that, but Aunt Odella woulda definitely told the girl to stand up straighter and to look people in the eye or she'd never survive in life.

"Willajean is going into the ninth grade," Mrs. Delaney announced as her daughter sank down on the davenport. "And she's real smart. What grade are you going into, Levi?"

Told her I'd be in the eighth grade in the fall.

"See, that's perfect."

Well, the word *perfect* landed like a dud rocket on the floor between me and Willajean. You could practically hear the thud it made coming down. The older girl's eyes cut over to me for one half second, glaring behind her wavy glasses, letting me know I wasn't anywhere close to her idea of perfect. You can be sure she wasn't mine.

Peaches wasn't much help either. Her teary gaze kept wandering toward the front window and she didn't contribute a word to the conversation. I think we were all relieved when our getting-to-know-you talk was over and we could go to bed.

I spent the rest of the night tossing and turning. Kept thinking about my daddy and replaying everything he'd said. Three years apart from each other and it felt like we'd only had three minutes to talk. We'd eaten a plate of turkey and green beans together, driven around Pendleton, and that was it. What if I woke up the next day and the 555th had shipped out again? What if those few minutes were the only chance we got to talk for another three years? I finally decided to give up on sleeping and switched on the light. Read some of *King Arthur and the Knights of the Round Table*, which I found on one of Robert's shelves. Hoped Robert— wherever he was in the war—wouldn't mind.

In his barracks on top of the hill, my daddy must've been kept awake by all the same thoughts. Next day, before we'd even sat down to breakfast, he stopped by again. "Can't stay, but I wanted to say hello and bring you a treat for this afternoon. It gets real hot here," he said, passing a ginger ale to me through the open car window. "That's your favorite, right?"

Nope, it wasn't, but I took it and didn't mention a word about cream soda.

My daddy said he hoped there'd be some free time on the weekend. "Fingers crossed, me and Cal will be able to come back Saturday afternoon or evening sometime. We'll all go fishing," he added, not sounding too sure of the time—or the fishing. Seeing as how it was only Wednesday, the only thing you could be sure of was the long wait.

28. A House of Cards

Now, you'd think with my father's orders to keep quiet about the balloon bombs and how careful he was when he first told us the story—rolling up the car windows and such—that it woulda been a deep dark secret in the town too.

Well, it didn't take long for me and Peaches to realize the paratroopers at Pendleton Air Base must've been the only ones who were trying hard to keep their lips sealed. The rest of the town knew the whole story already, and didn't mind sharing it with whoever they met. Honestly, if loose lips sink ships, Pendleton woulda been sitting at the bottom of the Pacific.

On our first morning at the Delaneys'—not long after my daddy dropped off the ginger ale and left again—me and Peaches were sitting with Mrs. Delaney and Willajean, finishing our breakfast, when Mrs. Delaney brought up the subject of balloon bombs. Right in the middle of spreading a thick layer of apricot jam on her toast, she turned to me and said: "I wonder if your daddy and the other fellows are going to keep looking for those Jap balloon bombs all summer?"

I'm telling you, me and Peaches almost toppled over like a house of cards.

I don't think Mrs. Delaney noticed our panicked expressions as she spilled out every drop of information she knew, not even trying to keep her voice down—how she'd heard the balloons were made of some kind of rice paper and had Japanese markings painted on them. She said the folks in Pendleton had been warned the balloons could drift over anytime the wind was strong outta the west and explode and start raging infernos and who knows what else. "So they tell us," she repeated. "But we think it's all rumors, don't we, Willajean?"

Willajean hardly glanced up from a *Modern Screen* movie magazine she was studying. Just nodded.

"Don't you think if big white balloons were floating through the air, somebody in this town would have seen proof of them?" Mrs. Delaney asked me and Peaches, but we didn't dare open our mouths. I was convinced the U.S. Army was probably getting ready to haul us off to jail as traitors at that very moment.

"Well, we haven't seen any trace of them. In fact, I was chatting about it with my neighbor yesterday," the landlady continued, "and we were saying to each other how it's nothing but stories they create to scare folks during war . . ."

So, the neighbors knew about them too.

Couple of hours later, me and Peaches were standing inside Rexall's in town buying some toothpaste and soap when the lady clerk asked if we were family members of the crazy colored soldiers up at the airfield, the ones who jumped out of airplanes and hunted for enemy balloons.

Heck, we couldn't believe it. Twice in one day we'd been tested.

"No ma'am, we live outside of town and don't hear much word about the war," Peaches replied quickly.

"Don't have a radio either," I added.

Peaches gave me a sharp sideways look.

The clerk kept pushing. "Where do you folks live?"

Peaches answered real smoothly, "Southern Pines."

"Never heard of it."

"It's a small place."

I swear I was sweating bricks by then.

Thankfully, the nosy clerk lady ran out of questions to ask and got another customer, so we could leave before we landed in more hot water. The two of us didn't dare to speak another word to each other until we were halfway back to Mrs. Delaney's house, when Peaches turned to me and said the West scared her already and all we'd done was eat breakfast and buy toothpaste.

Despite everybody else's doubts about balloon bombs, part of me felt honor-bound to stick up for my father and his mission, no matter how nuts it seemed. I didn't go around spilling the beans about it like everybody else in town. My father had asked us to keep quiet, so I did. But MawMaw Sands was right about how hard it is to believe in things you can't see. I tried to keep an open mind, but it wasn't always easy to do.

The Keeper of Secrets basket ended up on one of Robert's bookshelves. When I was unpacking, I cleared off a spot among all his trophies and schoolbooks and stuck the basket in the center. Gotta admit it looked kinda mysterious sitting there. Sometimes, I'd glance up at it and wonder if Maw-Maw Sands herself would believe the balloon-bomb story? Seeing how certain she was that a shooting star landed in her yard and grew into a tree, I figured she probably would.

I kept some of my own secrets inside the basket for safe-keeping: the dead scorpion, a couple of buckeyes, and a bunch of my father's letters. Left the scorpion right on top for anybody who might get the dumb idea of nosing through my belongings.

With George and Robert in the Pacific, I guess it's no surprise Willajean and me ended up being thrown together like leftovers in the basket of life. It being June, she had no school. And I was on my own as long as the men were busy with their training. So, Mrs. Delaney insisted on both of us sticking together for the duration.

"Willajean would be glad to show you around the

neighborhood," she said, clearing the breakfast table after me and Peaches had spent our second morning with the family. "Won't you, Willajean?"

The girl looked like she'd rather be executed on the spot.

I tried telling Mrs. Delaney that I'd be fine on my own. Told her I came from the big city of Chicago, so wandering around a small place like Pendleton was no problem.

The lady ignored me and kept working on Willajean. "How about if you walk around the neighborhood with Levi this morning while it's still pleasant outside and show him the river, and the downtown, and come back here for lunch? All right, Willajean?"

I don't think Mrs. Delaney ever got an answer, but it didn't seem to matter because she pushed us both out the door anyhow. Willajean started down the street ahead of me with her arms locked tighter than a person heading into a hurricane. Her long legs were scissors. Hard to tell who the heck she was most mad at—me, her mother, or both.

Now, Aunt Odella always raised me to be a gentleman no matter what, so I tried to be polite and talk to the girl. Not leave her in the dust, which is what I wanted to do.

"You lived here all your life?" I called out.

"Yep," Willajean said over her shoulder, not bothering to turn around.

"Seems like a nice place."

"Yep."

The neighborhood was an older one with narrow clapboard houses crowded close together. The lucky ones had a small fenced yard or a lonely tree, but most of them didn't. There seemed to be a lot of skinny-rib dogs wandering around the place, I noticed.

"This a white neighborhood or colored?"

"White."

"They friendly?"

"Some."

Good grief, you woulda thought there was a shortage on words.

I pointed out the strays. "They belong to people around here or just run loose?"

Willajean's eyes flickered in my direction for the first time and she said one sharp sentence. "Why do you want to know?"

Heck, I didn't know what to say. I didn't have any reason other than trying to be polite. Girls were a complete mystery. I was starting to understand why me and Archie mostly stayed away from them. I shrugged. "Just asking." Decided to stop talking altogether.

"You want to meet them?" Willajean's expression warmed up a little as she pulled a wax-paper bundle out of the pocket of her sweater.

Then all the strays in the neighborhood came running.

By the time she'd opened the paper, there were four dogs yapping around us and slobbering on our shoes. Each of the strays had a name, she told me. She'd named them all after poets—there was Robert Frost, Lord Byron, Edgar Allan Poe—and a sad-eyed beagle named Emily Dickinson.

"Why not?" Willajean said as she let the dogs lick every last scrap from her light brown fingers. "Something wrong with poetry?"

I began to get the feeling maybe stray dogs were the only things Willajean had for company. We passed a couple of kids playing ball in the street and none of them bothered to raise an arm to wave. Later, we walked past a bunch of high school girls downtown and they stared straight through us like we were walking windows. Since Pendleton was a small town, I thought for sure the girls would've known Willajean, but they didn't say one word to her. Don't know if it was because we were colored and they weren't, but it made me feel real grateful for having a gang of friends back in Chicago, even if Archie could be a knucklehead sometimes. Couldn't imagine growing up in a lonely place like Pendleton with nothing but hungry dogs and dead poets as my friends.

Well, I guess I was so caught up with feeling sorry for Willajean and picturing the sad-sack life she probably had that I never noticed the snake curled up on the road ahead of us, just outside of town. Which is a good lesson for life—before you start worrying about somebody else's problems, you better keep an eye on your own.

Willajean nearly yanked my arm outta its socket as she yelled, "Rattlesnake!"

Let me tell you, she could find a voice when she needed one—I practically shot out of my shoes. After leaping off the road, we were relieved to look back and see the snake wasn't a deadly-sized one, maybe just a foot or two long. Don't think it woulda killed us, but I'm glad Willajean didn't let us find out. I tried to tell her thank you for saving my life, but she kept walking. Guess she wasn't a big fan of compliments.

West of town, there were big outcroppings of rust-red rocks along the Umatilla River. Willajean told me it was a place her brothers liked coming to all the time before the war. If Archie had been there, we coulda spent days climbing the rocks—although, knowing Archie, he wouldn't have been happy until we tackled the most dangerous parts and nearly died. Willajean said people called them the Pendleton bluffs.

The two of us ended up climbing one of the lower outcroppings to get a better view of the river from the top of it. Willajean might've been a girl, but I'll give her credit for not letting that fact stop her from scrambling up the big rocks in a skirt and unfit shoes.

"You turn around and close your eyes while I'm coming up there," she ordered me. She skinned one of her shins pretty good, but she made it to the top. It was a peaceful view from up there with the Umatilla River, the town, the patchwork of wheat fields, and the distant mountains. I said it reminded me of sitting on the tar rooftops of Chicago. Only without the tar, or the rooftops, or Chicago.

"What do you think so far? Do you like it here or not?" Willajean said, picking at the bits of scraped skin on her leg.

I shrugged. "Haven't been around long enough to know."

"Well, I hate it."

There was a long silence as I tried to come up with something polite to say about where she lived, some kind of compliment. "The dogs around here seem nice" was the best I could do.

Which made Willajean burst out laughing. Let me tell you, she had a startling-loud laugh for a quiet girl. I mean— spit flew. Honestly, I was kinda proud of myself for being funny for once. Archie was always good at cracking up girls, but I never had any luck. All they'd do was roll their eyes at me and wander off. Maybe this proved there was some hope for my sense of humor yet.

After she finished laughing, Willajean said being stuck with me wasn't as bad as she first thought. "When I first met you, all I kept thinking about was my brothers, and how you weren't them, but you're all right, I guess. You want to bring some soda pops and books and come up here again tomorrow if it's nice?" she asked, sounding desperate.

I only said yes because I didn't want to hurt the girl's feelings—and because it seemed like it was my patriotic duty to stand in for her brothers. Plus, the bluffs looked like a good place for spotting any Jap balloon bombs that might decide to float across the sky. You could see for miles.

As we were walking back to her house, Willajean told me she thought she might've seen one of the balloons herself once. "It was in March. I was coming back from taking some letters to the post office and I saw a round dot—almost like a silver coin drifting above the mountains over there," she said, pointing east. "Then there was a tiny flash and it was gone. Didn't want to tell anybody what I saw or they'd think I was plain crazy."

For the next couple of days, I sat on the warm rocks above the river, hoping to see the same kind of dot in the sky. Willajean sat in the shade farther away with her nose in her books.

It was easy to be fooled by the sky, I soon found out. Time and again, I'd whip my head around, sure I saw something move outta the corner of my eyes. Only it would be a flock of birds, or an airplane, or something ordinary like that. Clouds played the biggest tricks. I saw more *Jap balloon clouds* than you can possibly imagine. Often, in the afternoon, a bunch of small clouds would start drifting out of the west, looking exactly like a fleet of distant balloons, and my heart would start to hammer. All the blood would rush to my head. I'd picture myself being an army hero—winning all these badges and medals for being the first citizen to spot an enemy balloon attack. Could see President Truman pinning the honors on my jacket as my daddy proudly watched.

Then the balloons would get closer and be nothing but dumb clouds. Didn't take long before I was sick of looking at the color blue.

From what I could tell, my daddy and the other paratroopers weren't having much luck finding the enemy balloons either. Think they were all getting fed up, from the way they sounded on Saturday when my daddy finally picked me up for the fishing trip he'd promised. We'd just finished clearing the plates off the table from supper—Peaches was on the porch rocking Victory, who'd started fussing—when my daddy and Cal pulled up to the house in Graphite, which was packed to the doors with men and fishing rods.

Cal leaned out the car window and said, "How about it, Peach—you mind if I go along with the fellows for a little while tonight?" Then he waved an arm at me. "Come on, Legs, your daddy says you're riding with us."

I don't think Peaches was too happy to see Cal choose fishing over her, but I was glad to be free of the house for a few hours. Being around a bunch of ladies all the time is no picnic, let me tell you. Earlier in the day, me and Willajean had been walking back from the river when she said to me, "Do you think I'm nice-looking or not?"

Heck, what was I supposed to answer? Willajean Delaney wasn't any picture of beauty. And probably never would be. So I said everybody had good and bad sides to them.

"What are my good sides?"

Well, I tried telling her how she was smart and knew more about poetry than a lot of girls and how she was kind to stray dogs—which must've been the wrong things to say, because she took off down the street and left me in the dust. Hadn't said a word to me since. That's why I was glad to climb into that automobile with all the troopers on Saturday night. At least they wouldn't be asking me for my opinions on their looks.

I got squeezed into the front seat of Graphite, between my daddy, who was driving, and the trooper they called Killer, who had legs the size of cannons. Cal had it worse in the backseat. He was sandwiched together with Tiger Ted and Ace and another big-shouldered fellow they called Brothers. Poor Graphite was dragging bottom when we left.

We ended up on the Umatilla River, not far from the Pendleton bluffs. Some other troopers were already there with their lines in the water.

Now, except for going catfishing with Uncle Otis once or twice when I was real little, I'd never been fishing before. Had no ding-donged idea what I was doing. My father pushed a pole into my hand and told me to go ahead and give it a cast. Well, the bait ended up landing in about two inches of water in front of my feet.

"Try again." My father pulled in the line and handed me the pole. I gave it one more cast and nearly put the bait in the back of my head. You could hear some of the fellows snickering. "You fish for a while." I gave the pole back and plunked myself down on the edge of the river, ignoring my father's offer to show me some of his casting tricks. Had enough of being everybody's spectacle. Told him I felt like sitting and watching instead.

After an hour or so, I think my daddy and the other men forgot I was there. They weren't catching any fish—not getting many bites either—and that was making them mad. Lines were getting snagged in the rocks and they were losing hooks and bait as fast as they put them on. And the bugs were getting real bad. As the sun started sinking, the troopers' spirits did too, and things got uglier. They started complaining about how the trout were no different than balloon bombs. Neither one was real.

Killer, who'd been drinking way more than most of them, started sloshing around in the river, smacking his pole on the water, yelling, "Hey, where are all them Jap balloon bombs?"

If there were any fish still hanging around in the shallows, they woulda been long gone after he was done. Cal tried to tell him to hush up. Then the one called Ace joined in—telling everybody how the army was gonna give them all fishing poles next.

"They took away our guns and handed us shovels. Told us we're gonna be putting out forest fires instead of fighting the Japs. What next? They gonna say fires are too dangerous for us, and hand us each a fishing pole? Tell us we're fighting trout?" Ace's rude laughter bounced off the rocks, echoing. "Hey, what do you think, Boots, we gonna be jumping outta airplanes with fishing poles and nets next, huh?"

Cal said a little louder that people should cool off their heads and talk about something else. "This ain't the right place or time. We're on a nice fishing trip with Legs and his daddy." His eyes darted toward me, so I think he was mostly saying those words for my benefit. My daddy stood on the riverbank saying nothing, just casting his line into the water and chomping hard on a wad of gum. The way he was acting reminded me of the times at school when people came up and tried thumping me in the stomach just to see what I'd do. *You like some kinda soft pillow, nothing can touch you.*

The troopers kept pushing, insisting how the whole mission was probably one big lie and how the army wanted them to fail. They were gonna die in the forests of Oregon, they said, without ever having seen the war. The bottles kept tipping back and things got more sloppy. Mosquitoes were eating us alive. Finally, my daddy had enough of being a punching pillow, I guess. He whipped around, his dark eyes throwing sparks.

"All of us volunteered for the airborne. All of us got the same wings and jump boots and patches as any other trooper in the service and agreed to follow whatever orders we get. No matter what color we are. Drop and gimme a hundred, everybody." My father's soft voice snapped with heat. "Even you, Levi. And whoever says one more word against the mission we've been ordered to do will find himself carrying one of the mortar baseplates on his back all day tomorrow."

What? Couldn't believe my father was giving me orders when I hadn't said one word against anybody. I wasn't a paratrooper. I was just sitting there minding my own business, swatting mosquitoes. Feeling pretty steamed, I flopped over in the grass to join the other fellows. Except for the ripply sound of the river, the air was dead quiet.

Once we started snapping out those push-ups, I'll admit to being kinda proud about being included. Felt like I was one of them. We were a smooth army machine popping out one push-up after another.

That good feeling lasted for about five seconds.

I was sucking bugs at thirty push-ups and almost face-down in the dirt at fifty. Never did get close to one hundred.

"Your boy's got a ways to go to catch up with us, Lieutenant," Killer joked, not even breathing hard after he'd finished. Of course, if Archie had been there, he woulda shot an impolite comment right back to defend me, but I didn't have the guts to say a word. Killer coulda flattened me with one finger. My father kept quiet too. Hard to tell if it was outta pure embarrassment for me or if he was looking out for his own skin. I began to regret coming along. It would've been better if it had just been the two of us catching nothing, instead of half the U.S. Army being there with us, you know?

Thankfully, the conversation moved on from my weakly push-ups to Tiger Ted's story about the time he'd fought Joe Louis. You could tell the men had heard the story a hundred times before and still enjoyed every detail. Tiger leaned against Graphite's back fender and the other fellows stretched out on the grassy dirt, passing around some of the snacks they'd brought. Pork rinds were a big favorite of theirs. I wouldn't touch them.

"Now, we're talking Joe Louis." Tiger popped a handful of food into his mouth. "Joe Louis versus me."

The men laughed—although Tiger wasn't any twig himself.

Tiger explained how the match was his commander's idea. "I was on a base in Louisiana and my commander was a mean son of a gun from Texas who hated Negro soldiers. Didn't even bat an eye when he called me into headquarters and gave me a direct order to fight the greatest boxer in the world. Told me Joe Louis was coming to the base, and he wanted to do an exhibition match with somebody. Commander said the *somebody* would be me. Said it was my patriotic duty to entertain the fellows before they went off to war."

Tiger shook his head. "Of course, I figured it was gonna be lights-out for sure. Thought I'd be lucky to escape with my head still attached to my body. But what was I gonna do? Commander gave me a direct order. Nothing I could do about it. So, I stepped into that ring and gave it my best

shot. Left jab here. Right jab here. Little duck and sidestep."
Tiger showed off some of the moves. "And I'll be darned if I
didn't hold my own against Joe Louis. We went two rounds
without a knockdown. Proved something to everybody—
even myself—that night. Joe Louis said I was pretty good for
a fellow right off the street. An amateur. Of course, I didn't
tell him I'd been a professional boxer before the war—or
how I was a middleweight champion back home. Just asked
for his autograph, shook his hand, and got my grateful butt
outta there."

The men all clapped.

Then Cal started another story about the time when a
new paratrooper at Fort Benning, Georgia, landed on the
chimney of a house during a training jump and busted it all
to pieces. "I mean, there were bricks and kindling from here
to breakfast. That poor fellow was picking toothpicks outta
his army underwear for weeks." Cal had all of us rolling, acting out the landing and the toothpicks.

The stories kept getting swapped around, one after
another, until it was dark and we drove back to Pendleton.
Nobody mentioned another word about the mission the rest
of the evening, but I noticed Killer and Ace kept their distance from my daddy, sitting on the edges of the group and
not glancing his way much. Even with all the laughter and
joking, you could tell the bad feelings were waiting right
below the surface, swimming around like the trout we never
caught.

29. Firecrackers

As June slowly dried up and turned into the white-hot month of July, everything in Pendleton seemed to crumble along with the days. The tall weeds that people called cheatgrass got brittle and sharp as needles. The dirt roads outside of town cracked along the edges like overbaked cookies. Spiderwebs grew on everything. I swear if you fell asleep on the Delaneys' small front porch, you'd wake up to find yourself wrapped up in webs, tighter than one of Maw-Maw Sands's baskets.

Got a short note from Aunt Odella at the end of June describing how the weather in Chicago had been real warm too and how she was gonna take deviled eggs to Uncle Otis's barbecue this year, even though she hated making them.

Every Fourth of July, Uncle Otis invited anybody and everybody to a big barbecue at his house. Didn't matter if you were related or not, all you had to do was show up with something edible. One time, there was so much food on the tables in his yard, they collapsed. His wife did too. It was a real mess. You didn't know what to save—his wife or the good potato salad somebody had brought.

Now, I kinda hoped Aunt Odella would have written a few words about how everybody back home was missing me and wishing I was gonna be at the barbecue—but she didn't. I read over the note a couple of times, thinking I might have overlooked something, but there wasn't much to overlook. If you squinted hard, you could see the pale pencil lines she'd put on the paper to keep her penmanship straight. That was about it. I stuck the note in MawMaw Sands's basket and decided Aunt Odella wasn't the world's best letter writer.

In Pendleton, the Fourth of July was more about noise than food, it seemed like. People bought armloads of whizbangs and rockets from the Chinese who'd been living in the town for years—ever since they built the railroads, Mrs. Delaney told me. I swear every man, woman, and child in Pendleton must've had their own Chinese arsenal. For weeks after the holiday, the streets of downtown were littered with burnt paper tubes and blackened fuses popping under your feet, no matter where you walked.

Probably the only people in the entire place who weren't allowed to shoot explosives into the sky were the paratroopers at Pendleton Air Field. Which burned them up, of course. But the army didn't want to take the chance of any kind of trouble starting between the town and the soldiers, the commander said, so they kept the whole battalion stuck at the base for the Fourth. No passes into town allowed.

Me and Peaches decided we'd join them for the holiday and try to raise their spirits a little with two homemade pies. Then Mrs. Delaney asked us to take Willajean along. You could tell she didn't want to come, but Mrs. Delaney insisted. To make matters worse, Willajean's mother put her in a church dress and white gloves, and gave her a ladies' pocketbook to carry. The girl looked like a Sunday-school teacher.

When we got up to the base, most of the troopers were sprawled outside the barracks in their white undershirts and army trousers, looking bored and hot as they pitched dice and round metal washers in the dust. Somebody said my daddy was trying to get a movie projector started inside the mess hall, but he wasn't having much luck with the projector or the people. Honestly, the whole place felt as if a slow fuse had been lit underneath it, and it was only a matter of time before everything exploded like Chinese fireworks.

Peaches must have sensed the uneasiness in the air because her voice sounded extra cheerful and extra loud. "Happy Independence Day!" she shouted, giving everybody a bright smile as she popped out of the automobile with Victory in her arms when Cal dropped us off. You could see a handful of other guests scattered around too—a couple of soldiers' wives and girlfriends. Lucky for Willajean, some of them looked as overdressed and out of place as her.

"Don't forget the pies we brought, Levi," Peaches said.

Instead of giving the pies to Peaches, I made the mistake of handing them off to Ace, who was sitting on a wooden crate nearby, tossing washers into his army helmet. Of course, he didn't even lift the wax paper to take a peek at what flavor the pies were. Or say a polite thank-you. Just walked off with Peaches's hard work, saying he'd put the food in the mess hall for later. I know she was hurt. Then Victory started howling as if she wasn't in a celebrating mood either, and you could see people glancing around for somewhere else to go. The holiday was a collapsing table with everything sliding downhill fast.

Thankfully, one of the fellows came to my rescue. Mickey, the young trooper I'd met on the first day, wandered over and invited me to join a game of horseshoes with him and some of the other men. "We're short a person on our side," he said. "You want to pitch some shoes with us?"

After I told him I'd come over, a shadow moved behind me and I knew Willajean was standing there awkwardly like a lost extra in a movie. Mickey's eyes glanced past my shoulder, clearly wondering who the Sunday-school teacher was, and I knew I didn't have any choice but to introduce her. "She's one of the Delaneys who live in Pendleton. Her brothers are both serving in the navy." I tried to make the story quick.

"Nice to meet you, miss." Mickey stuck out his hand. "You can come to the horseshoe pits and watch, if you want. I'll find you a chair."

It went better than I expected. Mickey drew people like flies, no matter how reluctant they were. Willajean started out hunched over a book she'd brought along, as if she was hoping to disappear, until he convinced her to keep score. "You gotta help us keep the other team honest," he said, trying to joke with her. "Look at them. You can tell they're a bunch of cheats." It wasn't long before she took off those dumb white gloves Mrs. Delaney'd made her wear and warmed up a little. Smiled a few times. Stuck her book and her pocketbook under her chair and forgot about both of them.

The whole gang of us had a great time drinking sodas and pitching horseshoes until it got too dark to see them landing in the dirt. My daddy joined us after giving up on the projector. We matched up officers versus enlisted, North versus South, West versus East, jumpers versus legs.

Second Lieutenant Battle and his son were two of the best, let me tell you. I wondered if maybe I'd finally discovered the one talent in the world I'd got from my daddy— pitching horseshoes. Who woulda thought? Never played horseshoes before in my life, but both of us had dead-on aim. Got more three-point ringers than anyone.

After dark, everybody gathered outside the mess hall, dragging out chairs and tables, to watch the flashes of fireworks over Pendleton. Being on a hill, the airfield turned out to have a view that couldn't be beat, so I think everybody was starting to feel better about being stuck at an army post for the Fourth. Mother Nature was putting on a good show herself, lighting up the night clouds with bright bursts of summer heat lightning. Don't know which was more impressive—Mother Nature or what the people of Pendleton shot into the sky.

The scene woulda been almost perfect if it hadn't been for what Ace spotted later on. We'd been watching the fireworks for an hour or so when he noticed a faint glow in the direction of the Blue Mountains to the east. Now, if it had been close to daybreak, you woulda thought the orange glimmer was the edge of the sun barely coming up, but it had only just set. "That's a damn fire way out there, isn't it?" Ace pointed. A bunch of the troopers around him jumped up on the chairs and tables to get a better view, and the fuse that had been smoldering under the whole day suddenly flared up like a hot match. Curses went flying.

I could feel my daddy's shoulders rising next to me. Standing on the other side, Cal was quiet. I figured it was a good thing Victory was with Willajean and Peaches, who had wandered off in search of our pie pans to take home. If the baby had been listening to the troopers' language, who knows what her first words might've been someday . . .

You could tell the fellows weren't too happy to see the fire, that's for sure. Nobody mentioned a word about whether or not a Jap balloon might've caused it, so that possibility didn't seem to be tiptoeing through anybody's mind. Only thing they cared about was the flickering orange line in the distance.

"Whole war, the army's been looking for ways to get us to give up and quit," somebody said behind us. The voice sounded familiar. It might have been Killer or Ace. I remembered the scene they'd made at the river when we were fishing.

"Well, they finally got their Christmas wish, haven't they?"

"Hell, if they wanted to, they could drop us straight into the flames right now and finish us off for good, couldn't they?" There was a jeering ripple of laughter.

"Naw"—somebody else interrupted. "Remember, we gotta land our parachutes in the trees first. Then whoever makes it out of the treetops alive gets to try fighting off a raging inferno with his ax and a shovel. Then if you're still in one piece after all that—*congratulations, soldier*—the army will fly you back here to Pendleton for whatever screwball mission they can dream up next."

"That's what we signed up to do." My father spun around, addressing the shadowy crowd behind us. "None of us got dragged into the paratroops, did we?"

"We signed up to die for our country, not for a bunch of damn trees and balloons nobody's seen, Lieutenant," somebody nearby shot back. A lot of the troopers stalked away to the barracks—including my daddy, who wasn't going to let that comment go, you could tell. The air around us popped with firecrackers and heat.

"That true, Cal?"

In all the arguing, the men had forgotten about Peaches and some of the other wives and girlfriends being there, I think. She must've come back and overheard the whole scene because her voice rose like a trembling balloon behind us. "That true about you landing your parachutes in trees?"

It was too dark to see her eyes filling up with tears, but you could tell they were. Right away, Cal went over to her and whipped his arm around her shoulders, insisting it was nothing for her to worry about. The few troopers who were left nearby jumped in fast to agree with him. "We're the best there is," they said, patting her back gently, acting embarrassed by what had happened. "Hooking the trees is nothing. We've already done it a half-dozen times and we're still in one piece. Don't listen to what some of the fellows are saying. Landing in trees is safer than rocking a baby, and there's still plenty more training to do before we start jumping into any fires. They don't know what they're talking about."

But Peaches was still sniffling hard when we left.

Two weeks later, I was lounging in bed early one morning. Light was just coming through the cracks in the curtains when I heard a rumbling roar pass overhead. The sound shook the walls of the Delaneys' house, making the yellow paint shiver. One shadow roared over the rooftops, followed by another, and another. Without even looking out the window, I knew the planes flying over us were C-47s from Pendleton Air Field and the men were heading out on their first fire call.

30. Seeing Underwater

Emerald Jones, the company cook, brought the official word about the mission a few hours later. We were still cleaning up the breakfast dishes—although nobody had eaten much of Mrs. Delaney's bacon and eggs—when Emerald knocked on the screen door. "Thought I'd swing by and drop off a couple of messages Cal and Boots left for you," he announced, trying to give us an easy smile. "Nothing to worry about. The fellows will be back home before you know it." He pulled out the folded notes from his front pocket and held them toward us. By then, Peaches was a train wreck.

My father's note was scrawled in his usual squinty handwriting: *Fire call. Gone a couple of days. Keep an eye on everybody. So long, Daddy.* Cal had written Peaches a long love note that made her cry a waterfall every time she read it. Trust me, he shoulda left his message on a hankie. It woulda been easier.

* * *

If I thought the six days crossing the entire United States took forever, it was nothing compared to the six days we had to wait for word from the men. Felt like eternity going backward. Peaches hardly left her room, and Mrs. Delaney fussed over her and Victory worse than a mother hen—tiptoeing around the house, keeping all the curtains closed for their peace and quiet, making sure nobody slammed a door. Every morning me and Willajean would escape after the breakfast dishes were dried. Willajean wasn't Archie, but she was all I had to talk to while the troopers were gone. I'd fidget around the kitchen, waiting while she gathered a bunch of smelly scraps for the Poets before we left. Then we'd feed them on the way to the river.

She could say some crazy things sometimes, though.

One day she told me how she was sorry my father had to leave on the fire mission. How it was too bad both of us had goodbye fathers.

"What do you mean by that?" I fired back, feeling like I had to come to my daddy's defense.

"Ones who are always leaving for somewhere," she said. "That's all."

I'll admit, I never put two and two together and thought about how me and Willajean had that part of our lives in common. It was true I'd only seen Mr. Delaney a few times in the month or so I'd been there. He was working day and night for the Union Pacific Railroad because of the war.

Despite Willajean's strange ways sometimes, I have

to give her credit for sticking with me during the six days the men were gone. Every morning—no matter how hot it was—she'd climb up the bluffs with me and watch the sky. Tried to tell her she didn't have to come. All I was doing was keeping an eye out for the C-47s returning home. Or any balloon bombs that might happen to drift over—although I'd almost given up hope of that ever happening. Mostly I was trying to keep busy with something useful, so I didn't have to picture all the things that could be going wrong on the troopers' mission.

Each time Willajean would shrug and say how she didn't mind sitting with me for a few hours. Usually she'd bring a book. By midafternoon, when even the trees had crawled into the shade, we'd head back to the Delaney house to find something cool to drink and to take our turn in front of the porch fan.

That's where we were sitting when the airplanes finally came home. All of us—Mrs. Delaney, Peaches, Willajean, and me—were crowded in front of the whirring fan, drinking lemonade, when Mrs. Delaney suddenly said, "You hear something?" Bolting upright, she plunked her glass on the porch railing. "I don't think that's a train. Sounds like airplanes to me."

Sure enough, it was.

I swear none of us moved or breathed until we heard the backfiring sound of Graphite finally coming up the street an hour or so later. Then Peaches made a spectacle of herself, running down the steps and kneeling in the small rectangle of dirt that was the Delaneys' front yard. Raising her arms up to the sky, she begged and hollered, "Please, Lord Jesus, please let that be my Cal coming back home safe and sound."

Me and Willajean stayed where we were, and just stood up to get a good look as the car came around the corner.

Honestly, I don't know how the driver could see to make the turn. That old Ford was packed to overflowing with people. As soon as its bald tires rolled to a stop in front of the house, my daddy, Cal, Tiger, Mickey, and a couple of other troopers bailed out wearing the biggest smiles you've ever seen. Didn't seem to matter that their army fatigues were a mess and they stank like a campfire. They were grinning from ear to ear. Cal came tearing up the walk and swept Peaches into his arms. Left smudges all over the nice dress she'd put on to welcome him home. But she didn't seem to mind one bit.

"Hooo girl!" He swung her around like a carnival ride. "We made it home, sugar pie. Yes sirreee, we did."

My daddy strolled up to the porch, smiling too. "It went almost picture-perfect," he said. Real proud, you could tell. "Couldn't have been better. Got the fires out and all our men back home safe."

The fellows were heading down to the river for a swim. My daddy said that's all they'd been thinking about for days in the smoke and heat—taking a plunge in the cool river the minute they got back. And then sleeping for a week. Peaches and Mrs. Delaney insisted they had to eat too. "After everybody's done swimming, you come back here and we'll stuff you full of chow again," they said.

Well, I sure wasn't gonna stick around the house cooking with the ladies, so I headed down to the river with my daddy and Cal. By the time we got there, it looked like half the U.S. Army was already swimming. The men had found a spot where the Umatilla River took a slow curve, making a deeper pool on one side, and that's where everybody was splashing. The shrubs and tree branches along the riverbanks nearby were decorated with more things than a Christmas tree. Ladies woulda been blushing, let me tell you.

Daddy and Cal peeled off their duds down to their army underwear, sending up powdery clouds of dust as the uniforms hit the ground. "Come on, Legs, take the jump with us," Cal said, waving one arm. My daddy was already on the water's edge. "You don't wanna be the last one standing in the door."

Now, up until that very moment I'd only waded in a couple of nasty city creeks with Archie before. You know, if there'd been a hard rain, we used to go walking in them, tossing rocks and such for fun. So when my daddy had talked about cooling off in the river, I figured he meant splashing around in the shallows, in water below your knees—not swimming in the darned river itself.

Heck, I couldn't swim a lick.

From where we were, you could see most of the men already standing in water up to their shoulders. Good God. It made me realize how many big things my daddy and me still didn't know about each other. Things that could kill you. My father turned around, waving an arm at me again.

"Can't swim," I mumbled real low to Cal.

"Honest?" Cal glanced back at me, surprised. Then his eyes darted toward my daddy, who was still waiting impatiently on the riverbank. Cal must've guessed what a tight spot I was in. "Well," he said, "no time like right now to learn. I'll stick to the shallows with you. Come on."

That river felt good on my toes, I gotta admit. I slowly eased in up to my knees, but the rocks on the bottom were slick, so you had to be careful where you stepped. Cal wandered within an arm's reach of me, not giving away my secret, but my daddy gave up waiting and splashed out to join the other men, who were whooping and hollering in the middle.

The air hummed with loud voices, as if the troopers had suddenly been released from a long vow of silence. They'd done something nobody else thought they could do. They'd jumped into trees with parachutes and put out forest fires with nothing but shovels. It was like boxing Joe Louis and coming out alive. I swear the stories that went flying around the river woulda sent Peaches to bed for a week if she'd been listening. I heard the fellows jawing about which troopers had hooked their parachutes onto the highest branches and who got down to the ground without a scratch. Heard how one team cleared a half-mile fire lane through a forest and scared off what they thought was a bear one night. Another team hiked fifteen miles over a mountain to get back to civilization.

Tell you what, it made me feel ashamed to be standing there in the shallows like a sissy girl with my arms crossed over my goosebumpy chest, after hearing all the brave things they did.

Told Cal I wanted to try going out deeper.

"Up to you," he said.

Pretty soon I was standing next to my daddy and the other men, in swirling water up to my waist. Thought I might die of mortal fright, my heart was thumping so bad. Couldn't even see my feet below me anymore. They'd disappeared.

"Want to try ducking your head under, Levi?" my father asked, giving me a look that said my secret was out. Suppose it didn't take a U.S. Army officer to figure out why I was half dry when everybody else had rivers trailing down their dark skin. "The water feels pretty good," he added.

Heck, what could I say? My daddy could jump into trees but his son was too chicken to get his head wet?

"Hold your nose." Cal gave me a friendly wink. "Me and Boots will make it quick."

Of course, you know all the other troopers overheard the conversation and came over. Killer, Brothers, Tiger, Ace—

they were all standing around. Nothing like having a big audience watch you drown yourself.

Once I had my eyes clenched shut and enough oxygen in my lungs to last until next week, I leaned forward as Cal and my daddy pushed my shoulders underneath the river's surface. When the cool water hit my face, my eyes popped open by themselves—just outta sheer panic, I guess—and I couldn't believe you could *see* under the water. There were yellow-green rays of sunlight coming down and the blurry outline of the rocks on the bottom. And legs. My legs. I was looking around—thinking, *Son of a gun, this is pretty neat that you can see underwater*—when they yanked my shoulders up and I was back in the open air, rubbing water outta my stinging eyes. My whole body felt cool and fizzy, as if I'd been turned into a bottle of ginger ale on a hot summer day.

"You feel all right?" my daddy asked, looking worried.

And I thought how nice it was to be worried about for once. Maybe I'd just stay there all day and soak up that worry like a big sponge. Thirteen years' worth of worry.

Couldn't keep a slow grin from easing across my face, though. Man oh man, I was proud of myself. Big Man had conquered the Mississippi, that's what it felt like. "I'm feeling fine" is what I said—which made everybody lose interest and go back to whatever they'd been doing before, since it looked like I wasn't gonna die after all.

I'm telling you, that afternoon on the river with my daddy and the other troopers is something I'll never forget.

I remember how the sun sank behind the bluffs near the river, turning the rocks a warm coppery color like pennies before the war. I remember the way the light danced on the rippling brown shoulders of the men as they skipped rocks and sailed an old tennis ball back and forth through the air, higher and higher against the blue. Tiger and Ace put on a boxing show, waist-deep in the water, that woulda impressed the daylights outta Joe Louis. Somehow Mickey managed to catch a fish with his bare hands—scooped up a little rainbow trout by the river's edge. All of us watched the silvery colors flash in his palms, everybody oohing and aahing. It was something magical, the whole afternoon. I think everybody woulda stayed there forever, if they'd had the chance. But the next spark was already smoldering somewhere.

It wouldn't be long before another fire was starting.

31. Revelations

As the bone-dry days of July drifted into the beginning of August, I swear the air itself seemed to have turned to smoke. When the wind was blowing in the right direction, the eye-watering smell of something burning could jolt you outta a sound sleep and make you think your own bed had caught fire. Almost every morning, we'd hear the big airplanes climbing into the sky over Pendleton carrying another group of troopers on a fire call. Sometimes the calls were nearby—the Blue Mountains or one of the big forests to the north in Washington State. Sometimes they were as far off as Montana or Idaho.

Hardly anybody bothered to look up when the airplanes came and went anymore, because all of us knew it had nothing to do with Jap balloons or the war in the Pacific. It hadn't rained in weeks. Every night the sky was lit up with lightning from distant storms that never arrived, and the troopers said most of the forest fires they saw were started by lightning. Only my daddy still insisted there was the chance that some of them could've been caused by enemy balloons. "I'm not giving up yet," I heard him tell Cal, who laughed and said he was as stubborn as the Japs.

Word was the Allies were planning to invade Japan soon. On the radio, there were daily news bulletins about waves of B-29 Superfortresses bombing Japanese cities in preparation for a land invasion. Honestly, people in Pendleton didn't seem to be paying much attention. When the grocery store in town ran out of summer melons, it created a bigger stir than the war news. Customers got into a fistfight. The police had to be called. You couldn't get through August without melons, folks said.

I think the paratroopers at the airfield were too tired to care what was happening in the Pacific or to worry about how they were being left out again. Most of them hardly stirred from their bunks between fire calls. Tumbleweed coulda rolled through the barracks. Nobody had any spare time to cool off in the river or go fishing for trout like they'd done before. Cal and my daddy would stop by for a quick visit and fall fast asleep at Mrs. Delaney's kitchen table while you were talking to them. Their eyelids would start to droop, their shoulders would sag, and it would be lights-out. We'd have to shake their arms to get them to wake up.

Then, on August 6, the biggest bomb in history was dropped on Japan.

And that news woke us all up.

* * *

When President Truman made the announcement over the radio, it caught everybody off guard, let me tell you. It was a Monday morning. Cal and my daddy had been gone for a couple of days on a fire call. Me and Peaches were helping Mrs. Delaney pickle some tomatoes, and the whole kitchen reeked of vinegar. Willajean was sitting at the table with a clothespin on her nose, writing letters to her brothers.

I remember how the radio was on, playing music. One minute we were listening to some patriotic tunes—and the next minute President Truman's voice was interrupting to announce how the Allies had dropped a bomb on Japan that was two thousand times stronger than any bomb ever used in wartime.

"What?" Mrs. Delaney spun around. "Willajean, turn up that radio."

As the president kept talking, all of us were so still, you woulda thought we'd been turned into pillars. "The bomb has harnessed the power of the universe," the president's voice of doom continued, "and it will bring down a rain of ruin from the air, the likes of which has never been seen on this earth."

Right then, I thought poor Mrs. Delaney was gonna collapse. The eyes behind her glasses glazed over and her body started swaying. Peaches's hand flew toward her elbow, trying to catch her. I grabbed a chair and she sank into it. Man oh man, it was close. A few more inches either way, and she woulda been facedown.

The president kept talking about the bomb that had been dropped on Japan—an atomic bomb, he called it. But Mrs. Delaney had stopped listening by then. She was staring toward the kitchen window, where the curtains were hanging limp as laundry. No wind. "The world's ending," she whispered weakly. "The apocalypse is coming."

I'm telling you, her faraway voice gave me the creepy-crawlies.

"Now, Mrs. Delaney, you know that's not true," Peaches said, hands on her hips, her righteous voice taking over from the radio. "The president of the United States wouldn't come on the radio to tell us the world is ending. It's a beautiful morning, everything outside looks fine and dandy, nothing different at all. Here, put this cloth on your forehead to calm yourself down, and stop worrying about nonsense." She ran a towel under the spigot and then held it toward Mrs. Delaney, who waved it away.

Mrs. Delaney was an avid Bible reader. She studied her scarlet-edged copy faithfully every night, and the Book of Revelation seemed to be one of her favorites. "Never hurts to be prepared for what's coming," she'd tell us, whenever she sat down to read. Which probably explains why she was convinced the end of the world had arrived.

"We've gone and let out the four horsemen, God help us, we have," she repeated, rocking back and forth as if she was in a trance, eyes staring. "The sun's going to go out next and the stars are going to fall out of the sky and fire and earthquakes are going to consume us."

"Now, you hush up, Mrs. Delaney." Peaches's voice was firmer. "The world hasn't ended yet. No need to go scaring everybody over something that hasn't happened." Meaning me and Willajean, of course, although I think she'd given Peaches the end-of-the-world jitters too. When a train thundered past the house a few minutes later, all of us jumped about ten feet.

It was Peaches who switched off the radio and ordered me and Willajean out the door. "Get some air. Don't want you listening to all this bad news. Here's some money for some ice creams." In the hallway, she dug some change outta her purse and handed it to us without even looking at it. "Go on now."

Me and Willajean stepped outside like we'd been sent into a minefield. Doom was coming. A brown sparrow darted in front of us and the thought crossed my mind that the ordinary sparrow could be the last bird we ever saw. Couldn't help looking around at all the possible lasts: last bird, last wilty geranium, last spiderweb, last pillowcases on the line, last empty milk bottles on the steps. The sky was the same washed-out blue it had been for weeks, but the color felt like a trick—a peaceful camouflage curtain, hiding something unknown behind it.

"You afraid?" Willajean asked me, eyes blinking behind her glasses. "Because I am."

"Naw," I said, keeping my voice easy.

"What if they drop one like that on us?"

"They won't."

"How do you know? Why couldn't they?"

Willajean was too smart for her own good. Sometimes I wished she'd just stop thinking.

"Tell me why they couldn't, Levi. Tell me some reasons why not."

While I was trying to come up with an answer, tears started coming down Willajean's face, and pretty soon the girl couldn't breathe from all the hard crying she was doing. We had to stop walking and I dug around in my pockets trying to find something to offer her, but all I had were the pennies and nickels from Peaches and crumpled bits of paper.

Willajean's words poured out along with her tears. "I want to be a poet like Emily Dickinson someday and write poetry everbody reads, and live in a nice house that isn't yellow, and save all the dogs in the world, and have a hand-some fellow who loves me and thinks I'm pretty, and marries me . . ." The torrent of words kept going. "It isn't fair, all those people in the Bible got to live as long as they wanted— why does the world have to come to an end while we're living in it?" She turned toward me, her glasses steamed up and her face a mess of tear trails. "I know I'm not pretty at all or your girl or anything, Levi, but do you think you could kiss me just this once?"

What? Under the word *shocked* in the encyclopedia woulda been a picture of my face right then. Kiss Willajean Delaney? In the middle of a neighborhood street?

"Please, Levi, nobody's ever kissed me. I'm going into high school and nobody's ever kissed me and I don't want to die without being kissed by somebody."

Her face looked so certain of our doom that the same worries started running through my brain. What if the world ended and all the time I spent getting ready for my future—wearing Vaseline on my hair and going to school and all—was wasted too? What if my life was over before it was started?

I know it probably sounds crazy, but just in case Willajean Delaney was the last girl on earth I'd ever meet, I decided I'd better kiss her. Not on her lips, of course. I got my limits, you know. Even if I was sure the world was ending right then, I wouldn't kiss Willajean Delaney on the lips. I planted a fast kiss on the side of her face. Well, closer to her ear than her cheek. It was strange to be that up-close to a girl's face, though. I could smell the strawberry jam Willajean always put on her toast for breakfast. Her cheek wasn't as soft as I woulda thought either. Not like a sponge cake, which is what I was expecting—more like an apple. Not that I went around kissing apples much.

After I kissed her, Willajean's eyes lit up, even with all the tears. "Thank you, Levi."

"Sure," I said, stuffing my hands in my pockets and

double-timing it down the street. Told myself maybe love is kissing somebody you don't like, just to keep the world from ending.

Lucky for me, the world was still there the next day. It was a big relief to know Willajean wasn't gonna be the last and only girl I ever kissed. I think all of us felt grateful for getting another hazy August day on earth when we got up the next morning. With the Delaneys' yellow house already starting to boil, the four of us ate breakfast on the porch and listened to the radio, which didn't tell us much. No more atomic bombs had been dropped, so that was good news. But the Japs hadn't surrendered. Nobody seemed to have any idea what would happen next. Felt like the world was holding its breath.

"Wait till the men hear all this news when they get back. They aren't gonna believe everything that's happened," Mrs. Delaney kept saying over and over, like a stuck button on a jukebox—until Peaches finally changed the topic to ants and how they were crawling up her bedroom wall, which sent Mrs. Delaney running off in search of them and left us in peace.

Late that afternoon, the troopers finally came back from their fire mission. I was on the back steps, peeling potatoes, when the C-47s soared over town. "Peel faster, Levi," Peaches called out from the kitchen window, "or we're never gonna get them potatoes mashed in time to feed the boys if they're hungry."

After the planes disappeared, we went back to our work. Didn't give them a second thought. About an hour later, we heard the familiar rattling sound of Graphite in the distance, and we went out front to meet the fellows like we always did. Peaches was particular about the routine. She always wore the same dress, stood in the same spot, and held Victory up, so she could watch her daddy coming down the road. Mrs. Delaney and Willajean fixed lemonade and cookies. I had the job of standing on the porch and telling everybody when Graphite turned the corner.

This time, what seemed strange was the slow way the car made the left onto the Delaneys' street. Nobody said a word, but I think all of us had the same feeling of something being wrong. When the automobile got closer and it was clear my father was driving and Cal was next to him, all of us took a deep gulp of relief. Heard Peaches whisper a hallelujah. But the grim look on my daddy's face straightened us right up. "Cal's all right," he said stiffly, as he got out of the car and came around to the passenger side. "Just got banged up some."

Even before my daddy got there to help, Cal was doing his best to ease out of the car by himself. "Busted an arm this time," he said to all of us, pointing at the sling that crisscrossed his chest. "And messed up a couple of ribs pretty good." Then his brave smile seemed to crumble and his shoulders started to shake. Peaches pushed the baby into Mrs. Delaney's arms and flew toward him. My father leaned over too, resting his hands on his legs, like he was trying to compose himself. It took me a minute to understand what Cal was saying to Peaches as the two of them held each other as careful as glass. His injuries were nothing, that's what he kept repeating. "I'm fine," he said over and over to Peaches.

Finally my father filled in what Cal couldn't. "We had a couple of jumpers hurt pretty bad." He paused, staring down at his boots. "And we lost one of our men."

We were prepared for bad news, but none of us were expecting to hear those terrible words. In all the dangerous jumps they'd done, the 555th had never lost a man. It was the one thing they were most proud of. Being unbeatable. Invincible. Lucky. I remembered how Uncle Otis used to tell customers that the only thing separating the lucky from the unlucky was time and a good haircut.

Their luck had run out, my daddy said.

Peaches was the one who finally asked the question nobody else could. "Which of the troopers was it?" she said, looking in my father's direction for the answer.

I know it's probably a mortal sin to say this—but part of me hoped it would turn out to be one of the fellows we didn't know real well. Or somebody like Ace, who wasn't well liked by anybody who did know him.

It was a hard slam in the stomach when my daddy said it was Mickey. I heard Willajean gasp behind me.

Mickey. My father couldn't be right about the name. That's the first thought that went through my mind. There *had* to be a mistake. It couldn't be Mickey, the soldier who hardly looked old enough to be a paratrooper. The kid who'd pitched horseshoes with me and Willajean on the Fourth of July. The one who'd caught a rainbow trout with his bare hands in the Umatilla River. It was like hearing the sudden news of the atomic bomb dropping and realizing that anybody's life could come to an end in an instant. It made death seem real close to all of us, you know what I mean?

My father's face was an unreadable mask—a silent movie—as he stood by the car. Couldn't decide whether I ought to go over and put my arm around his shoulders or not. Didn't want to start us both crying. Mrs. Delaney touched my arm and whispered that she and Willajean would go inside and make some strong coffee for everybody's nerves. Think they must've tiptoed up the porch steps behind us, with Mrs. Delaney still holding tight to Victory.

But my father didn't stay. He told me and Peaches that he wasn't ready for talking about what had happened yet. "If Cal wants to talk about it, that's up to him. I have a responsibility to Mickey's family first" was all he said before he walked stiffly back to the car. He was the picture of aloneness as he drove away by himself, and I felt as if I was watching the last person on earth leave. Wished I'd known better what to do.

Later on, Cal told us more of the story, although I'm not sure any of us wanted to hear it. Willajean ran upstairs, saying she didn't want to know how Mickey died—that she wasn't gonna believe it was true. I guess the rest of us felt duty-bound to stay. We sat around the kitchen table with the supper preparations scattered where we'd left them. A pan of potatoes on the range. A wilting pile of greens on the counter. Mrs. Delaney poured us cups of coffee that were strong enough to take rust off a car. Nobody drank more than a sip or two.

Cal said the trouble had happened when they were landing. The drop zone had been tight with trees and rocks. "A couple of us busted bones and got cut up by branches as we were coming down," he said. "It was a real tricky spot to land on."

But Mickey got the worst of it, he said, getting tangled high in a hundred-fifty-foot fir tree. He'd been trying to lower himself to the ground with his letdown ropes when something happened.

Cal had to stop talking and gather his emotions before he could continue. "Could've slipped, or lost his grip on the rope, or who knows," Cal told us, his voice dissolving more with each word. "Nothing any of us could do to help him. Nobody could've survived the fall from the height he was at." The men had spent two days walking through the mountains to bring Mickey's body to a town where it could be flown back to Pendleton.

My father was taking it hard, Cal told us. "Boots is having a real tough time of it." His eyes shifted toward me. "I think he's blaming himself for okaying the tight drop zone and letting everybody jump. Says if it hadn't been for him, we wouldn't have had jumpers hurt and Mickey wouldn't be dead. I tried to tell him anybody who jumps into the sky with a parachute strapped on his back takes the chance of dying."

Peaches jabbed her finger in Cal's direction. "And you ain't doing it ever again, Calvin Thomas. Not ever. Don't care what the Japs do in this war or how many forests burn up. You ain't jumping again. Not if you plan on staying married to me."

"We'll see," Cal answered.

"Nope, we ain't seeing nothing."

Then, in the middle of all this sadness, the two of them started razzing each other like old times. Peaches with her arms crossed and her eyes giving that prickly stare. Cal poking at her knotted arms, trying to make her laugh. You could tell Mrs. Delaney didn't know what to think about them. I used to see the same thing at funerals with Aunt Odella. How a roomful of people could go from a bottomless pit of grief to laughter in the span of a few minutes. Sometimes I wished I was the same way.

* * *

Guess my daddy kept his emotions inside too. The only way you would have known how hard he was taking Mickey's death was if you'd seen what happened the next day.

I was standing in the hallway when I heard Graphite drive up and the frustrated slam of a car door. Cal was fast asleep next to the fan in Mrs. Delaney's front room, where we'd been trying to give him some peace and quiet after all he'd been through.

Without even thinking, my daddy called out Cal's name before his feet hit the front-porch steps. Poor Cal jumped up so quickly, he was lucky not to snap a few more ribs. I don't think we were supposed to hear what was said between the two of them on the privacy of the porch, but being only a few feet away, I couldn't help it.

You could hear my father's soft voice shaking with fury. "Just met with the colonel. He said I can't escort Mickey's body home for burial. Tried to tell him it's my responsibility to do that for Mickey and his family. I was Mickey's commanding officer on the mission and he was just a kid, couple years older than my own son."

My ears burned, listening.

"Who's the colonel want to send?" Cal asked.

My father told him none of the officers were being allowed to go. "Colonel says he'll only approve sending two enlisted men. That's it. Says there's no need to waste an officer on an errand like this one."

A bunch of cusswords about the colonel ricocheted through the screen door, and then there was a long space of silence. I eased my back against the wall, worrying they'd guessed I was there.

But Cal's voice spoke up again. "You want me and Peaches to escort Mickey's body back home? You know we'd be willing to do that for anybody. Me and Peaches would see to it that everything was done right and honorable for him, and we could give his folks a hand with whatever they needed."

My father didn't answer.

"You know I won't be jumping again for weeks, maybe months," Cal continued. "So I'm no damn use to the outfit right now anyway. I'll just be pushing paper or counting pencils or who knows what. Colonel shouldn't care a scratch about me going—probably be glad to get rid of me. Afterward, me and Peaches could go and stay with her folks in Georgia until my arm gets healed up." Cal tried joking. "By then, the war will probably be over, and I'll have cracked enough bones to be let out of the service anyhow."

"An officer always looks after his men. It'll be on my conscience forever, not taking him home," my father said.

"It'll be there no matter what you do, Boots. You know that as well as I do. All of us are family."

Guess my father must've decided Cal was right. And convinced the colonel too. The next day, Peaches and Cal were packing up to leave. From the way Peaches was humming to herself and talking to baby Victory about all the people she'd meet in Georgia, I don't think she was too unhappy about going home. Mrs. Delaney made a big fuss over the two of them, saying how much she was going to miss being like a granny to Victory. "It's been years since I had any little babies around here. I got so used to her."

Cal and Peaches tried talking to me before they left. After we had listened to the news broadcasts about the second atom bomb being dropped on Japan, we went and sat on the porch steps in the dark. It felt almost like old times back in Southern Pines, if you could ignore the trains roaring past every so often. Cal insisted he and Peaches would be real upset if I didn't look them up again someday and come for a visit. How I was always welcome, no matter where they were.

"You think you and your daddy'll go back to Chicago once the war ends?" Peaches asked. I told her I was sure we would, since that's where we'd both come from. Started picturing all the familiar places—Hixson's and movies at the Regal—and realizing how I'd missed the whole darned summer. Aunt Odella's last letter said Uncle Otis was having wife troubles again, so I woulda found out the inside scoop if I'd been there to get one of his razor cuts. And believe me, I was in desperate need of one. There wasn't enough Vaseline in the world to help my head.

Cal said wherever I ended up in the world, I had to remember not to become a B-boy again. He called it an army term for somebody who's always getting left behind. "You gotta stick with the people you got, no matter what. Don't let people keep taking off, and don't you sit around waiting on them to come back."

I told him it wasn't something you had much choice about usually.

"You always got choices," Cal said.

When the eastbound train pulled into the station early the next morning, everybody in the unit turned out in their good dress uniforms to pay their respects as Mickey's body was sent home to his family. The troopers lined up in motionless rows of olive green on both sides of the station. Standing anywhere near the men, you could smell the faint scent of wood smoke drifting around them, but their uniforms were pressed and spotless. The boots and brass shone in the sunshine.

Willajean and Mrs. Delaney came to the train station in somber black and navy dresses, and they put me in one of Robert's church suits. We were all melting in the sun as we stood together with the other army families and friends.

When the coffin got loaded onto the train and the entire 555th saluted, I don't think there was a dry eye on the platform. Man oh man, it squeezed my throat hard when I saw the coffin pass by my father, who was trying his best to hold his salute, but you couldn't miss the crumpled look that went across his face when it did.

I kept thinking about that trout and remembering

how alive that fish was. How it had flapped and sparkled in Mickey's hands. No matter what, I just couldn't believe those hands were silent inside that box now.

Before getting on board the train, Peaches and Cal came over to where I was standing. Peaches was holding Victory, but she gave me a hug with her free arm. "Don't you go getting into any trouble without me around keeping an eye on you, Levi, you hear? Remember, I got four brothers, so I know all the tricks."

Cal shoved a paper bag into my hands. "Peanuts," he said gruffly, trying not to get teary, you could tell. "Don't eat them all this afternoon." He patted my back. "Sure we'll see you around again, Legs."

"You will." I tried to sound sure. Although the honest truth was, we had no idea if that ever would happen. My eyes burned like the dickens, watching them leave.

As the train started pulling away, the two of them waved goodbye and Peaches held baby Victory up to the window so we could see her. I don't know if Peaches and Cal noticed it or not, but baby Victory suddenly gave us one of the sweetest smiles you ever saw. Everybody who was watching started waving and smiling back—troopers, officers, everybody. Now, Aunt Odella probably woulda said a baby named Victory giving a dazzling happy smile was a sure sign of the war coming to an end.

And it was.

Four days later, Japan surrendered.

32. When Sugar Went Flying

Word of the surrender spread faster than a wildfire around Pendleton. One minute, it was an ordinary kind of afternoon—people going about their business, automobiles rolling down the street, birds chirping, flies buzzing—and the next minute, things were flying. Handfuls of loose change. Hats. Purses. Shoes. People just threw whatever they were carrying straight into the air. I heard later that the owner of the local five-and-dime tossed the contents of all his candy jars into the street. Gumdrops, lollipops, licorice—you name it. Sugar went flying. Wish I'd been there. Willajean and Mrs. Delaney were shopping at Rexall's, and they said it was a real sight.

Before I heard the news, I was sitting on the Delaneys' porch feeling real blue about Peaches and Cal being gone, when Graphite suddenly came tearing down the road. Didn't know the old heap could go that fast. But there it was, speeding down the street way faster than the wartime speed limits allowed—bald tires going *thump thump thump* on the gravel. Pulling up to the house, my daddy threw open the door, waving at me to climb in. Tiger Ted was driving.

"War's over!" Tiger shouted. "Come on, Legs, we're going for a ride."

The car was already packed with troopers, but I squeezed into the front with the door handles denting my knee.

"Have a roll!" Daddy shoved a roll of toilet tissue into my hands. What the heck was I supposed to do with it? "Throw it!" he hollered, a huge grin busting across his face. "Let those babies go."

Before I could even get my roll started, Graphite was careening back and forth down the street, horn blowing, and we were sending toilet paper flying out the windows in fluttering streams of white. All over town, you could hear church bells ringing and horns blaring. People were standing in their yards, waving U.S. flags and flapping bedsheets and towels and who knows what-all at everybody driving past. It was like being in a crazy parade of joy. Don't know how I'd pictured celebrating victory if it ever came, but I sure never imagined it would be riding around trailing toilet tissue behind me. We must've had two dozen rolls in the old Ford, and we used up every single one papering the town before heading back to the airfield to reload.

As we pulled through the gates of the air base, the guard suddenly closed them behind us. Which kinda took us by surprise, you know, since the war was over.

Then he padlocked them.

One of the troopers tried razzing the soldier, asking him if the army was afraid the Japs were gonna sneak into Pendleton and steal our toilet tissue. The guard didn't look like he appreciated humor much. "Colonel's orders," the fellow snapped, and headed back to the guard shack.

Later on we found out the real reason.

Once people ran out of safe things to launch into the sky, it seems they turned to unloading whatever ammo they could find to make a bang. They shot off pellet guns, hunting rifles, pistols, fireworks, Civil War relics—you name it, you could hear things exploding all over town. Guess the army didn't want to take the chance of any of that spare ammo getting unloaded on the colored troops and starting trouble, so they decided to keep the men at the airfield for their own protection, they said. A lot of the soldiers were real steamed about it. Same thing had happened on the Fourth, and they hadn't forgotten about that treatment either. Ace insisted he was gonna sneak out—he said nobody would keep him behind a fence like a Jap prisoner, not when he'd fought for our country and almost died for it.

He might've tried to get out too, if it wasn't for the celebration meal Emerald cooked up later on. I swear there couldn't have been anything edible left in Oregon after seeing how much the cook put together. Slabs of beef and heaping mounds of mashed potatoes, boatloads of gravy, and one entire table of nothing but cakes and pies. Plus, one dessert Emerald set on fire. The men joked how the army'd probably make them parachute onto desserts next. We ate until we were way past stuffed. Anybody who tried to climb a fence after that meal woulda been a fool.

After chow, a few of the troopers wandered over to the old piano in the corner of the mess hall. One of them started banging out a tune and the others started dragging over troopers to help sing, until there was a whole crowd gathered around. Let me tell you, the army has a few songs ladies should never ever hear. Probably made the piano blush.

Of course, my daddy had to get pulled into the fray. "You got a good-sounding voice," he said, giving me a rib poke after we'd joined in on a couple of numbers. "Guess you didn't get that from me, huh?" A smile crossed his face, but it faded quick because both of us started thinking about Queen Bee Walker, I guess—which made the moment go from happy to sad faster than a song.

The whole night was full of the same ups and downs. Like MawMaw Sands said, life can be a crazy mix of sweetness and pain. Only four days after we watched a coffin get loaded onto a train—we were singing songs and celebrating victory over Japan. At the same time we were celebrating, Mickey's heartbroken family was probably making plans for his funeral. Some of the troopers said if the war had ended a few days sooner, maybe they wouldn't have gone on that fire call and Mickey would be alive to see the victory. It was still hard to understand why it had to be him who was lost.

Everybody agreed it was a shame Cal wasn't around for the celebration, because no doubt he woulda been the life of the party. I know me and my daddy were both kinda lost without him. We wandered from the piano to the poker games, but my father only played a couple of halfhearted hands before he said, "Let's bug out of here and get some air."

We found a spot outside the operations shed, where you could perch on some oil drums and get a good view of the flashes of fireworks and gunfire still blasting all over town. It was a clear August night, with the moon almost full. It floated above us like a pale Jap balloon—trust me, it didn't take much imagination to see the connection. Reminded me of the big moon I'd seen outside St. Louis and my dream about chasing it with my father. Pictured us in that dream again, climbing mountains of sugar, trying to touch the darned moon.

Swear my father must've been reading my mind because, at that same moment, he sighed and said, "Sometimes I think we might as well have been chasing the son-of-a-gun moon in this war."

I asked him if he meant the balloon bombs. "You still think they were real or not?"

"I don't know," my daddy said, shaking his head. "Keep trying to tell myself the Japs could've stopped sending them for some reason, and that's why we never came across one— but sometimes I wonder, what if it all turns out to be lies? What if we were out here for nothing? What if I was a fool to believe what the army told me? How will I live with sending a young kid to his death?"

Even with the celebrations going on around us, you could feel the gloom surrounding him. All his lieutenant shine was gone.

"Why'd the army never send any of you to the war, do you think?"

It was a question that had been nagging at me for a while. After all, Mrs. Delaney's sons had been sent to the Pacific. Archie's brother had been sent to Europe. Why not the troopers at Pendleton?

Answer was simple, my daddy said. "Army couldn't keep us separate from white soldiers in battle. When you jump out of a plane, you come down in the middle of everything. Whoever you land next to, you fight next to. Nobody in the army wanted to take the chance of us landing next to them. Thought all our training would change their minds, but it didn't, I guess . . ." His voice trailed off into silence.

"Maybe someday it will change." I tried to sound hopeful.

My daddy sighed. "Who knows. Feel like I've spent half my life chasing after things or trying to change them. Chased balloon bombs and decent work. Chased people who I thought loved me. After your momma ran off, I spent all my time looking for her. Every town I traveled through, I'd search around for her name."

Wasn't sure I'd heard him right at first. Had he said he

went looking for my mother? Always thought she'd vanished into thin air and was never seen again. Never heard anybody in my family tried to go in search of her.

"Finally found her in Detroit. Couple of years after she ran off, I saw her name on a poster outside a club when I was driving around selling those encyclopedias I used to peddle," my father continued. "It said QUEEN BEE WALKER HERE TONIGHT." He pointed at the words as if they were written on the night air in front of us.

I held my breath waiting to hear more.

"So, I parked in front of the club, trying to decide what to do. How could I get her back? What could I say to change her mind?" My father glanced over at me. "I sat there for who knows how long, but I couldn't come up with anything. Not one word. So I reached for one of those fancy encyclopedias I sold. The *L* volume. Wanted to see what it told you about love. Always gave people the line that anything you needed to know in the world was inside those books. And you know what I found out?"

I shook my head.

"I found out love isn't in the encyclopedia. You look up *love* and there is nothing written there except for a few words telling you to look somewhere else. So you know what that made me realize, Levi?" He paused and stared up at the night sky. "It made me realize there are things in this world even the smartest encyclopedias can't help you with. Love.

Death. War. Why some people treat other people the cruel way they do. You need to look somewhere else for answers to the tough questions like that."

My father gave me an uneasy look, like he suddenly realized he'd gone on way too much. "Anyhow, I stared at the poster outside the club for a long time before I decided maybe there was nothing to say, maybe some things were better left alone. After that, I drove back to Chicago and gave up selling encyclopedias for good. Figured I needed to try something new in my life."

"You never talked to her?" Thinking if it had been up to me, I woulda gone inside for sure. Just to have some proof she was real, you know what I mean? And to find out why she'd left us. Woulda told her it was a big mistake to put those three words on a napkin too. *I Am Levin*. What dumb words to write. They had cursed me forever.

My father said no, he never talked to her.

"I decided it was better to move on," he said. "Had you and me to look out for, and finding work wasn't easy back then. I played for some of the traveling baseball teams and sold insurance. You had to do whatever you could to make ends meet. Then the war came along and I signed up for the army after Pearl Harbor, figuring I'd do something bigger with my life and serve my country. I'd be part of the first colored paratroop battalion and do something nobody else had done. Somewhere in between all that—the war decided it didn't want me, and you grew up too fast."

Heck, I had no idea what to say after hearing his sad speech. I tried pointing out to my father how he'd always been good about writing letters. "No matter where you were, you always wrote."

Couldn't tell in the darkness, but I'm pretty sure my daddy rolled his eyes. "Letters aren't being a father."

"Better than nothing."

"Not much better."

I tried something else. "You sent me a scorpion."

A sneaky grin passed across my daddy's face. "You still remember that gift?"

"Still have it."

"You pulling my leg?" My daddy glanced over at me, grinning wider. "You kept it from Odella all this time?"

I nodded.

"Well, that's something," he said, still smiling.

I had the feeling maybe I'd cheered him up a little.

Digging around in his pocket, my father came up with a crushed pack of Wrigley's and tore it open. "Have a piece," he said, passing a stick to me.

Sitting there in the darkness with the smell of spearmint drifting on the air around us, I decided life can be a real strange circle sometimes. Three years ago, I'd been a pesky kid begging for some chewing gum instead of missing my father. Now the two of us were sharing a pack of Wrigley's and I was listening to my father go on and on about how much he'd missed *me*.

I couldn't help wondering if my life woulda been any different if he'd talked to Queen Bee Walker all those years ago. Maybe they woulda fallen in love again, who knows. Or maybe she woulda taken off and left us twice in one lifetime. Guess there is no way of knowing if something is gonna be a Hollywood ending or a flop, right?

Sat outside with my father, talking and watching the celebrations, until way past midnight. Saw two shooting stars zip across the night sky, although I didn't see either one land and sprout into a tree like MawMaw Sands said. Despite the big party everybody below us in the town seemed to be having and the happy crescendo of noise coming outta the mess hall, I could tell my daddy was still wrestling with the idea of the war being over. More than a couple of times, he said, "All I want is for the people down there to know we did our part for our country. Don't want to go home feeling like we did nothing."

Maybe the stars were listening that night. Or maybe MawMaw Sands was right all along about believing in things you can't see. Turns out my father didn't have to wait very long to get one of the things he wanted. The next morning, everybody woke up to the news that something about Jap balloon bombs was in the headlines.

33. Headlines

Word reached the airfield as the men were getting into formation before breakfast.

Nobody was putting in much effort that morning, I gotta admit, with the war being over and all. Uniforms were wrinkled and trouser legs weren't bloused real carefully. Everybody just threw on their jump boots and clomped out the door, laces dragging.

I'd only got a few hours' sleep. I'd slept overnight in the service barracks, breaking every army rule there is—and probably worrying the Delaneys half to death—but since the army had locked up the base, what else could I do? My daddy couldn't take the chance of sneaking me into the officers' quarters, so Emerald found me a bunk in his barracks and some of the other fellows were kind enough to short-sheet the bed before I got into it.

Of course, I shoulda known from all my daddy's letters that you can't trust the mess hall crew any farther than you can spit, but there I was—tugging and tugging on the blankets with sweat beading up on my forehead—until the men, who were howling with laughter by then, showed me what they'd done. Told them they were a bunch of fools before I yanked the blankets over my head to get some sleep.

Anyhow, the army cooks were already hard at work fixing breakfast and I was standing around yawning and watching the troopers line up in their halfhearted rows when the rumor reached us about something important being in the newspaper. One of the officers said he'd overheard a guard talking about the headlines, so my daddy said the two of us would take Graphite into town and buy a couple copies of the morning edition before it sold out.

The day had been declared a holiday for everybody, but from the looks of things, I don't think the town of Pendleton had one single explosive left. The whole place was covered in a hazy firecracker fog that morning and seemed to be sound asleep. After all the crazy celebrating that had been going on, I figured a lot of people would be putting salt in their Coca-Colas for their headaches and staying in bed.

Took us a while to find any newsboys selling papers. We drove up and down Main Street twice. Finally found a kid with two skinned knees and a runny nose. He hardly looked old enough to read what he was selling, and I don't think he'd ever taken money from a colored person before either. When my father held out the money for him, he just stared at us. Then, after snatching the coins outta my father's hand, he threw one copy at us and ran off. Good thing it wasn't a windy day or the news woulda been all over the street.

We sat down on a curb across from one of the barbershops in Pendleton to page through the paper. Other than the two of us, the red and white barber pole seemed to be the only thing moving. All the stores around us were closed. My father stretched out his legs on the empty pavement and unfolded the paper across them. As he turned the page, a headline on the inside of *The Oregonian* caught our eye. There, in two-inch type, were the words nobody ever believed we'd see: JAP BALLOONS FELL IN SIXTEEN STATES.

I don't think I'm giving away any army secrets if I tell you this was one of the few times in my whole life that I ever saw my tough father cry.

34. Leaving

They talked about the story for weeks afterward. Nobody in Pendleton could believe the Japs had launched thousands of balloons and they'd drifted across sixteen states. And it was an even bigger shock to find out one balloon bomb had killed five Oregon kids and a young preacher's wife on a picnic in May—the same day the men had left North Carolina to come west. Another one landed near a factory in Washington State making parts for the atomic bomb. "See, we came closer to being the Book of Revelation than we knew," Mrs. Delaney insisted when she read the news.

The newspapers said some of the enemy balloons had traveled as far as Michigan and Texas, where people who saw the strange ghost-white orbs floating across the sky thought they were going nuts. By June, the Japs had given up sending them. Which explained why my daddy and his men had never seen one—nobody knew the attack on the West had mostly stopped by the time the paratroopers got there.

A lot of the paratroopers at Pendleton cut out every newspaper article they could find about the balloons. They folded them carefully in their wallets and carried them everywhere. It was a small piece of pride, you know what I mean? Other soldiers brought home medals and ribbons from fighting overseas, but those headlines were all the paratroopers had to show why they'd jumped into forest fires and landed in trees and all that. For a lot of them, just having the proof they'd been part of something in the war was enough. They were ready to go home.

I saved one of the articles and stuck it in MawMaw Sands's basket to show off to Archie someday. Back in Southern Pines, I'm sure MawMaw Sands was sitting in her rocker, having a little laugh about the news. I could hear her saying, "I told you so, Levi Battle. Told you sometimes you gotta believe in things you can't always see." My daddy sent one article to Mickey's family and another to Cal and Peaches, in case they hadn't seen the news. He wrote on it, *Watch out for any stray balloons floating over Georgia,* which I think was a joke, although jokes weren't my daddy's talent.

Then he hopped on a C-47 again and went on another fire call.

Couldn't believe it when we heard the big airplanes roar overhead only two days after victory had been declared. We were in the middle of finishing up a late breakfast—

me, Mrs. Delaney, and Willajean were just sitting around watching the butter melt—when the planes from Pendleton sailed over the house, rattling everybody's nerves again.

"What in the world is happening now?" Mrs. Delaney leaped up and tuned in the radio right away. Think we were all wondering if maybe the Japs had changed their mind and taken back their surrender. But Bing Crosby and the Andrews Sisters were singing "Victory Polka" on the local station and everything seemed peaceful. "Must be another fire somewhere and that's where all the planes are going," Mrs. Delaney said, coming back to the table and whispering a quick prayer before she picked up her fork again.

Of course, Willajean had to bring up the idea of me being stuck in Pendleton forever. "What if the army stays here for good and Levi never gets to go back home?" she asked, sounding hopeful.

Didn't say it, but I thought, *I'll walk back to Chicago if I have to. No way am I spending the rest of my life in Pendleton, Oregon.*

Mrs. Delaney sounded pretty sure the rainy season would put an end to the fires in the West soon. "Couple more weeks of August left, and then the rain will be here."

As the last weeks of August dragged on, I spent half the time hoping the fires would stop before my father or one of the other troopers died jumping into them—and the other half worrying what would happen when the missions did end.

It didn't help matters that everybody else in Pendleton seemed to be getting ready for their new future after the war. Every day more soldiers came home. There were weddings, funerals, parades, you name it. Mrs. Delaney kept moving my things into smaller and smaller piles, saying she had to make room for when her sons, George and Robert, got back from the Pacific soon. One day, I figured, she was probably gonna put me in one of those piles too.

The whole country seemed to be on sale. Victory bargains were everywhere. Mrs. Delaney bought herself a brand-new kitchen range—probably with all the rent money she got from us. Willajean bought high school sweaters and new shoes and tried to convince me to sign up for school in September.

Heck, school was the last thing I was worried about.

I kept waiting on my father to say something, to give me some hint about what our future held. Was he staying with the army or moving on? Were we going back to Chicago or not? But the future coulda been a rattlesnake curled on the road in front of us, given how much my father avoided talking about it. When I tried tossing out a question here or there, he'd always answer how the fires and his men were his main mission. "Can't think about anything else while I've still got a job to do here."

Once, when the two of us were strolling around the airfield for something to do, he asked if I had any interest in following in his footsteps and jumping out of airplanes someday. "You ever think it would be fun to go up in the sky and see what it's like?"

Guess we still had a lot to learn about each other, because he seemed surprised when I said, "Nope. Never." Even if I convinced myself to fly inside an airplane someday, there was no way I'd ever jump out.

That was the closest we came to talking about the future.

The rest of the time, we stuck to what we already knew best. Between fire calls, my daddy taught me to play poker. We put in a lot of time at the horseshoe pits too, and one September weekend we finally caught some fish. Brought back three nice-sized trout for Emerald to fry. Those Oregon trout turned out to be our last taste of summer, because a few days later the rain arrived.

I heard the sound first. Early one morning. A drumming sound like woodpeckers hammering on the roof. Then I noticed how the bedroom curtains in Robert's room were fluttering. My long legs prickled in the sudden breeze and I realized the air pouring through the open window was chilly. What the heck had happened with the temperature? I yanked the blankets over myself. The whole bedroom was sunk in a dark gray gloom. Couldn't make any guess as to what time it was.

Still freezing, I unrolled a pair of socks and pulled on my trousers. The hallway was empty when I stuck my head outta the bedroom, so I figured it was still real early. Could see Mrs. Delaney out on the porch, where she liked to sit before the neighborhood woke up. When I pushed open the door, she turned to check who it was. "Morning, Levi. You're up early. Welcome to the rainy season." She gestured toward the watery scene in front of us where the rain was coming down in sheets.

I gawked at the sight as if I'd never seen rain before. Good grief, a few months in the West and I'd forgotten what rain looked like.

"You can almost smell the Pacific, can't you?" Mrs. Delaney said, taking a big breath.

The Pacific? It was miles away. To me, the air smelled more like fish. A chilly, fishy smell. Uncle Otis had once taken me to see a pier that jutted into Lake Michigan, and I remembered how the greenish waves crashing onto the pier kicked up the same kinda smell. Watching the rain fall beyond the porch roof, I felt those same greenish waves kicking up inside of me, because I knew it was only a matter of time before leaving came up in my life again. Mrs. Delaney could smell the Pacific and I could smell leaving on the air.

Sure enough, a couple of days after the fire missions ended and some of the cleanup was done, my father stopped by Mrs. Delaney's house with an envelope in his hand. The rain was still falling, soaking the shoulders of his uniform.

"Came to talk to Levi for a little bit, if that's all right, ma'am," he said to Mrs. Delaney, who was dusting all her knickknacks in the front room with the help of Willajean. I put down the mop they'd given me and reluctantly followed his wet footsteps into the kitchen. Any other time I'd have been glad to give up cleaning something, but not then.

When my daddy handed the envelope to me and I saw the handwriting on the front was Aunt Odella's, I was convinced I was going back to Chicago. "Open it and see what's inside," he said, biting down on his lips like he was trying hard not to smile. I opened the flap, not knowing what to think about how strange he was acting.

Stuck inside, there was a letter—and a small snapshot slid onto the floor. Picked it up and couldn't believe my eyes. There was Aunt Odella smiling and standing arm in arm with a man in uniform. Written on the back in precise lines were these words: *Odella and Paul Carter, joined in marriage, August 18, 1945.*

Let me tell you, I was speechless. Could hardly keep myself from going over to the window to check if chickens were plucking their own feathers and pigs were flying.

"Can you believe it? My sister falling in love with a navy man," my daddy said, shaking his head and grinning. "She shoulda picked somebody from the army instead."

I kept staring at the picture, still trying to believe it was true. How was it possible? How had Aunt Odella found love and a husband in a few short months? And what did that mean for me?

Right then, it hit me. I was holding the snapshot of my

future. My daddy was sending me back to Chicago to live with Aunt Odella and her new husband, Paul, wasn't he?

I don't think my daddy realized I'd already guessed what was coming next. He pulled out one of the kitchen chairs, sat down, and said we had some important things to talk about.

By then, I was hardly listening. Instead, I pictured what it would be like to be wrapped up in Queen Bee Walker's fur coat—how you couldn't see or hear anything from inside it. Didn't care what my father was gonna say to me. All I knew was we'd spent the last few months getting to know each other and now it was all for nothing. I could say goodbye to the poker games and horseshoes and fishing and you name it because I was about to be handed those same three son-of-a-gun words again: *I Am Levin.*

"I know all the people and friends you have back in Chicago," my father said. "When I was your age, I loved Hixson's and going to Uncle Otis's and all that. Still do." His fingers drummed on the table and his expression grew more serious like the tough news he had to tell me was coming up next. "Trouble is, you can see Odella's got her own life these days and there isn't much room for you and me back there in Chicago anymore."

My eyes swiveled in his direction. What was he saying? A dizzying hum of noise filled my ears. What did he mean about no room for us in Chicago?

"If I want to stay in the service, the army says they'll

promote me to first lieutenant and send me for special officer training this winter," my father went on, noticing nothing. "They want to recruit more paratroopers for our outfit, and they think I could end up being one of the top colored officers they have in peacetime. Who knows, if I keep moving up, maybe someday I'll get to be general. Wouldn't that be something if your daddy ended up being General Charles Battle?"

A proud grin crossed my daddy's face and you could tell he had his whole life planned out ahead of him like a road map. Only thing that road map didn't include was me.

See, Aunt Odella had been right all along, I realized—the war might have ended, but my father wasn't giving up the army and returning to Chicago anytime soon. The truth was, he couldn't stop chasing after bigger things in his life, no matter what he said. If he got to be general, he'd want to try for something else. The moon was always gonna be just out of his reach.

But his next words caught me off guard.

Clearing his throat, my father grew serious again. "What I'm trying to tell you, Levi," he said, giving me one of his eye-to-eye lieutenant looks, "is that I'd like to stick with the army and I thought maybe you'd like to come along with me this time and see what happens."

I'm sure I was blinking like a bird that had just slammed beak-first into a window as I tried to sort out what I'd just heard: He wasn't asking me to go back to my old life in

Chicago. He was asking me to start over somewhere else. He was saying give up Archie and my friends, Aunt Odella and Uncle Otis, the neighborhood I knew every crowded square inch of—even the school I'd gone to since I was a little kid—and come with him.

"So what do you think?" My daddy studied his big parachute-holding hands. "I know it's a lot to decide all of a sudden."

I had no idea what I thought. I tried to come up with something else . . . anything else . . . to ask.

"Do you know where the army's sending you?" I held on to a small scrap of hope that it might be a place *near* Chicago, right? On the other hand, it could also be somewhere miles away. Like the South. No way I was going back there.

Honestly, I thought it was a cruel joke when my father said, "Well, it turns out the army's assigning our battalion back to Camp Mackall in North Carolina."

What?

All I could do was stare. Out of all the son-of-a-gun places in the entire United States the army coulda picked—and my father was asking me to go back to *the worst place I'd ever been?*

It felt like getting a sudden stinging slap across the face. Could feel my whole face getting hot. How could my father even think of asking me to go with him? There was no way I'd do it. No way.

"Why would you want to go back there and put up with

all that?" My arms chopped at the air and my voice was louder than it probably shoulda been. "All those signs and everything all over the place." It was one thing to stay with the army, it was another thing to go back to the COLORED signs and water fountains and being treated like you were less than nothing, you know what I mean?

"Wherever the army sends us, that's where we go," my father said coolly, trying to keep up his tough lieutenant bluff—as if the army could send him off a cliff and it wouldn't much matter to him. Then he added with a trace more sharpness, "If I wanted easy in this life, I wouldn't strap a parachute to myself every day and jump out of airplanes, now would I?"

There was a long silence. A chilly, wet breeze ruffled through the kitchen. I think Willajean and Mrs. Delaney must've been listening in the front room, because they were awfully quiet.

My father's voice was softer when he spoke again. You might've been able to hear some disappointment in it if you listened hard. "If you don't want to come along with me, that's fine, Levi," he said. "I can talk to Uncle Otis or one of my sisters and see if they wouldn't mind looking after you, if it comes down to that. I'm not dragging you along with me if you don't want to go. You're old enough to make some of your own decisions these days. I thought you'd want to give this a try, but if you don't want to, that's all right. The choice is up to you."

More silence.

"And if I was to go back to Chicago, who would you have left?" The angry question flew out of my mouth before I could stop it. Think it took both of us by surprise.

"I don't know," my father said, looking confused by what I was asking. "The other troopers in the outfit, I guess."

"But not me."

"Right," he answered uneasily. "Not you."

More heat pushed behind my voice. "So you're saying you'd let me go back to Chicago and leave you with no-body?"

My father rubbed his eyes. "What I'm saying is, it's up to you."

Well, I couldn't do it.

No matter how much I wanted to stay in Chicago and no matter how much I hated the idea of going back to the South—I couldn't tell my father I was leaving him in the dust. Couldn't say those three words to his face: I am leaving. Even if he was ready to take off and follow the army wherever it went, I couldn't do the same thing to him.

Tell you the truth, realizing that fact about myself was one of the best things that coulda come out of the bad moment. When you are from a family of people who don't stick around, it's easy to start worrying if maybe you have that same quality. But all those years of picking up buckeyes—how I couldn't leave one behind—that shoulda been my first clue. Because now I could clearly see the one thing I didn't get from Queen Bee Walker. Or my daddy. Or the Battle family either.

Some people might've been able to put a goodbye note on a car seat and say, *I Am Levin,* but the honest truth was—I couldn't. When it came right down to it, I might've been born into a family of people who couldn't stick around, but I was somebody who did.

So that was the reason why I didn't have any choice really. Sitting there in the Delaneys' little kitchen with the rain hammering down like the Pacific Ocean outside, I had to act like a tough pillow, like nothing could bother me, and tell him yes—

"All right," I said, trying to keep my voice from falling to pieces. "I'll go along with you."

35. Sitting Still

Turns out, the decision to go along with my father would be the easy part, but the harder parts were still waiting ahead. We made plans to leave Pendleton at the beginning of October, and it was my daddy's idea to stop in Chicago before we went to his assignment in North Carolina. "I've got some furlough time," he said, "so we'll spend a few days there." Think he was trying his best to make me happy, but I was afraid seeing the place would only make me miss it more.

When she heard we were leaving, Willajean acted like her world was gonna end, even though her brothers were expected back home any day. I was packing up the last of my things one night when she came into my room with a folded-up piece of paper.

"Wrote you something," she said, holding it toward me, her eyes blinking nervously behind her glasses. "You can go ahead and look at it."

Well, I opened up the paper, and it turned out the girl

had written the world's longest poem for me—a poem all about stars and peace and everlasting love. Good grief, I had no ding-donged idea what to say.

"What do you think?" she asked after I read it.

I had no idea what I thought. Fortunately, I noticed MawMaw Sands's sweetgrass basket, which was sitting empty on the bed, waiting to be packed up, and I got a flash of divine inspiration. "I think you should have this basket for your poems." I pushed the basket toward Willajean. "It was made by an old African lady named MawMaw Sands, whose ancestors jumped off slave ships and lived in the Georgia swamps years ago, and everybody buys their baskets from her because they have things in them you can't always see. She gave me this basket before I came to Pendleton and now I want you to have it."

"What in the world are you talking about?" Willajean glared, hands on her hips.

"I'm just saying, sometimes you gotta believe in things you can't see, that's all," I replied, trying to sound mysterious. Swear I was almost as good as MawMaw Sands herself. "Since you want to be a poet someday, I thought maybe you should have something nice for keeping your poetry inside."

Willajean studied the basket, opening it up and looking inside. "It's pretty, but I wanted you to have the poem. I wrote the poem for you."

Heck, girls were impossible. I had to think fast. "Well, how about if you keep the basket and I keep the poem?"

Willajean gave me a melty-looking smile and she took off with that basket like it was a block of gold, telling me, "Thank you, Levi. Outside of my family, nobody has ever given me a real gift before."

I hoped MawMaw Sands wouldn't mind me giving away her gift, but I figured she probably already knew I would. Wouldn't be surprised if she was sitting down there in North Carolina on her viny green porch, making me a new one at that very moment.

I'll admit I hung on to the poem from Willajean for a long time after leaving Pendleton because it was the first poem a girl ever gave to me, and maybe someday Willajean would be as famous as Emily Dickinson, who knows.

The morning we left Oregon, the weather was clear and chilly, not a cloud in the sky. "Perfect jump day," my daddy said, glancing upward and shaking his head like it was hard to leave. Willajean was back in school, so it was only Mrs. Delaney seeing us off at the station. She was waiting on pins and needles for her boys to come back. I think she spent more time looking around the train station for the two of them than saying goodbye to us, but that was okay with me.

Now, if you've ever come back to a place that you haven't seen in a while, you know how things change. After all the wide-open spaces of Oregon, the city of Chicago seemed to have shrunk while I was gone. Everything felt smaller. Aunt Odella's apartment was a shoebox compared to where we'd been. When we arrived and she flung open the door to welcome us, I looked around the tiny space and thought, *Good grief, how could the two of us have lived here?*

Aunt Odella was the real story, though. She looked as if she'd gone back in time and found her younger self. "Levi, look at you," she said in this soft-edged voice when she opened the door. Swear even the voice sounded new.

When my father stepped through the doorway in his dress uniform, she started carrying on and crying all over his shoulders, which took me by surprise considering the way she used to be. I guess some people must get their waterworks later in life, because Aunt Odella couldn't stop boo-hooing and telling my father how proud she was of everything he'd done in the war.

After introducing us to her new husband, Paul, she heaped on about a hundred more praises, saying how my daddy was one of the few colored paratroopers in the army and I was one of the nicest boys in Chicago. "I raised him right," she said proudly.

Paul reached out to shake our hands. He had a weakly grip and sweaty palms, but he seemed like a nice enough fellow. Found out he'd met Aunt Odella in June at a church funeral, where else? And it was love at first sight. You could tell they were crazy about one another from the way they kept giving each other little smiles and looks when they didn't think we were paying attention.

It made me wonder if the cactus was right after all. Without all the heavy burdens on her two shoulders, Aunt Odella had changed into a bright cactus flower overnight. Like I said, she didn't even seem like the same person she was before. Which just goes to show you maybe there are times in life when change is what you have to do to survive. Despite what other people might've thought about my aunt sending me away so suddenly, I couldn't hold that choice against her—or anybody else, you know what I mean?

Archie stopped by for a visit while we were there, and I'll be honest with you, he had changed for the worse. We'd written a few words back and forth during the summer, so I'd heard the bad news about his brother being declared killed in action. Don't know if it was the pain of losing his brother, or me not being around to keep him on the straight and narrow—or both—but he'd taken up cussing and girls and just about every other bad thing you could name.

When he showed up to see us wearing one of those baggy zoot suits with a fedora slouching over his eyes, Aunt Odella turned right back into her old self. "Can't believe you are strolling around town looking like that," she said, hands on her hips. "Putting your family to shame. You can expect next time I see your momma or your granny in church, I'm gonna have a word with them." After he left, Aunt Odella shook her head and said it was too bad the way he'd turned out. I'll admit part of me was torn up to see him so different.

Fortunately, Uncle Otis hadn't changed much at all. Well, except for his wife—she had left and took the green battleship with her too. Uncle Otis had bought his first Buick because he thought maybe the problem was with his automobile, not his wife. Me and my daddy heard all the sorry details of his wife troubles while he was giving us our sharp-looking razor cuts. Then he started pestering us for the reasons why we were going back to the South.

"War's over. Can't understand why you're sticking with the army and moving south, Charlie. Why not stay right here where all your family is?" he said, talking to my daddy like he was my age. "How about if I give you that spot right over there." He pointed at the empty barber chair next to us. "Teach you everything I know about cutting heads. Let Levi go back to his old school and all his friends. This young man's got a good head on his shoulders, you know." As he patted my shoulder, the razor drifted dangerously close to my ear. "How about you? How'd you like to be a barber some-day?" he said, looking at me.

I shrugged and told him no, I'd thought about maybe working for a newspaper.

Uncle Otis shook his head. "Naw, you don't want to do that. All they tell is made-up lies. Be a barber instead. We give people the real scoop about the world right here."

My daddy grinned. "Nobody tells stories or cuts heads like you, Otis."

"That's true." Uncle Otis nodded solemnly. "Can't keep a wife to save my life, but I sure can keep Chicago looking good."

You can see how everybody in the family was doing their best to get us to change our minds. It wasn't easy to leave, especially when Aunt Odella handed us a bag of her good fried chicken and a framed picture of her and her fellow and started boo-hooing about never seeing us again. It was real hard.

But even with all the begging and bribery, me and my daddy stuck with what we'd planned to do. After spending almost a week in Chicago—which was both too long and too short at the same time—we bought tickets at Union Station and boarded the train again. Felt like I was repeating my own life. Same station I'd left from in May. Same destination. Only thing different was having my father sitting next to me, instead of a white lady with a cake box.

One whole day passed by our windows without much to worry about. We were on our second day of traveling—I think we were somewhere in Maryland—when we noticed a few of the folks around us getting up. Two colored servicemen carrying their army duffels on their heads left the seats behind us. A colored family near the front corner of the car stood up suddenly and left their seats as a whole group. "Must be something good cooking in the dining car up ahead this morning," my daddy joked. We were reading some penny comics and magazines we'd bought, not paying much attention to where we were, just having a good time. We'd already eaten breakfast at one of the train stations, so we weren't hungry.

I remember the shadow that was cast across our seats by the conductor who came to stand next to us. Think me and my daddy looked up at the exact same time. The conductor wasn't smiling. He had a thin face that coulda used a good shave and there were stains under the armpits of his wrinkled uniform, as if he was somebody who didn't care much about how he looked. "Time to get up and move forward," he said, pointing at the front door of our passenger car.

"Pardon?" My father set his magazine down slowly.

The man's voice got louder and slower, as if we were ignorant fools. "I said, it is time to get up and move forward to the colored car." Heads turned to look at us. All the faces around us were white. I suddenly realized there wasn't a colored person left in the whole car. And let me tell you, if the eyes of the passengers sitting near us had been machine guns, me and my daddy woulda been full of holes.

"I'm Lieutenant Charles Battle of the U.S. Army, sir, and I'm staying right here in the coach seat I bought and paid for," my father replied calmly. Very slowly he unrolled his magazine and began to read it again. My heart was pounding so hard, I thought my ribs might explode. Stared at my comics, not seeing a thing, just a dizzying blur of colors and words. The back of my shirt melted into the blue seat cushions.

"If you don't get up and go where you are supposed to go, soldier, I'll have you removed from this train."

Now, you gotta picture my daddy's square army shoulders and strong parachute-holding arms. His sharp dress uniform with its perfectly creased blouse and tie. The paratrooper wings and polished brass. Think you woulda needed a tank to get him off the train.

"I'm an officer in the U.S. Army," my father said, sliding out of his seat. As the train rolled down the tracks, he stood in front of the conductor in the swaying aisle. His head almost skimmed the ceiling. "I risked my life jumping out of airplanes and protecting this country from the enemy for the last three years. I saw one of my men lose his life for the war, and I have a right to this seat"—his hand smacked the cushions, making me jump—"as much as anybody in this country. And I'm not leaving it."

He sat back down, not looking at me. You could see a shine of sweat across his forehead and the veins on his temple standing out, thick as roots. With a slow, deliberate move, he reached toward the floor and picked up his magazine again.

I think all the air had gotten sucked out of the car by then, because I sure couldn't find any to breathe. I was convinced the conductor was gonna take us out of this world. Instead, he turned toward me. Even though me and my daddy looked alike, I don't think the conductor realized we were father and son. Most army officers didn't travel around the country with their half-grown children.

The conductor pointed his finger at where I was sitting, next to the window. "You, boy, get up and follow me to the front right now. You know better than to be here in this car. Let's go." His face was hard.

This was the point when I realized that deciding not to leave somebody—and deciding to stay with them—are two entirely different things. Deciding not to leave my daddy was the easy part because all I had to do was follow him. Choosing to stay with him meant accepting the consequences of whatever happened to us—good or bad—together.

"I think I'm gonna stay where I am," I replied, my voice not sounding too certain.

The conductor acted like he hadn't heard me. Or didn't believe me. Hard to tell.

"What did you say, boy?"

This time I found another voice. "I'm staying here with my father."

The conductor's expression was a flat plate of fury. The rest of the passengers still had their eyes aimed in our direction. You could feel the looks ricocheting around the car.

"You'll regret not leaving when you had the chance. You get farther south, they'll show you what's what." A mist of spit from the conductor's mouth splattered our faces. Then he turned and stalked out of the coach, keys clattering on his belt.

I know it probably sounds strange to say, but I believe that was the moment when the two of us—my daddy and me—felt like we were father and son for the first time. As we sat there in that southern train car splattered with spit, sweat pouring down our faces, I think both of us realized we were stuck together by what we had decided to do, no matter what happened next. We'd done a blackout jump together, as Cal would say, and there was no leaning back to close the door.

As the train rolled through town after town, getting deeper into the South, the two of us stayed side by side, waiting for whatever fate would come on board for us. Didn't dare say a word to each other, just stayed face forward, our eyes staring at the seats in front of us. At one point my daddy's hand reached over and squeezed my arm, like he was telling me to not give up hope yet.

We were on that train for what seemed like hours and we never moved one inch from our seats. Our spit dried up and our stomachs rumbled and pee backed up to our eyeballs, but we sat there like we were glued in place. Figured we'd never be able to unbend our legs again, after all that time. To this day, I don't know why nobody came on board to get us. Or why we weren't arrested at one of the stations and dragged off to jail.

We rode in a coach car meant for whites only all the way to Fayetteville, North Carolina. When we peeled ourselves outta the seats finally, it was early evening. We stumbled off the train at the end of a long line of white people who were in a speedy hurry to make it down the aisle before us, as if we had some dread disease that might be catching.

Nobody was waiting to arrest us once we set foot on the ground, though—which was a big surprise to us because we sure thought they would be. Same dumb signs still hung everywhere, of course. COLORED. WHITE. Black fingers pointed out the direction we were supposed to go. But we stood there on the platform, ignoring all of them. Turning quick, my daddy wrapped his arms around me in an army hug that just about squeezed the pee into my brain. His hands thumped my back. "You are one darned brave person. I am so proud of you. So darned proud of having you as my son."

"Well, I am too," I replied, which didn't make much sense, but that's what I said.

As we headed to the army bus stop with the sun setting behind us, I knew our old lives had come to an end. Things were changing.

The world was changing.

Me and my daddy—we'd been away from each other for a long time, rolling through our lives like lonely rocks. Leaving had been a curse hanging over both our heads, but we'd stood up to it on the train—looked it right in the face—and stuck together, no matter what harm coulda happened to us. And now that curse felt like it had finally been broken.

Maybe our new life together wouldn't always be easy—I was sure it wouldn't since me and my daddy were different people, you know, and we had a lot of catching up to do. Living in the South would be tough on both of us.

But as Aunt Odella always said, "The end of one thing is the beginning of something else." As I walked next to my father under the cactus-orange sky, you could tell the new beginning was already starting for us. Even if I did have to practically run to keep up.

Author's Note

Within the big stories in history, there are always many smaller ones—stories of ordinary people doing extraordinary things. I first heard about the black paratroopers of the 555th Parachute Infantry Battalion from a veteran who had been one of the famed Tuskegee Airmen, a group of black pilots in World War II. The few details he knew about the paratroopers and their mission intrigued me. He said the men of the 555th were sometimes known as the "Triple Nickles," and they had once been part of a secret operation to protect the United States from Japanese balloon bombs and forest fires during World War II.

My search to find out more about this little-known part of World War II led me to an eighty-seven-year-old veteran named Walter Morris, who was the first African American in U.S. history selected to become a paratrooper. In early 1944, Mr. Morris was part of a small "test platoon" of seventeen soldiers who became the nation's first black paratroopers at a time when few African Americans had ever flown inside a plane, let alone jumped from one. This small group eventually became the 555th Parachute Infantry Battalion, or Triple Nickles.

Now, it is a rare opportunity for any writer—any person—to have the chance to talk to somebody who was there, who was a *first* in history. Whenever I spoke with Mr. Morris, I was always a little awed—and *jittery*, as Levi would say—to be able to interview this humble man who played such a unique role in World War II. I felt it was important to bring the fascinating story of the 555th and their mission to life.

And that's where this book began.

Many of the names and places used in this story are real, including "Tiger Ted" Lowry, who once fought Joe Louis; the army cook called Emerald Jones, who washed out of the paratroops because he couldn't jump; and the troopers nicknamed "Killer" and "Brothers." Graphite was indeed the name of the paratroopers' official army heap, a 1937 two-door Ford.

Today, there is still a small town in North Carolina called Southern Pines, where some of the black paratroopers' families stayed during the war. If you look very carefully, you might find a trickle of a creek called McDeeds running through the middle of it. Our Lady of Victory Church still stands on the town's main street, although it now serves as a community center. You can also find the old train station, where Levi arrived in nearby Fayetteville.

While few trains are pulled by coal-burning locomotives

today, the experience of what it was like to ride in the "Jim Crow cars" in the South hasn't been forgotten by those who did. When I asked one black veteran what he recalled, he looked at me with an unflinching gaze and said, "I remember riding right behind the stinking coal car."

Although the characters of Levi and his father are fictional, the war experiences they describe are as realistic and accurate as possible. Many scenes in the book were adapted from details found in the written and recorded interviews of the men who were part of the 555th, including the final scene, in which Levi and his father refuse to move to the Jim Crow car, and the storekeeper scene, in which Levi nearly loses his life by asking for a Coca-Cola.

As the army's only airborne firefighting unit, the 555th made about twelve hundred individual jumps into forest fires during their service in the western United States, from July to October 1945. You can watch army footage of the real 555th in action during the war and see the men "hooking the trees" and parachuting into forest fires on the unit's website: triplenickle.com.

Despite the hazardous nature of their work and numerous injuries, the Triple Nickles lost only one paratrooper during their mission. Tragically, just a few days before the war ended, a medic from Pennsylvania named Malvin Brown died in a fall from a tree during a firefighting run. Walter Morris was one of the soldiers who accompanied the soldier's body home for burial.

Although most of the paratroopers in the 555th never saw a Japanese balloon bomb, it is estimated that between six thousand and nine thousand balloons were sent from Japan during the war. Parts of the balloons are held at several museums, including the National Museum of the U.S. Air Force, near Dayton, Ohio. Historians believe some balloon bombs may still remain undiscovered in the West today. One was found in Oregon in 1978.

A few months after the war ended, the 555th left Oregon and returned to North Carolina, as Levi describes in the story. In January 1946, they were invited to join the 82nd Airborne in New York City for one of the largest victory parades in the United States. By the following year, the 555th had grown to thirty-six black officers and more than one thousand men as they became an elite demonstration unit·for military training exercises and air shows across the country. In December 1947, they became the first black unit integrated into the regular army—long before integration happened in the rest of the country.

Lt. Col. (Ret.) Bradley Biggs, one of the 555th officers, wrote later that he didn't join the black test platoon to prove that he could jump out of an airplane, but "to prove it should have been done all along."

In 2010, Walter Morris and the 555th veterans were honored in a special ceremony at the Pentagon.

Acknowledgments

I am indebted to Walter Morris for so graciously sharing his time with me. I'll always remember asking him to describe the color of his World War II uniform and how he told me, "Just a minute, I'll go look at it." I'm grateful to the other paratroopers who recorded their recollections and left them in the care of our libraries and colleges so that future generations could learn from them. Material used for the novel included recordings by Bradley Biggs, Clifford Allen, and Clarence Beavers in the collection of Howard University (Moorland-Spingarn Research Center) and published interviews of Melvin Lester, Carstell O. Stewart, and Roger S. Walden.

Ted Lowry's self-published memoir, *God's in My Corner: A Portrait of an American Boxer* (2006), and Bradley Biggs's book about the 555th, *The Triple Nickles: America's First All-Black Paratroop Unit* (Archon Books, 1986), were invaluable resources, along with the Harry S. Truman Library online collections (trumanlibrary.org), the Oregon State Archives online collections, and the Veterans History Project collections of the Library of Congress. The Airborne & Special Operations Museum in Fayetteville, North Carolina, and the Pendleton Public Library also provided important information for the book.

My journey into World War II history began in another place and time entirely, and I'm grateful to Judith MacPherson Pratt, Kim Pratt, and the Ebel family for being part of my early journey, and to Revere Middle School for introducing me to the Tuskegee Airmen. Thanks to my family—especially Mom, Mike, and Ethan for their spectacular patience. I couldn't have written this book without the support of my editor, Nancy Siscoe; my agent, Steven Malk; and others: Marcy Lindberg, Jackie Kreiger, Laura Little, Matthew, and the knight. And finally, a big thank-you to the following students who read the first draft of the book: LeAnn Bannister, Sharlene Bannister, Adam Bennett, Sydney Bennett, Kaiya Epps, Amea Jefferson, Moussa Kesselly, Sheyenne McKie-Battle, Lashe Miles, DeSean Smith—and their amazing teacher, Rose Levine.